Thundering Meadows
Thundering Mountain Ranch
Book 3

Nicole Neiswanger

Calico

publications

Cover Design: Covers and Cupcakes, LLC
Publisher: Calico Publications, LLC
Digital ISBN: 978-1-960600-02-8
Print Edition ISBN: 978-1-960600-03-5
Large Print Edition ISBN: 978-1-960600-13-4

To my friend, Jessica Lane
Her invaluable input in this novel and all my
novels is what makes them better. She has an
uncanny ability to pull out the best in my work,
and helped make particular scenes downright
delicious. I can't thank her enough for her
friendship and support.

Chapter 1

Christmas Eve 1899

"All aboard."

James stood, stiffness in his bones from the hard wooden bench. Pinprick tingles ran down his back and across his shoulders from leaning against the jagged edges of the rough brick station house. Smoke from the engine swirled around him, enveloping him in its thick, moist heat.

Waiting for the train to arrive, he had sat mesmerized watching the snowflakes fall until the conductor broke the silence. A clean winter wonderland had replaced the once ugly, mud crusted platform. The snow was picking up in intensity and a peek at the sky made it clear it was going to get worse before it got better. He prayed the train made it to Helena in one piece.

He rolled his shoulders, the strap of his tattered knapsack slapping against his back as he moved toward the passenger car. He handed his ticket to the conductor, who checked it closely before waving him inside. His gloveless fingers reached for the frosty handle, pulling his weary frame up and onto the metal steps, each step more freeing than the last.

Emptiness greeted him as he moved into the cool train car. No body heat warmed the inside and the small stove was cold to the touch. Clearly there was no reason to keep a fire burning if no one sat in the worn red leather seats. He gripped the wooden backs, one hand at a time, as he made his way to the middle of the car, one seat as good as another. Placing his knapsack in one next to a window, he dropped onto the flattened cushion.

He tightened his thin coat around his gaunt frame, pulling up the collar in a useless attempt to keep what remained of his body's heat. Ice crystals formed from the frigid air inside the passenger car, but at least the four walls kept the wind at bay. He scrunched down and attempted to get comfortable for the long ride.

The engine chugged to life, steam billowing behind the frost covered windows. He ran a hand across the glass to remove the ice and saw a young woman and child run toward the train. The conductor held out his hand to help her scramble up and into the passenger car. She handed him two tickets, and he nodded, gesturing for her to take a seat. Breathing hard, her hot breath formed a mist in the frigid air. She rushed down the aisle. Her heavy coat opened revealing her belly, round with child.

The conductor pulled out a pocket watch and snapped it shut a moment later before stepping outside and shutting the door tight behind him. A few minutes later the train pulled away from the station, the lurch jarring but welcome as James was finally on his way home.

He wondered about the woman's man, but of course, it wasn't any of his concern. She had settled a few seats in front and to the left of his, dumping her two carpetbags onto the dirty floor. She had dropped her head in obvious fatigue before hugging her son to her side. He began to fuss, but she distracted him by pointing out the window and whispering in his ear. Within moments, he ceased crying, and she relaxed, closing her eyes.

He couldn't help but notice her reddish blonde hair streaked with bits of gold. It sat piled high, accentuating her pink cheeks, big green eyes, and plump red lips. Other than her protruding belly, she was small and petite in stature.

The train labored along the tracks, picking up speed, lulling him to a comfort he had long forgotten, and anticipation for a warm feather bed filled him. The simple things were what he'd missed. Everything else could be left behind. He closed his eyes and enjoyed his newfound freedom as he slipped into a restless slumber.

Metal against metal and abrupt jerking movements yanked him from his sleep. The train shook and rumbled as the engineer applied the brakes. The train shuddered to a stop, throwing him forward. He braced himself, but the young woman wasn't as fortunate. She'd wrapped her arms tight around her son, but the abrupt stop caused her to slam her forehead into the hard wooden back in front of her.

She slumped, unconscious. Her son screamed and tears poured unchecked down his rosy, red cheeks as he tried to wake her. "Momma," he hollered. "Momma!"

Jumping up, James hurried forward. Kneeling eye level with the young boy, he smiled. "It's all right, little man, let me check on your ma."

The boy popped his thumb in his mouth. His wet, dark green eyes were the spitting image of his mother's.

James checked the woman over to assess her injuries. She had a nasty gash above her eye, but otherwise appeared to be unharmed. Grabbing a handkerchief from his coat pocket, he tried to staunch the blood trickling from her wound.

She opened her eyes and screamed. She swung her arms and shoved him away, fright in her eyes. He sat back on his heels, startled, giving her room until she realized he offered no harm.

"Ma'am, you've been hurt. I'm only tryin' to help."

She quieted as soon as she saw her son. She softened her gaze before she turned to James. Her eyes were full of apprehension, but her tension eased as though taking his measure with one glance. "What happened? Where am I?"

"It appears the train had some trouble. When it stopped, you banged your head. Your son's unharmed, though. You protected him while at the same time allowing yourself quite the injury."

"Oh." She arched her lower back, and gripped her belly with her hands. She strained the muscles in her neck. She groaned in agony.

He cursed under his breath. She had just gone into labor.

James was the only one with her and the only one to help. He didn't want to do this, but he clearly didn't have a choice.

* * *

Rose gasped as sharp stabs slammed into her spine and radiated across her taut belly. She grabbed the armrests, riding out the waves until they subsided. She panted, popping her knuckles when she released her grip.

No, no, no! Why did this have to happen today, of all days?

Her head ached, and her waters had broken as evidenced by the watery mess running down her legs and soaking her drawers. Having her baby now was the last thing she expected when she climbed onto the train, fatigue across her body and mind from running. She wasn't due for another month, but with the stress and commotion over the last few weeks, she shouldn't be surprised the baby picked right now to make its appearance. She had wanted to be settled far away, but God had other plans. No matter what happened, she would endure. She had to, for her choices had been wrenched from her hands the day her husband passed.

Another pain started low in her belly and radiated up and across her tight skin. Putting her faith in both God and the brown-eyed stranger sitting in front of her, she breathed through the intense pains. The man had a kind face that was somewhat gaunt, but his clothes were clean though threadbare. He didn't appear to be squeamish and that would be of the utmost importance when the baby arrived, if he were willing.

Taking a deep breath, the latest contraction ebbed away. She only had a moment before the next one began. They were coming fast and furious. They said the second child always came quicker, and it looked like this baby would be here before she knew it. She clasped Tommy's hand, squeezed it, and smiled. He was everything to her, and she didn't want him to have cause for concern.

Something wet trickled along her hairline. Placing two fingers against the wound, they returned sticky with blood. She reached for her bag, but the man stopped her. He had a gentle touch as he pressed a worn but clean handkerchief against the gash.

"Let me, ma'am." He had a warm and comforting smile and a solemn but friendly gaze.

"Thank you."

"My name's James. It appears we might have a situation on our hands."

"You could say..." She bent forward and grimaced as another torturous ache wound across her belly. This baby was not waiting and was coming, and there was nothing she could do to stop it.

***

James watched as she dealt with the onslaught of labor pains. She stiffened in agony but didn't scream, just grunted and moaned as the discomfort of each one tore through her.

It was of little consolation that he knew all about how babies were made but didn't know the first thing about delivering one. As they say, fate waits for no one, and it mattered less what he knew or didn't know, as he was the only person who could help. He wouldn't leave this young woman to do this on her own, no matter how much the thought made his stomach drop.

The air in the car was cool, but despite that, hot, sticky sweat pooled under his arms, down his spine, and around his waist. He should find coal, but it'd likely have to wait as it appeared the baby was coming sooner rather than later. He didn't think he'd have time to think, let alone find any usable coal to start a fire.

He stood, removed his threadbare coat, and rolled up his shirt sleeves. His pounding heart felt as though he had ran ten miles through the desert. The reality of their plight surrounded him and weighed him down. He didn't have time to consider a way out of this. No doctor was going to arrive from the front of the train to rescue them, and they weren't anywhere near a town. The train had stopped somewhere between stations and with the blizzard raging outside, it'd be some time before help would arrive.

James reached for her young son and placed him in the seats across the aisle. The child would want to be close but needed to be out of the way. Fussy, the boy quieted with one look from his ma.

"Ma'am," he said. "Do you have any toys your son could play with while we… um… handle this?" He waved to her belly as though she didn't already know what they were dealing with. It was her belly that was tightening every few minutes and was going to be expelling a child at any moment.

"In my bag." Gasping through the next pain, it took her a moment before she continued. "There are wooden blocks and a stuffed bear. Tommy loves those." Out of breath, she paused. "They should keep him occupied." Her voice raised in pitch as a new labor pain took hold of her. She clenched her fists and bit down on her bottom lip. Her pretty face grimacing with obvious hurt.

James picked up her light brown carpetbag and unsnapped it. Riffling through the clothing near the bottom, he brushed his hands against a pair of silk stockings. Heat bloomed up his chest as he realized he was touching her intimate items, but lucky for him, she was otherwise occupied with the situation at hand and likely didn't see his embarrassment. James quickly found the toys and handed them to Tommy. His attention was focused on his toys and appeared content for now.

Nervous, he studied the woman. He had never delivered a baby or been around a woman heavy with child. He was going to depend on her to get him through this, which was a ridiculous notion because he should be the one tending to her.

After the next contraction, she gazed at him and shook her head as though she could read his mind and the confusion clear as a bright star in a dark sky. Holding her hands in the air, she asked, "Can you help me stand?"

He nodded, captured her slim hands in his, and helped her to her feet. She made quick work of removing her overcoat, but before she could sit, another series of labor pains roared through her. She gripped the seat in front of her, her knuckles turning white as the pressure from her hands would surely break the backs into tiny splinters. When it eased, she raised her eyes to his. Small beads of sweat had gathered along her brow and as she panted, wisps of her dampened hair fluttered across her cheeks. The large green ovals surrounding her black pupils showed all the emotions he too was feeling—fear, trepidation, and determination.

When she released the seat, he reached for her hands again and squeezed. In his own way, he would offer her comfort and the knowledge she wasn't alone, a small comfort it may be.

"We can do this, Mrs…?"

"Rose." She panted. "You can call me Rose."

"Rose, it's a pleasure."

"I'm not quite sure this is," she gasped. She hunched over once again and he couldn't help but notice her slim neck covered in a tangle of reddish curls and the slightness of her frame.

He stiffened as she grasped his hands, squeezing tight, near cutting off the blood to his fingertips. Her weight bore into him, and he held her as though he were the roots of a tall pine tree, preventing her from crashing into the lonely forest.

Her fingers dug into his palms, her sharp nails likely leaving marks. He grimaced and marveled at her strength but didn't let go. She held onto him as if he was her lifeline, and in a way, he suddenly was.

Chapter 2

Rose blinked away hot tears. Intense pain radiated through her belly, down her spine, and almost buckled her at the knees. It was so severe she doubled over. The only thing holding her upright was James's strength.

She was surprised she didn't rip his hands from his arms, and she clutched him until the pain eased. But it was only temporary, as immense pressure grew between her legs. The baby was coming now.

Rose was amazed at the handsome man standing in front of her. He was going to be the one delivering her baby, or at least she prayed he was. If this were any other time, she might have swooned at his good looks. Brown hair, the color of dark chocolate and a strong, angular jaw, she might have itched to run her fingers across it if it had been any other time in her life.

He was at least a foot taller than her, broad-shouldered, although he looked as though he hadn't had a good meal in quite some time, but the muscles under his ill-fitted shirt only enhanced his build.

Out of breath, she said, "It won't be long. The baby's coming." She wheezed. "Will you help me?" She could hear the desperation in her voice and asking a stranger was the last thing she wanted. But it was happening, and God help her, she needed him.

"Um," he gulped.

Still standing, she said, "Please!" Gasping for breath. "I can't do this alone. I know it's too much to ask, but..." She stopped as another sharp wave of pain hit her hard. Moaning, she dug her fingers into his palms. She was hurting him, but she couldn't seem to help it. After what seemed like hours but was only a few seconds, the pain receded, and she sucked in the frosty air. Despite the cold weather, her forehead was damp and wet ringlets stuck to her forehead and cheeks.

Nodding, he let go. She lifted her skirt and tugged at the waistband of her drawers. Struggling, she couldn't get them undone. Frustrated, she stomped her foot, which was a mistake, as it only caused the pressure between her legs to increase tenfold.

James brushed her hands away and made quick work of undoing the ties. They fell to the floor in a soggy mess. Stepping out of them, she gripped the seat in front of her as another sharp stab hit her. When it eased, she looked into his horrified face, but he didn't run and for that she was indebted. She wanted to laugh hysterically at his obvious dismay, but the urge to push was rising to a fever pitch.

She crouched on the floor in the space between the seats and grimaced. Not having the time to remove them, her skirt and petticoats would be ruined if they hadn't already been soaked through from her waters breaking, but it was nothing she could fix right now. She didn't even have time to remove her shoes. Spreading her legs wide, she settled on her hands and wished there was something to brace against. Not quite the image she wanted to display in front of this handsome man, but she would worry about the lack of propriety later.

Hot and sweaty, she would have been comfortable with less clothing on, but she feared if she did, she might undo the tenuous control James was holding onto. She could tell he struggled to keep his emotions in check and probably wished he was anywhere but there, and she couldn't blame him. She felt the same way, but it wasn't as though she could run from the baby begging to be released into his waiting hands.

It was time for her to bear down, but she had to school him on what to do, as he was clearly confused and frightened. Speaking quickly and determinedly, she said, "In my bag is a worn blanket you can use to clean the baby and then a soft baby blanket for later. You'll use that…" She gasped as the next pain started and nature took over. She pushed with all her strength, an unladylike guttural groan escaped from her lips.

James knelt in front of her and swept her skirts out of the way. He at least knew enough to do that, she mused, before all rational thoughts disappeared. She pushed and pushed hard. Nothing would stop the baby now.

* * *

Moments later, James held a squalling little girl in his arms. So tiny, he couldn't believe his eyes. He was in awe. Everything happened so swiftly. Rose heaved, strained, took small panting breaths and before he knew it, the little girl slid into his waiting fingertips. He hadn't the time to consider what he was seeing or what he was touching, but understood it was the way God had intended.

It was a wonder, a beautiful little miracle. Using the worn blanket Rose had suggested, he quickly cleaned the baby while being as gentle as possible before wrapping her in the soft blanket. He hadn't the time to warm the passenger car before she had slid into the world, and he didn't want her to catch a chill, as that could end a newborn's life faster than he could spit.

Rose schooled him between raspy breaths on what to do each step of the way. Her ability to give instructions while giving birth was quite remarkable. After placing the baby in her arms, James followed her directions and disposed of the remains of the birth outside in the snow. Standing on the steps of the car, he took a moment to breathe. In all the excitement, he had forgotten what put them in this position to begin with. Using the cold metal handle as a brace, he leaned forward to gaze down the tracks.

He wondered what had caused the train to come to an abrupt halt. Through the blinding snow, he stared in disbelief. It appeared the steam engine and the coal car had plumb gone off the tracks. He had heard of trains derailing but had never experienced it firsthand. Somehow, the car coupled to the coal car had stayed upright, thus keeping the remaining cars on the tracks. He realized that if any of the cars had twisted and fallen, their car could have done the same. Severe injury could've been the result. They had been lucky this night. A Christmas miracle in more ways than one.

Wondering if the engineer and conductor were all right, he considered braving the snowstorm, but hesitated. Growing in intensity over the last few hours, a blizzard swirled with a powerful fury and snow drifts were growing rapidly in size. With the train incapacitated, it could be days before anyone found them. He should return to Rose and her children, but he had to know if the derailment had hurt anyone. It wouldn't be honorable to leave someone injured. He had done enough damage in his life. This was at least something he could prevent.

He shouted to Rose he was going to the front

of the train to see what he could discover. She murmured a response. The words were muffled as the wind howled around him, whipping his hair around his ears and pulling at the collar of his shirt.

Stepping down the steps of the car, he struggled against the wind and snow and fought his way through the thick drifts to the engine. Freezing, he realized too late he should have grabbed his coat before making this foolhardy trip, but he couldn't go back now. He was too close to the finish line.

Reaching the engine, he grasped the rails and pulled himself up and into the cab, where he found the engineer and conductor. They appeared startled at the intrusion, but none the worse for wear.

"Sir, what are you doing up here?" the conductor asked. He had a small gash above his right eyebrow, but the injury didn't appear to be life threatening.

James put his hands to his mouth and blew into his palms to warm them before responding.

It had been frigid outside, and he'd been a fool to go through the snow without protection. It would just be another example of him making the wrong choice in his long, pitiful life. "I wanted to see if you were all right and to find out what happened. It was quite an abrupt stop."

The engineer frowned and ran his hands through his hair. Covered in soot from the coal, his bright blue eyes were in stark contrast to the black staining his face. "Damn track contracted from the cold and split. I didn't see it 'til it was too late. With God's good graces, we were goin' slow enough that the cars didn't overturn and completely drop off the tracks. Problem is, we can't go anywhere without help and the blizzard's gonna prevent rescue anytime soon." He looked at the conductor as though asking if he should continue.

The conductor nodded. "We're stuck. When we don't arrive at the next stop, they'll know something's happened. We're sure they'll send a search party when the weather clears."

"What do we do now?" James asked, placing

his hands under his armpits. The sharp pinpricks had eased, but his hands were undeniably cold.

"Not much we can do except wait it out," the conductor said.

"That's all well and good, but we have a problem," James said. "There's a mother in the passenger car who just gave birth."

"Well, that's the last thing I expected you to say," the conductor said.

"It surprised me but came fast and hard. She delivered it before I knew what was happening."

"Is she all right?" the conductor asked, his wide eyes filled with concern.

"Yes, she appears to be," James said, "but I ain't no doctor, and I only did what she told me. She and the baby are both alive, but the car is ice cold and if we're going to be here for a few days, it's necessary I keep it warm."

"There's plenty of coal and should last us 'til the rescuers get here. I should've started a fire in the passenger car, but we were in such a hurry to leave I plum forgot," the conductor said.

"Perfectly understandable. Do you have any

blankets I can use to keep the mother and baby warm?" James asked.

"There's bound to be something in the cargo car we can use. I'll see what I can find for you and the lady," the conductor said. Turning to the engineer, he asked, "Will you be all right up here?"

"Yep. Let me know if you need my help."

Both the conductor and James climbed out of the engine, the steps slick with ice. James almost lost his footing, wrenching his arm as he grappled for control. Once on solid ground, the two of them stumbled through the snow to the coal car. The conductor gave James a large bucket to hold the hard, black pieces, and then they left for the cargo car.

James's teeth chattered uncontrollably as he once again berated himself for not grabbing his coat. Perhaps the cold was penance for the multitude of mistakes he had made over the years. Although he had served his time according to the laws of man, he didn't know if he had served enough time in the laws of God.

He wasn't a religious man by any stretch of the imagination, but he had plenty of time to think over the last six years, and he wondered if he hadn't made mistakes that could never be forgiven.

Chapter 3

James stood above the waning heat coming from the stove and filled it once again with chunks of coal. After braving the blizzard conditions, he returned to the rail car with a bucket of coal and a stack of fresh blankets. There had been a crate full of the monogrammed blankets on their way to a hotel in Helena. The hotel wouldn't appreciate them borrowing from their stock, but better for hotel management to be irritated than freezing to death in a raging blizzard. The conductor was glad of it, as he too would make use of the blankets for him and the engineer.

The conductor also found them food—shriveled apples, a stale loaf of bread, and cans of beans and peaches. It wasn't much but it would keep the hunger pains at bay. Rose was going to need it more than ever if she was to keep the baby nourished. She also had little Tommy to consider. No one had planned on being on the train for more than a few hours, so they would ration the food as best they could until help arrived.

Rose was mighty appreciative when the conductor handed her the satchel of food. A beautiful smile lit up her face, her green eyes luminescent. She had a glow about her, likely from giving birth and the joy of having a sweet baby girl in her arms. The conductor blushed and tripped over his own feet when he went out the metal door with similar supplies for him and the engineer.

James melted snow over the hot stove for water and gave it to Rose to wash as best she could from the birth. She was weak, struggling to stand, and trying to smother her groans from any sudden movements, but she thanked him again and again for his help. When she was done with her ablutions, he created a cocoon of sorts near the warm stove and moved her and the baby there, bundling them snugly into the thick blankets.

Little Tommy had fallen asleep during the commotion. Tired from the late night and the excitement of his baby sister's birth, he had closed his eyes, his little bear tucked under his chin. James picked him up, taking care not to wake him. Tommy stirred but stayed asleep when James settled him on the seats across from his mother. Covering him with a blanket, he looked at the little tyke, his thumb snug in his mouth. His red hair was darker than his mother's, but there was no denying he was hers.

Remorse filled James that his past actions had prevented him from having a family. He was getting older, and with his criminal history, no decent woman would ever have him. Being alone was his future, but at least he was free now to make the best of his lot. He still had his sister,

Elizabeth, and he was lucky her husband, Ben, was letting him come to his ranch until he could make plans for his future.

Shaking off his maudlin thoughts, he checked on Rose. She rested in the seats with her new little girl tucked into her folded arms, but the thick blanket had fallen to the ground. He picked it up, brushed off any dirt from the floor, and placed it around her waist.

He rubbed his hands against his arms as he caught a chill from the metal door. It didn't seal all the way and was letting in the frosty air. He'd have to keep an eye on the stove to keep the coal from burning down and letting the car get too cold.

He grabbed the coat he had discarded earlier and pushed his arms into it, making quick work of doing up the worn buttons. His energy had faded. The stress of the past few days settled deep in his bones. He sat on a seat behind Tommy and Rose. Resting against the window, he placed his feet on the seat next to him. Closing his eyes, he fell asleep, his last thought of the joy he had in bringing a new life into this world.

* * *

A few hours later, Rose woke as the baby stirred in her arms. Unbuttoning her blouse, she settled the baby closer to her chest. The baby hadn't wanted to feed earlier, but it appeared she was hungry now. She rooted her mouth, and it only took but a moment for Rose to instruct her. She soon latched on, the sucking motion soothing and comforting, the first milk providing nourishment.

Leaning against the hard wooden seat, Rose rested her eyes as the baby suckled. She hadn't had a moment to take stock of what had transpired over the last few hours, let alone the last year. She'd gone from being a happily married woman with a husband she loved to a widow, heavily pregnant. The only things keeping her going were her children.

A logging accident had taken her husband in

an unforeseen and tragic way. Killed instantly, he didn't suffer, but it still broke Rose's heart to know her Joseph lost his life trying to provide a better life for them.

Excited about the birth of the baby, Joseph had taken the job at the logging camp to earn more money. He hadn't been a logger, but he mistakenly believed if his older brother Charles could do it, then he could do the same. He should have stayed working as a bookkeeper, but instead Charles had enticed him with a large bonus if he joined the team. Rose had argued with him, but Joseph felt strongly he had to do it with another mouth to feed. She hadn't been able to convince him otherwise once he got the idea into his thick head.

Charles believed a real man worked with his hands and because Joseph had sat behind a desk and used his brain, Charles never believed in him and told him he never measured up. Fifteen years older than Joseph, Charles made him feel inferior and believed their parents had coddled him.

Joseph had only been eighteen when their parents passed away. Charles tried to take him into his home and control him with a firm and rigorous hand, but Joseph had stood up to his brother and refused to quit the school his parents had enrolled him in. With the money his parents had set aside for his education, Joseph finished his schooling and went against Charles's wishes. Joseph had regretted the divide it had put between them and tried to mend the angst when he had come home to Smelter to work in the logging camp's offices, but it hadn't helped, and Charles never forgave him for what he considered a slight against him.

During the first few days after Joseph's death, Charles had been kinder to her than he'd ever been. This surprised Rose, but she accepted his caring words and leaned on him in her time of grief, but it soon became clear Charles had an ulterior motive, one which Rose was very much against.

Two weeks after Joseph was laid to rest in the family cemetery, Charles approached Rose and told her she was to marry him. As head of the family, he said he had a duty to make her his wife, and he believed Joseph would have wanted it. He had spoken to the minister, and the wedding was set for the following week.

Staring at him in horror, Rose was without words. She hadn't known what to say and Charles, in his perverse vanity, believed her silence indicated her agreement. Grinning enthusiastically, he bounced out the door.

Joseph would never have asked her to do this. He had known how she felt about his brother, and they had only stayed near Charles out of loyalty. There was no way she'd marry Charles, no matter what he believed. The man was cruel and treated those around him with disdain. She had always felt uncomfortable in his presence and would never agree to be his wife.

The following day, she left Tommy with a neighbor and went to the logging camp. Finding Charles during his noon break, she pulled him aside and asked if she could speak with him.

Believing his future bride was happy to see him, Charles stepped away.

Trying to be kind, she told him she wouldn't marry him.

"What are you blathering on about?" he roared. Red streaks climbed up his thick neck. He balled his beefy hands into fists and anger contorted his features. He was large, bulky, with thick muscles from his years working in a lumber camp, and he could tear her in half if he had a mind to. Fearing his reaction, she retreated, but he grabbed her arm, pinching her skin with his fingers. He pulled her toward him and spittle flew onto her cheek as he menacingly whispered in her ear. "You'll marry me, Rose McGaven."

"No, I won't." She struggled, pulling, but he only tightened his grip.

"You will," he said. "The minister agrees. You need a husband. Since you married my brother, you and your children belong to me. There's nothing you can do."

She ripped her arm from his grasp. "I don't have to marry you."

His anger came in waves like a roaring wildfire, eating up everything in its path, not caring what was there, consuming, devouring until all that was left was destruction. "Mark my words, you'll marry me. You're living in my house and if you dare to go against me, I'll take the house. I'll take everything you hold dear, and you'll regret crossing me."

Swallowing painfully, fear crawled up her skin and along her spine. "I don't understand. That is my home. Joseph would have wanted us to always be safe."

He sneered. "Joseph couldn't afford to give you a house. I bought and paid for it and it's mine, not yours. If you don't want to lose your children, you'll marry me. If you try to leave, I'll take Tommy, and when this one is born, it'll be mine as well."

"You can't take my children away from me." Tears clogged her throat.

"Can't I?" he said. "The law'll be on my side when I tell 'em how you've been hittin' your son, and how he cowers in fear whenever you're around."

"That isn't true. I would never hurt him."

"That isn't what the judge'll believe. You forget," he paused, "I grew up in this town, and I play poker with the only judge around these parts. His son and I are the best of friends. They'll believe anythin' I tell 'em." His eyes were wild and crazy. He fairly frothed at the mouth at his power over her. "You aren't from here and no one knows you. There's no way you could convince the judge you're a decent mother, so don't bother trying."

Gulping back sobs of fear, Rose didn't know what to do. She was an orphan and had been a governess when she met Joseph. She had no family, no one to lean on, no one to protect her. Charles was right. He was well respected and knew everyone in town. No one would believe her, not if he chose to tell everyone vicious lies.

Cowering, she nodded in acquiescence when he told her to prepare for their wedding. She left the logging camp with slow and sluggish steps.

Her mind raced trying to make sense of the position she found herself in.

Before she reached the home, she mistakenly believed was hers, she dried her tears. She didn't want her neighbor to believe she had been crying. Not knowing if the neighbor was in Charles's pocket, she forced a smile and retrieved her son. That night, after putting Tommy to bed, she contemplated her future.

Charles was an angry, hurtful man whom she could never love. The anger burning deep within him scared her. He'd harm her if given half the chance. Maybe not today, but one day. She survived an orphanage and losing her husband. She had to escape before he caught wind of any plans she might make, but she needed money, and she only had a few dollars left in her kitchen fund. Joseph had always given her what she needed, but she never understood what they really had for she never had reason to know.

The next morning, she went to the bank to see what was left in her account. Only a scant amount remained, not enough for her to get away, but she withdrew every penny, telling the bank manager she needed it to buy items for her wedding. Charles had already spread the news in town. By telling the gossiping bank manager the falsehood, she prayed if the information were to get to Charles ears, he wouldn't suspect her true intentions.

Unfortunately, if she couldn't come up with more cash, she'd never be able to disappear. Thinking through her options, she decided lying to Charles and telling him she couldn't wait to be his wife was her only course of action. If she told him she wanted an elaborate and lavish wedding to celebrate their union, perhaps he'd give her the funds she desperately needed. Once she had money in hand, she and her children could vanish.

That afternoon, she sent word to Charles and invited him over for a hot meal. Putting on her prettiest dress, doing her hair in the most flattering style, she set out to woo her brother-in-law with the sole purpose of getting his money. She hoped she could carry off the charade and hide her loathing. She had to protect Tommy and her unborn child, no matter the cost.

After welcoming Charles, she offered him a glass of whiskey and asked him to sit in front of the warm fire. She plumped the pillows behind him and gave him a wooden stool to rest his feet on.

She stood in front of him, clasping her hands in front of her belly, trying to look contrite and obedient. "Charles, I've thought about it, and after some thoughtful praying, I believe you're right."

He lifted his eyebrows. "About?"

He wasn't going to make this easy. Swallowing her repugnance, she attempted to look beguiling. "I was distraught the other day and didn't give you a fair chance. Losing your brother has been very difficult for me, as I imagine it has been for you." She shed a tear because losing Joseph had been difficult and wasn't a lie. Her next words, however, were nothing but lies. "You've always been so kind to me, and I know how much you loved Joseph."

He preened. "Yes, it has been difficult. Joseph was a weak man but tried hard when he put his mind to it."

She wanted to hurl a skillet at him. Joseph had been anything but weak, but she couldn't let Charles see how much his words bothered her. "You're so right." She stepped near him, brushing her skirts against his legs, and placed her fingers on his forearm, touching him lightly, trying not to cringe at the sweaty, dirt crusted skin that lay beneath. For this to work, she had to be believable. "I'd be honored to become your wife. My children need a good man to raise them, and I'm sure Joseph would've wanted this. It just took me a moment to realize the truth in your words."

A wide, salacious grin covered his lips, making her shiver with horror. He stood, grabbed her waist, and lifted her off her feet, swinging her around the room before dropping her, still keeping her trapped within his arms. He bent and placed his lips on hers, grinding them against hers in what he thought was an amorous kiss, but was nothing short of revolting.

Desperate to contain the acid in her throat, she forced her arms around his neck, so he'd never know he was the last person she'd ever want to kiss. He moved his hands along her back and forced her into him. She bit the inside of her cheeks to keep from crying out in pain.

Knowing she'd lose what contents remained in her belly if she didn't put distance between them, she put her hands on his chest and pushed him away as gently as she could.

Pasting a smile on her face, she patted his chest. "Now, now Charles. This isn't appropriate. I'm not your wife yet. We need to wait until it's official."

He grinned. "We can have a little fun before, don't you think?" He reached for her again, but she stepped out of his reach, and turned away from him, trying to act as though she was gaining her composure. She fanned at her face. If he continued to touch her, she might clench her hand into a fist and hit him as hard as she could.

"Charles, my dear," she said, looking over her shoulder. "I am a lady. I don't want there to be any vicious rumors about us before we are married. Our children deserve to have respectable parents, don't you agree? You're admired in our tight-knit community and if there's any hint of scandal, well..." She let the words hang. His desire to be respected and powerful was the one thing she could use against him.

He raked his gaze over her for a long and measured moment and then nodded. She'd play on his desires for as long as she needed, especially if it helped her get what she needed.

"But I require your help," she said, her gaze downcast, trying to be the demure woman he'd expect.

"Help?" He puffed up his chest as though she had just granted him the keys to the kingdom. "Of course, I'll help. What can I do?"

"Our wedding should be special." She batted her eyes, or at least she thought she did. The coy game was not one she played well and never had, but he was clearly only seeing what he wanted to see.

"Yes, yes. Exactly what we need." He widened his eyes with lust.

She dropped her gaze and fidgeted with a tendril of hair next to her neck that had loosened from her coiffure.

"Tell me, Rose."

"I… well…" She hung her lips in a small frown.

"Don't be shy. You're to be my wife." He oozed confidence and excitement. It was enough to make disgust crawl up her skin, but she couldn't lose sight now. He took her hands in his, running his fingers up and down her wrist as though he thought what he was doing was wanted.

"I don't have any money." She tried to pull them away as though she was embarrassed at her plight. "I don't want to shame you, but I don't know how I can give you… us… the wedding of our dreams without a few dollars."

"Oh, is that all?" He dropped her hands.

Charles reached into his shirt pocket and pulled out his billfold. "How much do you think you'll need?"

"I'm not sure. I want to make it very special. As you know, Joseph and I didn't have a large wedding. He didn't like to put his business out there, but with you, I feel you deserve more from me and well"—she looked at him from under her long eyelashes, her cheeks likely bright pink from lying through her tight teeth—"if I were to dream, I'd love to have the biggest and best wedding this town has ever seen."

He had removed a few bills but reached back in and extracted more. He took the cash and placed the green money into her hand, folding her fingers over the bills. She tried not to grin with satisfaction. She wasn't clear about how much he had given her, but it was plenty more than she could have wished for.

"Thank you," she said. "I'll do my best to make you proud." Realizing she was pushing her luck, she tried once more. "If I find I might need more, would it be too much to ask?" She tilted her head to the side.

He licked his wide lips. "Yes, yes. Anythin' you might want is no trouble. I'm happy to give you as much as you need. You're to be my wife and shouldn't want for anythin' at all." His yellow teeth showed in all their disgusting glory. "If you need more, you just let me know."

"I will." She shoved the money in her skirt pocket. She would count it later.

"Now I've got to go."

Her heart pounded in fear. She didn't know what she would do if he'd figure out her real motives for her flirtatious behavior.

"I wouldn't want to spoil your reputation. You get to plannin' that wedding of ours," he said.

"I will," she said, grinning.

He turned to leave, but before he did, she asked, "Charles?"

"Yes."

"One more thing."

"Of course, my dear."

"I'm afraid a week isn't enough time to plan

the wedding of the year. Would you be terribly upset with me if we postponed it for one week?" It took everything in her to not sound like she was begging.

"I don't know, Rose."

She didn't want to anger him, so she stepped forward and placed a hand on his cheek. "It isn't that I want to postpone it, but there is so much to do." She took a heavy breath and placed her other hand on her belly to remind him she was with child. "I get so tired with the little one on the way, but I want to make you happy. If I must rush things, I'm afraid it won't be as nice as it could be, that's all, I promise. I want to marry you and an extra week will be hard, especially with the thought..." She blushed more from the abhorrent thought of his hands on her. "Well, with the thought of us sharing our love intimately, if you understand."

His eyes darkened, as he brushed his lips against her hand. It was all she could do not to pull it away as he dragged his scratchy tongue against her palm. He thought he was passionate, but he truly was repulsive.

"I certainly do. I'll wait another week with the promise our wedding night will be one I won't forget." His hand dropped to the valley between her breasts and lingered there for a long moment.

She swallowed, trembling inside. "It will be, I promise."

He grinned, grabbed her shoulders and placed another slurpy kiss on her lips. After the door closed, she furiously wiped at her face, trying to remove the taste of him. She was afraid she'd never forget the putrid taste of him. Her plans had to be foolproof, otherwise she wasn't sure what she'd do. She'd never marry that man, ever.

Slumping into an armchair, she sat there for a few moments, calming her racing heart. She couldn't believe she had pulled off that charade. Pulling out the cash, she counted it and sighed with relief. She now held enough to get train tickets with a little left over. She wasn't sure it would be enough to begin a new life with her children, but she could find a job as a seamstress or a cook. If it wasn't, she'd survive. She always had and always would.

She hurried to her room to pack her bags. She wouldn't be able to take much, as she couldn't tip Charles off to her intentions. With a touch of luck, she could disappear without his knowledge.

Late into the evening, she packed everything she thought she'd need for herself, Tommy, and the new baby into two worn carpetbags. It was all she could carry and would have to be enough.

She placed the money she gained into a pocket of her satchel, where it should be safe, and set the bags deep in her wardrobe, behind thick coats and dresses. Charles would have no reason to look there and when ready to leave, she would take the bags and disappear with Tommy forever.

Chapter 4

The baby released, the popping sound pulling her from the memories of the past few months. A trickle of milk ran across her baby's sweet little chin. Quickly wiping both clean, she buttoned up her blouse and patted the baby's back to burp her. Once done, Rose tucked the soft blanket more securely around the little one. Warmer now in the passenger car, she prayed it'd be enough to keep her little girl from catching her death of cold.

With the labor pains catching her unaware and the birth coming soon after, she had lost sight of Tommy. Thankfully, James had the foresight to ensure his safety, and he'd been well looked after. It was a Christmas miracle to know someone as kind and considerate as James had come into her life when she needed someone the most. Things could've turned out quite differently if she'd been alone.

Wondering where James had disappeared to, she held the baby with one arm and used the other to pull herself to stand. She gripped the edge of the seat, using it as leverage, as her legs were still shaky, and she ached from giving birth.

She straightened the blanket on Tommy, his round face slack from sleep, and moved a lock of his hair. She ran her fingers against his pink cheeks. He shifted and turned but didn't wake.

Looking around the car, she found James sleeping soundly in the seats behind Tommy, his soft snores making her grin. A blanket cushioned his head between the seat and the window. His tall, broad body was shoved into the tight space, and he was likely quite uncomfortable. His other blanket had fallen to the ground, and he shivered, jerking ever so slightly. She crouched to pick it up, her body protesting each movement, but it was the least she could do after the considerate care he had given her throughout their short time together.

She dropped the blanket around his waist and then stopped herself from waking him. She shouldn't disturb him. He looked tired and likely needed his rest.

As she backed away, James's eyes opened and caught hers. He sat up straight, dropping his legs to the floor, hitting the ground with a thud, and shifted awkwardly.

"Rose," he said, rubbing at his eyes.

"I didn't mean to wake you."

"You didn't." He moved the blanket to the side and stood. "I should've been more vigilant. It's gotten chilly in here. I didn't mean to sleep so long." He straightened his coat and ran his fingers through his hair. "Pardon me while I tend to the fire."

Before he could move past her, she reached out and touched his arm. "You were a godsend for doing what was necessary and taking care of my Tommy as well. Is there anything I can do to properly thank you?"

"No, no. Your safety is thanks enough." He looked past her to the stove and twitched.

She wondered if she was making him uncomfortable. "My thanks don't seem adequate."

"Believe me, it is." He lifted the collar of his coat and shivered. "Are you feeling… Are you still sore?" The words came out in a rush, as if he didn't get the words out quick enough, he never would. His face was bright red with embarrassment.

"Nothing that isn't normal. No reason to be concerned. This birth was easy compared to Tommy's, and I'm sure I have you to thank." She lifted her lips into a grin.

He avoided her gaze. "I'm relieved to hear that. Are you staying warm enough? How's the baby?"

"It's chillier in here than I'd like, but she's as sweet as can be." She gazed at the angel in her arms and ran a finger across her tiny fists. The little hand grasped her finger even though she didn't open her eyes. "Do you have any idea when we might leave?"

"I'm afraid not. When I spoke to the conductor and engineer, they didn't know when help would arrive." He scooted around her and went to the stove. "Let me add more coal. I don't want you to catch your death." He added a few pieces of the black coal and stoked it with the poker. "The conductor has no way of communicating with the next station. The blizzard outside is fierce and it could be days before anyone comes."

Fear settled into her heart. She had only been on the road for a few days, and still wasn't far enough away from Charles. If she got stuck on this train for much longer, it'd make it easier for him to find her. She didn't know what she would do if he found her.

As soon as James mentioned they might be stuck on the train for a few days, Rose retreated within herself right before his eyes. He could see the fear seep into every bone of her body. She shuttered her eyes, slumped her shoulders, and shrunk in front of him. Her face grew pale, and he wondered what caused her to panic. He wanted to ask, but he didn't want to overstep.

Deciding her health was more important, he said, "What is it? What can I do to help?" The words tumbled from his lips before he could stop them.

Startled, fright filled her eyes, but she only gazed at him for a moment before dropping them to the now fussy little girl. She had tightened her hold on the baby when he had asked her the questions. Loosening her grip, she lifted the baby to her lips and murmured in her ear. The baby quieted at once.

"I didn't mean to upset you," he whispered.

"You didn't. You've been nothing but a big help. There are things that…" She stopped, her eyes downcast, avoiding his.

He wanted to comfort her. "You're safe here. No one can get to you."

Shock registered across her features at his clear insight into the fact she was afraid. Trying to put on a brave face, she forced a smile that didn't reach her eyes. Her emotions were simple to read. She appealed to him on a level he hadn't been prepared for and in a different time he would've wanted to explore, but those times were no longer available and hadn't been in some time.

"If I can help, I'd like to." He rubbed his hands together. Although the stove was blazing hot, it wasn't as toasty as he'd like. It was as though he could never get warm anymore, the chill settling deep into his bones.

"I appreciate the sentiment more than you'll ever know, but no one..." She stopped abruptly, her discomfort apparent.

"Why don't you sit near the stove where it's warm? I'll get you something to eat. You need to keep up your strength."

Trying to distract her, he broke off a piece

from the loaf of bread and grabbed an apple. Watching her shuffle to the seats where she'd been sleeping, something stirred within him, a warm feeling he thought was long gone. She was a stunning young woman, but her beauty was more than skin deep. He saw the way she gazed at her baby girl and the motherly looks she sent Tommy's way. Her husband was lucky, and a surge of jealousy pierced his gut but also a rage of anger. No man should leave his wife alone while she was so heavy with his child. Her husband should've been here to protect her and should be ashamed of himself for leaving her alone in this predicament.

James went to hand her the food and stopped as her hands were occupied with the little girl. He looked at her and she looked at him. They both laughed as they considered the dilemma.

He swallowed hard with the possible fear of rejection. "May I hold her while you eat?"

She nodded. He placed the food on a piece of clean linen and then lifted the tiny baby girl to his chest and held her close. He dropped his gaze. He still couldn't believe the miracle he held in his hands. His heart tugged, and he wasn't sure what to make of it.

He was in awe of her delicate features and tiny fingers and toes. Never had he held a child this precious in his arms, and protectiveness surged. There wasn't anything he wouldn't do to guard this little girl and her mother. Bringing the baby into the world and being near this woman in such an intimate moment had brought forth feelings he never thought possible.

He wasn't sure he could have them, though. They had just met, and he had no prior connection with this woman or her children, but he suddenly wanted to.

He let Rose finish chewing the bread. "Have you decided on a name?"

"Not yet, I have a few ideas but—"

"You want your husband to be with you when you decide?" he asked, interrupting.

Her smile faded, and tears filled her eyes.

He stiffened. *What did I say to make her cry?* "Did I say something wrong?"

"No." She paused for a long moment. "My husband, he… He passed away." She blinked furiously, but a tear leaked and traveled down her pink cheek.

"I'm sorry." He berated himself. *How could I've been so insensitive?* His jealousy overrode his good sense. "I didn't mean to pry."

"You didn't know. How could you?"

"Do you have somewhere to go?" he asked.

"No, not really." She picked at the bread in her lap, pulling it apart with her fingers, and dropping the pieces onto the piece of linen, none making it to her mouth.

"Can I help? There's something wrong, but you aren't willing to tell me, and why should you? I'm a stranger, but I want you to know if you need help, I'm here." He silently cursed when he realized he was pushing too hard, too fast.

"Where are you headed?" She ignored his questions.

It was clear she didn't want to confide in him.

He, of all people, should know that some things are best left in the past. He smiled. "To my sister's. Her husband owns a ranch outside of Helena. I was supposed to spend Christmas with them, but I don't think that's gonna happen, least ways not now." He frowned at fate spoiling his first Christmas out of prison in years.

"I'm sure she'll be disappointed."

"Likely." If he knew Elizabeth, she was likely worried sick that he hadn't made it on time. "But we haven't seen each other in six years, so a few more days won't hurt."

"Why so long?" she asked.

James hesitated. He didn't know how much he wanted to tell her. As soon as he told her where he had been, it would compromise their tentative connection. He wasn't sure he wanted to lose it.

She fidgeted self-consciously. "I overstepped. It isn't any of my concern."

"No, you didn't overstep." The baby stirred, and it gave him a moment to gather himself. "I'm afraid you won't want to have a thing to do with me and to be honest, I don't want to lose that." He moved his feet. "I like you more than I should."

Her face flushed red. "I'm not sure what to say. I'm flattered."

He had gone too far and took a small step back to give her room. "I've embarrassed you."

"No, I appreciate your honesty."

"Why don't you finish eating?" He paced with the baby, patting her on the bottom as though she had fussed, and he was trying to calm her. It was more to comfort himself. He was doing anything to avoid looking at Rose. A beautiful woman like her would have nothing to do with a no-account man like himself, and she didn't even know what he'd done or where he'd been. Once she discovered his past, she'd likely never speak to him again, let alone let him hold her new little one. Likely, this would be the one and only time he'd be in the presence of someone as beautiful and as pure.

The door to the car flew open and interrupted the awkwardness. James sighed with relief as the conductor stepped inside. A chilly breeze blew into the car and Tommy stirred from the frigid air. Sitting up, he cried out in fear. Rose jumped to attend to him, her movements stiff, but she didn't let that stop her. She pulled him into her arms and wrapped the blanket around him. She wiped the hair away from his eyes and kissed his cheek.

"Ma'am," the conductor said as he closed the door behind him. "Didn't mean to disturb him."

"You wouldn't have known," she said. "He was just startled and will fall asleep again soon."

"Do you have enough coal to get through the night?" the conductor asked.

"I reckon so," James said. "If'n we need more, I can always get more from the coal car."

The conductor shuffled. "Folks, I'm real sorry this has ruined your Christmas. With any luck, the snow'll ease up soon. As soon as it's safe to travel, I'm sure there'll be a search party sent to find us." He reached into his pocket, pulled out a watch, and glanced at its face. "We should've arrived at the station near abouts three hours ago, so the stationmaster will likely alert the authorities."

With that, he opened the door and stepped outside. The wind blustered, the blankets fluttered, and the flames in the stove flickered before the door latch clicked and everything dropped into its place.

Rose gazed at James. "I guess we better settle in, then. It could be some time."

Sighing, he said, "I think you're right."

Rose rocked Tommy until he once again fell asleep. Gently placing him on the seat, she made sure the blanket was secure around him before she reached for her baby.

Not wanting to hand her over, he hesitated for just a second before he kissed the soft skin on her head and then gave her back to her mother.

"Merry Christmas, Rose," he said.

She smiled with pink and rosy cheeks and glowing green eyes. "Merry Christmas."

Chapter 5

Christmas Day, December 25, 1899

James's eyes flew open, and he promptly squinted from the bright glare of the sun through the frost covered windows. The blizzard had stopped. He was still in the passenger car of the train, and it was Christmas morning.

Shifting on the seat, he groaned. He creaked and cracked as the bones and muscles snapped back into place. As he became fully awake, the events of the previous day came rushing back. Worried about the safety of the children, he stood, stretched, and marched to the stove.

During the night, the fire had burned low. He had every intention of waking every few hours to add more coal, but instead he had slept hard and peacefully for the first time in six years. Surprising, as the seats were not meant for comfort. Unfortunately, his dreamland peace wasn't safe for Rose and the children. With any luck, the thick blankets they found in the cargo car would have kept off the worst of the icy air.

Shoving more coal into the stove, he stoked it until heated air flowed from it once again. Wiping his hands free of the black coal dust on a well-used rag, he peered at Rose and the baby. They were both sleeping quietly. Rose's hair was a tangled cascade of curls across her shoulders and down her back, her dark lashes laying against her pink cheeks. He dropped his shoulders in relief, as they appeared to be well and good.

Wood hitting wood hit his ears. It was little Tommy playing with his blocks. Tommy grinned at James, but went back to his toys, seemingly unconcerned with him or his mother.

"Are you hungry, Tommy?" he whispered, not wanting to wake Rose.

Tommy bobbed his little head. Reaching for the bag of food, James pulled out a chunk of bread and tore off a piece. Tommy grabbed the bread and took a big bite. With a full mouth, he asked, "Milk?"

"Buddy, I don't have any. There's water, though."

His smile fell and big tears formed in his eyes. "Want milk," he screeched.

Tommy went from quiet and content to a toddler throwing a fit. If James hadn't seen the transformation himself, he might've thought he had done something to the little tyke.

"Shh. You don't want to wake your momma, do you?"

"Milk!"

Squatting to his level, James tried to reason with him, but Tommy wouldn't have it. He threw a wooden block across the room, and it hit the stove with a large thunk. He cried inconsolably, the bread falling out of his mouth.

Rose stirred. The baby in her arms woke and emitted a large cry of displeasure, adding to the cacophony of sounds coming from Tommy's lips.

Rose simultaneously tried to comfort the baby and Tommy. "What's wrong, sweetheart?" She nudged James out of the way.

"Milk." He hiccupped, big tears falling down his face.

"Oh, sweetheart. I know you want milk, and we'll get some for you as soon as we can. But for now, can you drink the water instead?" She placed her hand on his cheek and brushed back his tears. She then pulled him to her side while holding the baby in her other arm.

Gulping back his sobs, Tommy quieted at once.

James watched in amazement as she calmed both of her children with her quiet resolve. His heart softened, and he wanted this woman permanently in his life. He just didn't think he'd ever have the chance to do it.

Astonished at his feelings, he wondered where they had come from. He was forty-three and wasn't getting younger. He wanted a family. Rose didn't know him, and he wasn't a man any decent, respectable, and god-fearing woman would want, but perhaps he could pretend it never happened and never mention it. If she never asked, he wouldn't have to explain. He could suggest their pasts didn't matter and the only thing that did was their future. Maybe, just maybe, he could have the dream he had always wanted but had to give up when he was thrown into jail; a ranch, a wife, and a passel of kids.

Before the dream could take hold, the reality of his situation struck him like a ton of bricks from a falling building, smashing to the ground, dust flying everywhere, smothering him 'til his breath caught.

He was being impractical, foolish. This beautiful, caring mother wouldn't want to spend the rest of her life with him. He was a good-for-nothing, had nothing to his name. He was a criminal who had made countless poor decisions and could never offer her anything good or wholesome. Instead, he'd be lucky if he'd be able to find a steady job once anyone discovered his past.

He needed to remember that and work hard to make sure Rose and her children survived. Once they were safe, he could continue to his sister's home and pay off his debt to her husband. Maybe then he could begin to pay back the wrongs he had done.

* * *

Seeing the look in James's eyes, Rose was confused. He was disheartened, so sad, as though he had lost a vital piece of himself. It reminded her of how she must've looked the day she had lost Joseph. Devastated and inconsolable where nothing anyone said or did could make it better.

She didn't understand the change in his bearing. Tommy had only wanted milk. Maybe he didn't understand children. No man would be upset because a three-year-old cried. It had to be something else, but he didn't know what.

James scooted around her to his own little nook and settled into the seat, a small piece of bread in his hand. He hadn't been eating much, and she worried he was leaving most of it for her and the children. That was generous of him, but he needed food, as much as they did.

She yawned. She hadn't slept well the night before, but it was another night in a long line of nights where nightmares and uncertainty about her future interrupted her rest. It had taken some time before her eyes had grown so gritty, she'd fallen into a fitful sleep, waking every few hours to feed the baby. She didn't feel rested and the next couple of months would be difficult once she was far from Charles's reach. She wouldn't have anyone to help her, but she told herself she'd survive once she was safe from his clutches.

Early in the morning, long before the sun rose and when the snow swirled around the train cars, so blinding she feared they'd find themselves buried underneath the onslaught, she walked up and down the aisle, rocking her baby gently in her arms. Every step was painful, cramping in her belly, but the pain was welcome as it was a reminder she had made it this far.

Stopping in front of the seats where James had laid to rest, she stared at the man who had become her hero, her savior. A very handsome man, he stood well over a foot taller than her petite frame. His hair begged to be touched. It curled at the nape of his neck and she itched to run her hands through it. It looked so soft. She didn't think it was right that a man should have hair that looked so good. He had strong rugged features, but there was a gentleness in his dark brown eyes that tugged at her heart.

She still loved her husband, but something about James warmed her from the inside and made her feel safe. If this had been a different time, a different place, she might have pursued him, but she had two children to think of. Chasing a man who'd been forced to deliver her baby might not be the best idea. No longer an idealistic young woman with stars in her eyes, she was a thirty-two-year-old woman with two young children to care for and a brother-in-law who would ruin her if given the chance. She couldn't afford to explore a future with this man. Her focus had to be on escaping the clutches of her brother-in-law as fast as she could.

She had never expected the strange turn of events over the past few days. She had hidden in the depot, waiting until the last moment to jump on the train in the off-chance Charles had somehow traced her movements. After leaving Smelter, she had gone from town to town, taking random train routes to get far from him. A frightening reminder of what she had been through when she had left the orphanage after her brother had died in her arms. She had believed once she had married Joseph, she would finally be safe from all the things that had befallen her in the years before, but she had been mistaken. Tragedy seemed to follow her like a rat after scraps on a dirty wooden floor.

James, being on the train to Helena, had been fortuitous indeed, for if he hadn't been there, then the night could have had a far different outcome. Although he had been there for her, she couldn't expect him to take on her problems with her brother-in-law as well as the responsibility she brought with her.

Disappointment spread through her and it surprised her. She didn't know him well and didn't know his true nature, but deep in her heart where her treasured hopes rested, she had no doubt he'd be gentle with her if given the chance.

Chapter 6

Restlessness throbbed inside James. He had sat on the floor and played with Tommy, entertaining the little boy, but when he had taken his nap, James had paced from one end of the car to the other. He was trying to pass the time, but instead it crawled by almost as bad as it had been every day for the last six years.

Not being able to leave the train car was eerily similar to the prison he had left behind. He had been there for far too long and thought he had escaped imprisonment when he stepped out from behind the prison walls. The only thing keeping him from jumping headfirst into the deep snow and crawling away on his hands and knees was seeing Rose. She was a boon to his battered soul, but any relationship with her was so far out of reach, he might as well be behind bars again.

He stopped at the frosty metal door and pushed it open, looking outside as though he could will the train onto the tracks. The train was going nowhere until help arrived. They didn't have the men or equipment to do what needed to be done.

His nerves were going to get the best of him, and he feared his anxiousness was going to rear its ugly head and he'd likely scare Rose something fierce. He hadn't been around civilized folks in some time. He might have become hard and heartless to those with sensitive hearts, so he had to be careful with his words and his actions.

Suddenly needing to get out of the suffocating and stifling hot passenger car, he grabbed his thin coat, shrugged into it, and told Rose he'd be back soon. Not giving her a chance to respond, he stepped outside and closed the door tight behind him. The crisp, icy air stung his warm cheeks, but at the same time soothed his wounded spirit. He took in a healthy breath to calm his racing heart.

Frost covered the trees and snow blanketed every bit of ground foliage as far as he could see. A dark heavy cloud surrounded and blanketed the mountains, their peaks barely visible. As pleasing as it was, it could be days before they were rescued.

He trudged through the thick snow to the engine to see how the conductor and engineer had fared the night. He pushed slowly through the snowdrifts, each step difficult as he sunk through the snow as high as his knees. With the thick accumulation, it took him longer than the night before and longer than he would have expected. Finally, reaching his destination, he climbed up the metal steps and into the cab. The two men were troubled, concern over their plight written on their faces.

James's blood grew cold. There was a bigger

problem than the train derailing. He looked at them and instead of extending any pleasantries, he asked, "What's wrong?"

The conductor tried to smile. "Not a thing, sir. You should go back to the passenger car. Nothing you can do up here."

"Gentleman, I don't mean to be rude, but I don't believe you. Might as well spill what's on your minds."

The conductor looked at the engineer as if to ask, *should I tell him*? The engineer shrugged.

The conductor sighed. "The snow's deep. It's gonna take time for help to get here. Not sure we have enough coal or food to last us for the long haul."

They shared the same fears. "I figured as much. We'll conserve what we can." He shoved his hands into his coat pockets to warm them. "We can do a few things. Perhaps we should all stay in the passenger car to conserve coal. I'll give my food rations to Rose and the children. I can live without for a few days."

"I can set a few rabbit snares. We might

catch one or two," the engineer said, trying to get into the spirit of positivity instead of thinking about what was likely going to be a very dangerous situation if help didn't arrive soon.

The conductor looked side-eyed at the engineer.

The engineer chuckled. "Don't need to look at me like that. I didn't grow up on a train, ya know?"

The conductor laughed. "I didn't expect to see you out snaring rabbits."

"There might be a thing or two you don't know about me," the engineer said. "I don't share all my secrets."

"I guess not," the conductor said. "Well, let's grab our things and go to the passenger car. It's bound to be more comfortable sleeping there instead of the hard floor in here."

Within a few minutes, they had put out the fire in the engine, grabbed their few belongings and the blankets they too had grabbed the night before, the knapsack of food, and followed James. They might not have much, but between them, they'd ride out the time until help arrived or die trying.

* * *

They spent the next few days sleeping, eating, and helping Rose with the children. They kept each other entertained with songs, stories, and simple games. The engineer had even pulled out a pack of playing cards and the men played a hand or two of poker.

They used pieces of coal as their currency and laughed and teased one another, even convincing Rose to play a hand or two. Grateful for their help, Rose discovered the true meaning of Christmas with the selfless acts of the three men, but deep inside, her worry intensified. Every day she didn't run gave Charles a greater chance of finding her.

Late Thursday afternoon, they heard the sounds they had been waiting for, horses and men coming to their rescue. Nerves were strung thin with anxiety over the dwindling food and their ultimate safety, and from the relaxed shoulders and wider grins, the men were grateful it was coming to an end.

The men stepped outside to greet their rescuers, while Rose readied the children. It was imperative they were on the next train. She should have healed enough to continue. It wouldn't be easy, but at least she could put more distance between her and Charles.

As she buttoned up Tommy's coat, the door to the car opened and James walked in, his face grim.

"Is everything all right?" she asked.

"It seems we have a situation." He avoided looking at her and instead focused on the window behind her.

"And what's that?" she asked as she straightened her thick coat.

"There's someone here who's…" He stopped, as if unsure how to continue.

Looking at him in confusion, she waited for him to find the right words.

When he didn't speak, she said, "What is it? What's wrong?"

"He's claiming you ran off with his son."

Dread circled her spine and curled around her like a thick vice, squeezing, squeezing until she was left with little hope. Charles had found her. It couldn't be.

"That's ridiculous. My husband passed away."

"He's brought the Marshal with him and is insisting you turn Tommy over to him at once. He's claimin' you're not in your right mind and Tommy's in danger of being in your care."

She dropped into the seat next to Tommy. She shook and struggled to hold on to her composure. *How had he found me so quickly?* She thought she had covered her tracks. Rose didn't know what was she going to do. She wouldn't let him have her son and once he found out about her baby girl… Well, the thought was too difficult to complete.

James squatted in front of her. "Who is this man? Let me help."

She wanted to trust him but wasn't sure if she should. There was no way he could possibly help her. Her choices were limited. Either trust James or take the chance Charles would take her children. He would do it, too, of that she had no doubt. Charles would force her to marry him if she wanted to keep her children, unless she could find another way.

She decided to take a chance. With her voice cracking under the strain, chills traveling up and down her spine, and her eyes brimming with tears she told him who Charles was and what he wanted from her.

Chapter 7

As James listened to Rose and what had occurred over the last few months, he was stunned into silence. Her brother-in-law was a vicious, vindictive man who only wanted one thing, but threatening to take her children was unconscionable and pure evil. James *wanted* to protect her.

Rose sat terrified in front of him, unrestrained panic causing her chest to heave. She trembled and she shifted her eyes between him and her children. He wanted to pull her into his arms and comfort her, let her know everything would be all right. *But how can I?* He had no rights when it came to this woman and her children.

Taking it slow, he cupped her cheek. She lifted her long eyelashes as she searched his face, as though hoping he'd solve all her problems. And he would, he decided, if she'd let him. If there was one thing he couldn't abide was a man taking advantage of those less fortunate than themselves. He might not have done much right in his life, but this was one thing he could do, if she was willing. "I want to help. If you'll let me."

Hope sprang into her eyes but disappeared as quickly. "I'm not sure how you can. Charles has the Marshal on his side. If I don't marry him, he'll take my children."

"I don't think he has as much power as he'd like to believe."

"I don't understand." Questions burned in her eyes. "He's friends with the judge in Smelter and they'll believe anything he'll tell them."

"He might've convinced those in Smelter, but we're not in Smelter. The Marshal appears to be reasonable and doesn't seem to be in too much of a hurry to believe him." He paused and shifted to stand. His idea was ludicrous, and he'd be insane to suggest it, but he had nothing to lose and perhaps everything to gain. "He can't make you marry him or take your children if you're married to someone else."

Rose stared at him, trying to understand, but he stood silent, waiting until the light came on in her eyes.

When she didn't immediately protest or run screaming out of the train car, he continued, "I realize this is unexpected and we don't know one another, but I have a proposition for you."

"What are you proposing?"

James took a deep breath. It was now or never. She would either agree or slap him upside the head. He wasn't sure which, but he'd never know unless he asked. "I don't like what he's doing to you. You need a husband so he can't take your children."

Her long, slim fingers fidgeted with her black skirt, the buttons of her blue blouse, and then down to her skirt. She was silent, her eyes downcast.

With a rush of breath, he said, "I propose a marriage in name only. I won't ask anything of you that you ain't willing to give. I'd like to give you a home where you'll feel safe. You can have as much or as little as you want from me, and I'll never force myself on you." She raised her head in shock. "I'm getting older, and I'm afraid I'll never have any children of my own. Over the last few days, I've come to care for your children and the birth of your little girl was something I'll never forget."

She visibly gulped, and darted her tongue out to lick her plump lips.

Desire rushed through his limbs. She likely had no idea what she was doing, but he wanted to kiss her and to make her his.

He shoved his thoughts into the dark recesses of his mind. This was not the time or the place. He hadn't proposed a traditional marriage and whatever dreams he had were still on hold. This was strictly a way to protect her from the vicious man she was running from.

"I realize this isn't what you wanted or planned, but I'm afraid the Marshal's hands are tied. Charles says you've no way to care for your children. Since Tommy's his nephew, he says the judge agreed Tommy is to go with him. I think I can stop the Marshal. I can tell him you've agreed to become my wife, and we're on our way to my sister's house for the wedding. It might be enough to sway him, as my brother-in-law has a lot of influence and is well known in Helena."

As he looked at her, he couldn't begin to read her thoughts. He worried he had either pressed her too far or not hard enough. This was the only way he could think of to save her from the erratic and delusional man pacing outside the train. It had been all he could do to convince the Marshal to keep Charles outside when he came inside to talk to Rose. They didn't have much time. She had to decide and decide soon.

* * *

Rose was shocked and confused by James's proposal. She didn't understand why would he suggest such an arrangement. He didn't know her. They had only met a few days before. He said it was because he wanted to protect her, but she thought there might have been something more. Everything he had done since they met had been nothing but altruistic, so she didn't want to believe he had ulterior motives. If there was one thing she had learned, however, it was she couldn't trust anyone.

James appeared earnest and hopeful. She didn't want to give him unrealistic expectations, but his suggestion could get her out of the plight she found herself in. He had given her a choice, but she had to decide if it was the one she wanted to take. If she agreed, she had to clarify that it was just for his name, nothing more. She wasn't ready or prepared for a husband in the true sense of the word. She was still in mourning over losing Joseph so suddenly and violently.

She had nowhere to go, not with giving birth days before and a three-year-old son to care for as well. With no means to run, no horse or carriage and no family to protect her, she could either give in to Charles's demands, accept James's offer, or let the Marshal decide who was telling the truth.

She remembered how James delivered her baby, his kindness and patience with Tommy, and his general concern for her wellbeing. It wasn't much to build a relationship on, but it had to be better than a lifetime with Charles. Maybe in a few months when the pain of losing Joseph wasn't so sharp, she could explore what tender bond she and James had developed. But did he feel the same way toward her, or was he just doing a chivalrous deed?

"Rose, before you answer, consider this."

He paced and picked up her fussy baby girl, rocking her as though she belonged to him. A longing to be protected and loved pierced through her so deep, her fluttering heart exploded with the possibilities.

"If things don't work between us or it at any time you feel we should end this, you'll be taken care of. I'd still like to be involved in your children's lives, but I don't want you to feel as though you don't have options. Think of this as a temporary means to get out of your brother-in-law's clutches. If we decide we want to stay married, we will. If we don't, then we'll find an amicable solution that'll benefit you and the children."

She was surprised, but also not surprised, at his thoughtfulness. Most men wouldn't offer such a solution, as it had nothing in it for them. Could he really be that selfless?

"What if you find someone you want to marry? I don't want to stand in the way of your happiness."

An expression she couldn't read crossed his face before it disappeared. "I don't think that'll be an issue. I know you've no reason to trust me, but I hope I can offer a solution you didn't have before."

What do I have to lose? This was more

palatable than marrying Charles or losing her children, so giving caution to the wind, she murmured, "Yes. Yes, I'll marry you."

He smiled and joy lit up his eyes. He touched her shoulder but pulled away as though he realized they were nothing more than two passengers thrown together in a difficult and tenuous situation. "Everything'll work out, I'm sure of it. I'll go outside and inform the Marshal of our plans. He may want to speak with you." The baby squeaked. He murmured something in her little girl's ear, quieting her almost immediately. "I don't want you to lie, but he needs to believe we were planning on getting married, so be prepared."

He was clear. Her life and her children's lives depended on this. She had to be convincing.

James handed the baby to Rose and went outside. The door stood open, and a bitter cold breeze blew in, an ominous foreshadowing of the dangers a few feet away. Rose tried to calm her racing heart. She couldn't appear petrified. Instead, she had to be a woman in love with a man she had just met, as the alternative was too horrifying to imagine.

A few minutes later, yelling and cursing could be heard from outside the passenger car. Charles's furious voice rose as he tried to convince the Marshal her children were his.

A moment later, Charles barreled inside. Pushing Tommy behind her and placing the baby next to him on the seat, she stood her ground, protecting them from the evil man coming toward her.

His jaw was tight. He flared his nostrils like a bull ready to attack and balled his hands into fists. He stormed toward her, his coat flapping behind him, and the buttons on his stained brown strained against his large belly. Disheveled, he looked as though he had thrown on the first shirt he could find in his determination to find her.

She didn't see it coming. He slapped her across the face, the force swiveling her head to the side. She was certain if it hadn't been attached, it would have flown across the room. It took every bit of strength she had not to fall to the ground from the power behind his anger.

An animalistic roar bounced off the walls of the passenger car. James grabbed Charles by the neck and threw him against the outside wall, Charles's bulky body slamming into it. While James had appeared gaunt, he was remarkably strong if he had moved Charles with such speed and force.

Tommy cried out in fright and gripped Rose by the legs, grasping and pulling his tiny arms around her. Her face hurt, and she'd likely bitten her cheek as the taste of blood filled her mouth, but she would protect her children, no matter the cost. Charles would have to kill her before she would let him get his hands on them.

"Don't go near her," James yelled in fury.

Charles shoved at James, and he stumbled but didn't fall. Charles's hand curled into a fist. He reared back, but before he could hit James, the Marshal stopped him.

"Enough!" He blocked Charles's fist as he

stepped between the two men. "This isn't how we'll settle this, Mr. McGaven."

"But it's how I'll settle it." James tried to push around the Marshal.

The Marshal held them apart. His muscles bulging under the strain of trying to keep the two men from pummeling one another. "If I have to lock you both up, I will," he barked. "This ain't the time or the place."

Both men's chests heaved in anger, but the passenger car had filled with other men. Charles's crazed eyes looked around and forcibly relaxed. James caught her gaze and something in her eyes must have convinced him to stop as he retreated, holding his hands out in surrender. The Marshal had stopped them from engaging in an all-out brawl.

Rose scooped up her baby, placed her against her chest, and huddled on the seat with Tommy at her side. He had clambered onto the seat and wrapped his hands around her neck, whimpering in fear. She murmured into his ear, calming him as best she could while her face rang from the force of Charles's blow. Considering how frightened she was, she wasn't sure how much of a comfort she could be to her children, but she had to try. They came first. She'd tend to herself later.

Tensions rang high, but the Marshal moved Charles away from them and James strode to Rose, squatting in front of her.

"He hit you." He brushed his fingers against her tender cheek. She winced. A nasty bruise would soon develop, of that, she was sure. "Are you all right?" James asked, trying to convey with his eyes how precarious their situation was.

James's strength and resolve gave her the courage to stand up to Charles.

"Will you hold the baby?" She placed the baby in James's arms before he agreed.

He held the child with care, tucking her into the crook of his arm. Rose pulled Tommy onto her hip and didn't let go. Standing next to James, she faced the Marshal.

"Keep him away from me, please." She nodded toward Charles. "He's not my husband or the father of my children."

The Marshal narrowed his eyes, but they appeared kind. "I understand, ma'am, but he claims your children are at risk."

"At risk from who?" she said. "He hit me, and I'm the one that is a danger to them?" A trickle of blood from her lips dripped to her chin. She used a handkerchief to wipe it away. Her cheek smarted from pain, but she held onto her composure with a strength she didn't know she possessed.

"Yes, ma'am. I understand, but he says you've no family to help. He's insisting the boy is his nephew, and he's responsible for him. He's claiming the judge in Smelter granted him rights to take the children."

"That's preposterous, sir. I have someone to help me with my children and they are *not* at risk. James is my fiancé, and we're on our way to his sister's ranch to get married. Mr. McGaven has no claim on me or my children." Taking a risk Charles was lying, she said, "Does he have papers granting him any rights over my children?"

The Marshal turned to Charles and waited. Charles blustered for a moment and made excuses for why he had nothing with him. He argued he did in Smelter and could prove it. If the Marshal would give him the children, he would take them with him and prove his rights.

The Marshal pressed his lips together. Rose realized his position was perilous. The Marshal had no way of knowing if Charles was telling the truth. She regretted the Marshal had to make this decision, but she wasn't giving in without a fight.

James stepped forward. "If it helps, Marshal, my brother-in-law is Benjamin Seymour of Thundering Mountain Ranch. The ranch is outside of Helena. We can send a wire to the Marshal in Helena so you can verify who I am."

The Marshal swallowed, grabbed his shirt collar, and pulled it away from his throat as if he was choking. The mention of Mr. Seymour caused him to pause. She wondered if that would be enough to convince him to let her be.

The Marshal stuck a thumb in his vest pocket and strode back and forth, reaching one hand toward his thick mustache. He smoothed the edges before seeming to decide. He halted, looked at James and then at Charles. "Mr. McGaven, I'm afraid if you don't have any paperwork from the judge, you don't have any legal standing to take these children."

"That's ridiculous," Charles blustered, displeasure reddening his face. "I ain't gonna let 'er leave. She stole those children, and I'm aiming to take 'em with me. The judge'll have your head if you don't do as I say."

James stiffened behind her, but the Marshal stood his ground. "Unless you can provide proof, she and her children are free to go."

Anger rolled off Charles in waves, and Rose knew this wouldn't be the last time she would see or hear from him. She was deathly afraid of what that could mean. He wanted her and would do anything in his power to get her under his control.

He zoomed his gaze on her, and he sneered with lustful contempt. "This isn't over, Rose. Those children'll come home with me. Maybe not today, but they will. I'll be back with orders from the judge, and there's nothing you can do to stop me. We all know you weren't planning on marryin' that man, and I'll prove it." He stormed out of the passenger car, the door slamming behind him, a jarring reminder of what she had narrowly escaped.

She sagged in relief, leaning against James's sturdy form. He rested his hand against her waist, strong behind her, keeping her from collapsing. She had been granted a temporary reprieve, but it wouldn't last. Charles would return.

The Marshal said, "Ma'am, sorry for the trouble, but he insisted he come along when we got word the train hadn't made it to the next train station. I didn't know what his intentions were until we arrived, and he discovered you were on the train." He pinched the bridge of his nose and then removed his hat. "I don't know if he's telling the truth, but it might be wise to get yourself a lawyer as soon as possible." The Marshal fingered his hat as if trying to decide what to say next. "I'm not one to question what goes on between a man and a woman, but something tells me this marriage is a ruse to protect your children. I highly suggest you make sure it isn't before he returns."

"Thank you, Marshal," James said as he stepped forward to shake his hand. "I appreciate you going out on a limb here for my fiancé. We'll be at my brother-in-law's ranch if Mr. McGaven comes with his proof. By that time, we'll be married and will have secured a lawyer."

Rose knew the Marshal doubted them, but he seemed to be a kind man who recognized Charles was not who he claimed to be. Perhaps he realized if he didn't give her a chance, he'd make a bigger mistake.

Rose touched the Marshal's arm. "Thank you."

The Marshal nodded and tipped his hat. "Well, let's get you folks out of here. I'm sure your family is worried sick."

As the door closed behind him, Rose raised her eyes to James. "I can't lose my children," she said. "He'll take them from me if he can find a way. What am I going to do?"

James placed his hand on her shoulder and squeezed gently, his touch comforting. "I'll do anything and everything to protect you and your children. If it's the last thing I do, you'll be kept safe from him for the rest of your life."

She wasn't sure she believed him, but he was all she had. Her trust had to go somewhere, as tenuous as it might be. Grabbing their meager belongings, James helped her, Tommy, and the baby out of the train and onto the waiting horses that would take them to the nearest town.

Charles sat on his horse, glaring at them menacingly, but James stayed by her side the whole way, his presence a comfort in a tumultuous situation. Holding onto the belief James would keep his promise that their marriage would be in name only, Rose hoped she wasn't making a mistake.

She prayed they could fight Charles and keep him at bay or else she might be in for something unexpected and truly horrifying.

Chapter 8

The next twenty-four hours were a flurry of activity. They made it to the nearest town, consisting of a train station, a bank, a general store, a two-story boarding house, a few small houses with worn picket fences, and a weather-beaten, once white church on one end of the road standing across from its rival, the obligatory saloon. There was more action in and around the saloon than there was at the church where a few members of the flock stood, singing enthusiastically but not loudly enough to drown out the piano music and laughter billowing from inside the saloon.

The railroad provided them with rooms for the night and with tickets the next morning to Helena. Charles disappeared once they arrived in the small town. James wasn't sure they had seen the last of him, but for now his concern had to be in getting Rose and the children to Thundering Mountain Ranch where they'd be far from his clutches.

James sent a telegram ahead of their arrival to let Elizabeth and Ben know he was fine, but there were complications. He didn't give details and asked if Ben could meet them at the train station. Once there, he'd explain the strange predicament he found himself in, but one that had the potential for a brighter future, at least for himself, and he hoped for Rose. He didn't quite believe he had found a readymade family mere days after he was released from the worst six years of his life, but he was determined to make it work. He had a chance to do something positive, and he was going to make the best of it.

They arrived in Helena weary as hungry

prairie dogs and travel-worn as battered boots put out to pasture. Tommy and the baby were fussy and beyond tired. Stepping off the train, James held Tommy with one arm and Rose's bags in the other. His knapsack was draped across his shoulder. It wasn't much, but luckily, she hadn't noticed. He wasn't ready to explain his past yet. That would be a discussion they could have later, after some rest and much needed food.

Peering around the platform, James spotted Ben, but Ben didn't appear to recognize him. Dropping their bags, he waved and hollered Ben's name. The throngs of people were thick, but at last, Ben smiled and maneuvered through the sizable crowd. Holding out his hand, Ben said, "James, I'm so glad to see you. We've been worried."

James shook Ben's hand and grimaced. "Yes, it's been a rough few days. My tardiness was a little out of my control."

"Understandable. Elizabeth was certainly

relieved when we received your telegram." Ben glanced at Rose and the children, questions in his eyes, but was smart enough to realize that now was likely not the time to ask for too many details. "Who do you have with you?"

"Ben, this is Rose, her son Tommy, and her new baby girl."

"Ma'am," Ben removed his hat and bowed his head slightly. "It's a pleasure."

"Thank you, sir." Turning to James, Rose asked, "Is there someplace we might sit? I'm not feeling too well."

"Ben?"

"Yes, follow me." Ben picked up their bags and went to the station house.

James placed his hand on Rose's waist. She took a few hesitant steps, swayed, and then started to fall. James immediately placed Tommy on the wooden floor, caught her around the waist, and grabbed the baby before Rose dropped her. He stumbled but kept her and the baby from falling.

"Momma!" Tommy screamed and then placed his thumb in his mouth while he cried big tears.

Ben hadn't taken but a few steps when he turned. He immediately clutched the baby so James could help Rose.

James swept Rose into his arms, looked at Tommy and said, "It's all right, son, your momma is only tired. Why don't you go with Ben and your sister, and I'll be right behind you."

Rose looked at Tommy, held out her fingers as if she could comfort him from a distance. "Listen to James, sweetheart," Rose said. "I'm sleepy and James here is helping me. Please go with Ben. We will be right behind you."

Tommy stared at Ben and then at them before following Ben reluctantly, looking over his shoulder to make sure James followed.

When Tommy turned away, Rose pushed at James's shoulders. "You can put me down. I just lost my balance."

"Nonsense," he said. "You're exhausted. Let

me carry you inside, where we'll get you a bite to eat and a cool drink." She stared at him with her big green eyes before she relaxed. She put her head on his chest and tucked her hands snugly against him.

She fit perfectly in his arms and weighed next to nothing. Clearly not eating well, the stress was taking its toll on her slight frame. He wanted nothing more than to shield her from harm and prayed he'd have the opportunity to do that. Unfortunately, he would have to rely solely on his brother-in-law and had no one to blame but himself.

Walking inside the station, he went to the bench where Ben waited with the children. Carefully placing Rose on the wooden bench, she reached for the baby.

She rubbed at her eyes. "I don't know what's wrong with me. I didn't mean to stumble. I think I'm a bit weak from everything that's happened. Thank you for keeping an eye on them."

Ben smiled. "My pleasure, ma'am. Let me

see if I can find you something to nibble on. James?"

"Rose, will you be all right while I go with Ben?"

She pulled Tommy close and brushed strands of hair from his cheek. "We'll be fine, won't we, darling?" A soft smile passed over her lips.

Tommy smiled around his thumb that was permanently stuck and nodded enthusiastically.

Knowing they would be fine for at least a few minutes, James followed Ben to the cafe.

"What's going on?" Ben asked once they were out of ear shot of Rose and the children.

James removed his hat and scratched at an itch before slapping it on. "I guess I should explain."

"Yes, please do. I didn't expect you to arrive with a woman and two children." Ben's piercing and questioning eyes made James squirm.

James owed a lot to this man who had stepped in when his sister Elizabeth needed someone the most and had kept her safe from harm when he had been unable to do so.

"Didn't expect it myself," James said. "It's a long story, but suffice it to say, we need to get married as soon as possible."

"What?" Shocked, Ben stopped and grabbed his arm. "Why do you need to get married? Are you the father?"

He smirked at the ridiculous notion. "No, I couldn't be. You know where I've been for the last six years."

"I do, but who is she?"

"She was on the train with me. When it derailed, she went into labor, and I helped deliver her baby."

"You didn't?" Ben shook his head in disbelief.

"I did. Shocked even myself. When the rescuers arrived, she found herself in a pickle. I offered to help, but it'll be a marriage in name only." Although if he were truthful with himself, he wondered if he treated her with respect, perhaps after some time she would trust him enough to explore a relationship that was more than what they had first agreed upon. "I have little to offer except my name. And frankly, I'm not sure that's worth much."

"Where's the father of her children?" Ben crinkled his forehead.

"She's a widow and her husband died a few months ago. Her brother-in-law is threatening to take her children and is tryin' to force matrimony on her. We thought if we got married, he'd have a difficult time convincing a judge he has any rights to 'em."

Ben rubbed his temples. "Does she know about your past?"

"No." James shook his head and sighed. "Not exactly."

"Are you going to tell her? I think you need to." Ben pressed his lips together with obvious disapproval.

"I realize that, but she doesn't need more stress. She just gave birth to a baby and is petrified she's gonna lose her children. I can protect her from him, especially with your help. I know I have no right to ask and will be imposing on your hospitality, but she recently lost her husband. I can't let her lose them, too."

Ben stared at him hard, assessing James. It had been six years since they'd seen one another and they hadn't been on good terms, considering the secrets James had kept from Ben and his subsequent imprisonment.

Ben sighed. "What's your stake in this?"

"Nothin' really. I've made a mess of my life. Perhaps this'll make amends for some of what I've done."

Ben said nothing more. James was grateful Ben didn't question him further, as he didn't know what else to say. What he was doing made little sense. He put himself in the middle of a situation that wasn't any of his concern, but he couldn't seem to stop himself and didn't want to. He was in the middle of the mess, and he didn't want to be anywhere else.

✳ ✳ ✳

Hours later, Ben drew on the reins, the horse's hooves slowing as they came in view of the main ranch house. Rose groaned softly. Her neck was cramped from leaning against the hard planks of the wagon. Tommy was draped across her numb legs, and the weight of the baby made her arms ache. James had sat next to Ben on the wagon's bench, and they talked in low voices on the trip to the ranch.

Ben had apologized profusely about the uncomfortable wagon, as he hadn't been aware there would've been anyone other than James. He had glared at James when he said that, and she had hidden a grin at the look of consternation on James's face. They had a history, but she wasn't sure what it involved, and it certainly wasn't her place to ask.

She assured Ben it wasn't a problem. She told him that she and the children would be perfectly comfortable in the bed with the thick woolen blankets he had stored under the seat. Ben explained he and Elizabeth had gotten caught in a blizzard once. Since then, he stowed blankets for any weather emergencies.

What she hadn't anticipated was how long or how bumpy the ride would be. She ached something fierce as the wheels hit rut after rut on the snow-covered route. She was desperate to close her eyes and not wake for hours, but with a newborn, that wasn't possible.

The sun had dropped behind the mountains by the time they reached the ranch. Pinks, oranges, and purples streaked the dark midnight blue sky. Daylight was short this time of the year, but they had made it before the sun fully set. Her head bobbed with fatigue, and she slept in small bits, waking only when the baby or Tommy stirred.

Before leaving Helena, they stopped at the courthouse where Rose was married once again, but this time to a perfect stranger. Her eyes were gritty, and she could've stood a good washing, but she found an inner strength and stood proudly before the judge when he pronounced them man and wife. Somehow, marrying James was the right thing to do. He stood tall and dedicated next to her, not crowding her but supporting her in a silent, but sensitive manner.

Right before the ceremony, Rose had pulled Ben to the side, the baby nestled in her arms. "Mr. Seymour."

"Please call me, Ben," he said. "We're soon to be brother and sister."

"I realize this is sudden and awkward, but I'm eternally grateful for what James is doing to help me and my children. I… I can't lose them." Her chest hurt from her thumping heart. "I'll do my best to make him a good wife."

Ben smiled at her. His solemn dark brown eyes were kind. He would be a good brother-in-law, of that, she had no doubt. With any luck she had stumbled into a warm and giving family.

"You don't have to explain. He told me some of what you're facing." He brushed away a strand of the baby's light reddish hair. "We'll do everything in our power to protect you. I do have some influence. If your brother-in-law tries to get you into court, I believe we can fight him."

Tears of gratitude pooled in her eyes. She placed her hand on his forearm and squeezed before saying a very quiet but grateful thank you.

Ben smiled and patted her hand. The door to the judge's chambers opened, and she swiped at the unshed tears. She gave him one last tentative smile before joining James.

That was hours ago and they had finally arrived at Ben's ranch. The massive front doors opened, and a tall, slim woman with a dark brown braid across her shoulder stepped outside, the lamplight spilling out behind her. She ran down the steps, a thick grey woolen shawl held tight and a wide smile on her face. She stopped when she realized Ben and James were not alone. Her gaze scanned the weary group.

James moved Tommy off Rose's legs before grasping her around the waist, taking care not to knock the baby from her arms, and lifting her with ease to the ground. He waited until she was steady before picking up the sleeping Tommy. He held him close, the blanket securely wrapped around him.

With his hand against the small of her back, James led her to the woman who had to be his sister and Ben's wife, Elizabeth. Elizabeth looked between them with a confused but welcoming smile. James had told Rose a bit about his sister while they had traveled on the train to Helena. He insisted Elizabeth would welcome them, but Rose was still hesitant. Elizabeth wouldn't have been expecting the extra mouths to feed, and Rose prayed they wouldn't be an imposition or a burden on the family.

James's hand dropped, his warmth disappearing as he reached for Elizabeth and gave her a quick hug.

"I'm so glad to see you. We've been worried. You look healthy," she said.

"You're not a good liar, Elizabeth," he said, chuckling. "I feel bad that I worried you, but as you can see, we've arrived safely. Let me introduce you to…"

Rose watched as James struggled with what to say to his sister.

Helping him, she said, "I'm Rose." It gave

him a moment to gain his composure. She hoped this wasn't a sign of him regretting his decision.

Ben interrupted the awkwardness. He put his arm around Elizabeth's waist and pulled her close. "We can explain later," Ben said. "Let's get them inside where it's warm. They've had quite the trip and are exhausted."

"Of course. I should've realized. Come inside." She gathered her skirts and led the tired group into the sprawling ranch house.

They traveled down a long hall to a large room, where a warm fire blazed. Plush armchairs and sofas were scattered around the room, making it quite homey. Thick brown rugs covered the wooden floors, and it was clear the room was lived in and made for comfort. James placed Tommy on a sofa near the fire and tucked the blanket around him. With all the excitement, he was plum exhausted.

Rose tried to remove her coat, but her arms were limp and she struggled. Seeing her discomfort, James took the baby and helped her before leading her to a chair next to Tommy.

Elizabeth grabbed a quilt and handed it to her. "Are you hungry? There's hot stew and fresh bread."

"That'd be most welcome, thank you." She wasn't sure she'd be able to eat for fear of falling asleep at the dining table. She looked at James. "But if I could, would it be terribly rude of me if I slept first? I'm afraid I'm a bit tired. Perhaps I could dine in a few hours?"

He grimaced. "Yes, I should've realized."

"You wouldn't have known. I just need to lie down for a few minutes and then I should be all right."

James looked at his sister with a question in his eyes.

Elizabeth tilted her head. "Let me show her to…" She shifted her eyes to Ben.

"The guest room at the end of the hall. We can work out the details for everyone else later," Ben said.

Elizabeth held out her hand. "If you'll come with me, Rose, I'll show you to your room."

Rose stood, took two steps forward, and started once again to collapse. She was a blundering mess and was close to tears. James grasped her waist, the baby held in his other arm. Elizabeth gasped and made quick work of taking the baby so he could steady her. She was mortified at her inability to even take a few steps.

"I'm so sorry," she murmured.

Elizabeth gazed at her with concern. "Should we send for a doctor?"

"No," Rose said at the same time James said, "Yes."

"Please don't trouble yourselves on my account," Rose insisted.

Ignoring her, James said, "She gave birth a few days ago and I'm not a doctor. I failed to consider if she might need one. I'd be grateful if there's one close."

"Please don't go to the trouble. I'm just a little tired," Rose said.

"Maybe, but let's have the doc look you over."

She sighed but agreed. She didn't have the energy to argue.

"Elizabeth, if you wouldn't mind," James said.

"Whatever she needs. Let's get her to her room. Follow me."

Elizabeth led them to a guest room on the main floor. James placed her on the bed, careful with his movements, as though she were an invalid. Her eyes were heavy, and she struggled to stay awake, but she had done more than she should've over the last few days. Finally, her eyes closed and blackness pulled her away.

Chapter 9

James was barely holding it together. He had given her his name, but he wasn't sure that was enough. He'd blundered by not calling for a doctor immediately. Then compounded that by not telling his own sister he was married to her. He was sure Ben would tell Elizabeth what he knew but felt sure he had embarrassed Rose with his missteps.

The last few days had been strenuous and difficult. He wasn't a doctor. He was a criminal, a no-account who could have endangered his wife during the birth.

His wife.

How strange and right that sounded.

Once he had placed her on the bed, Rose's eyes fluttered closed, and she fell asleep immediately. He put another log on the fire and groaned with fatigue. The last few days had been exciting, terrifying, exhilarating, and the possibilities as well as the dangers whirled through his mind. He didn't know if he was strong enough to protect her from her brother-in-law. *Am I the man she deserves?*

He had made several mistakes in his life, and he wanted to start anew. Sighing, he observed her in her slumber. Her hair had fallen from its pins and lay in a mass of tangled curls. He picked up a strand of her hair. It was silky like reddish orange corn husks as it fell through his fingers.

He couldn't believe how lucky he had become. Two children with a woman as beautiful as any he had ever met and as kind and loving as his sister, Elizabeth. He yearned to know more of her, but feared what she would think once she got to know him. He wasn't sure he would be worthy of her, but he could be making more of this than he should. He might be foolish to even assume she would want to stay married to him. He had suggested a marriage in name only and that might be the only thing she'd ever want from him. He needed to remember that.

He stood, hesitating on what to do now and in the future, when she fluttered her eyes open. She startled and gasped, shrinking away. James stepped away, holding his hands up in surrender, not wanting to scare her further. She blinked a few times, looking confused and cautious.

"I didn't mean to frighten you," he whispered. His voice was dry and husky.

"You didn't." She pushed strands of hair from her face. "I shouldn't have fallen asleep." She struggled to sit. "Let me wash and try to feed the baby. I'm sure she's hungry.

"Don't you worry," James said. "I've no doubt Elizabeth has everything in hand."

She swung her legs over the side of the bed.

"Please, you're exhausted and need sleep," James said.

"I'm a little tired, that's all."

"I think it's more than that. You just had a baby. I'm not a doctor, and I'm not altogether sure I did everything a doctor would've done. I'd be more comfortable if he looked you over. Besides, Elizabeth will watch over the baby and Tommy's already down. Why don't you sleep?"

Her eyes drooped with fatigue. "I shouldn't."

"Yes, you should." His voice was stern. "You're safe, Rose. There are plenty of people here to help and trust me, they want to."

She sighed, but seemed to agree, albeit reluctantly.

"Do you need help with your… Your clothes?" His cheeks reddened and his heart hastened, even though his question was innocent enough.

"No." She avoided his gaze. "I can manage. Is my bag in here or would you mind fetching it for me?"

"No, it's likely still in the wagon outside, but

I'm sure we can find something." He opened the wardrobe drawers and found an old worn shirt that would hang to her knees.

"How about this? Would it suffice?"

"Yes." She held out her hand and their fingers touched, sending a surge of awareness through his skin.

"Is there anything else I can get for you?"

"No."

"All right, well, get some sleep." He stood awkward and silent, staring at her for a moment, needing to say or do something, but instead he headed for the door.

As he opened it, he heard her soft voice.

"James?"

"Yes." He looked over his shoulder and wrapped his hand around the bronze door handle.

"Thank you."

It was as though a whisper of wind fluttered across his skin, sending goosebumps down his spine. "You're welcome, Rose." He turned his lips into a smile before wishing her a goodnight.

James slowed his steps before he finally left and let the door click softly behind him.

*** * ***

The next morning, the doctor arrived, his hair standing on end, his coat flapping, and his thick black leather bag in his pudgy hand. He apologized profusely for not arriving sooner, but Ben told him they were grateful he could come when he did. James showed him to Rose's room and then stood outside pacing, one thought after another racing through his mind.

He had slept fitfully the night before, worrying over whether he had harmed Rose while delivering the baby. What if he had waited too long to get her the care she needed.

After what seemed like hours but wasn't near that long, the doctor emerged. He waved for James to follow and grabbed his coat hanging from a hook next to the front door before stepping outside.

Stopping in front of his black carriage, the

doctor cleared his throat and smiled encouragingly. "She's healing quite well from the birth." The doctor shrugged into his coat. "Don't you worry son, your wife'll heal soon enough."

"What about her milk? She's right worried about that," James said.

Rose had confided in him on the train ride to Helena. She was struggling to ensure the baby was getting enough and feared she wouldn't be able to care for her little one.

The doctor placed his hand on James's arm, his short stubby fingers thick and heavy. "She needs plenty of food and rest. I suspect her milk'll come in soon, likely within the next day or two. What she doesn't need is to worry. Be supportive and give her plenty to drink." He placed his bag on the floor of the carriage and opened a storage box. He searched through it for a moment, pulled out a brown glass bottle, and handed it to James. "If you're worried, you can give the baby some of the Horlick's Malted Milk. It'll be a good supplement for the baby until her milk comes in."

James looked at the small container and raised his eyebrows. "Is that all?" It didn't seem enough.

The doctor smiled. "Yes, that'll do plenty. The milk will help keep the baby satisfied for now."

"But what if it still doesn't come in?"

"It will. She's healthy and strong. If she's still concerned, tell her to have the baby try to feed. The baby won't get much more than first milk, but the sucking motions should help encourage it to come in. She truly doesn't need to worry. I have no doubt that in a few days, all will be well."

"Thanks, Doc."

The doctor tipped his hat and heaved his round body into his black carriage, the springs groaning under the weight. "If she needs anything, send word, but she'll likely be fine. I see no need to be concerned." He picked up the reins, and then as if something suddenly occurred to him, he said, "And I might also caution you against tending to your own… Well, your own male needs for at least a few weeks until she's healed properly. It's perfectly normal for her to be sore for a few weeks, so don't worry yourself on that account."

The doctor gave him a stern, yet steady look to assess whether James understood his well-meant advice as intended, but James was too taken aback by the suggestion of his *male needs* to utter a response. Apparently, James's dumbfounded speechlessness was satisfactory enough for the doctor as he flicked the reins and with a jerk, the horse pulled away. The carriage wheels carved a path through the snow that had fallen through the night.

After the doctor left, James breathed for the first time in hours. She'd at least recover physically. He just wasn't sure if she would heal from the trauma her brother-in-law had inflicted. She was scared and even though Ben offered them a haven, James wasn't positive Rose believed she was safe. He supposed there was always a chance Charles could get to the children, but he wouldn't let him, not without a fight.

His doubts crept in as he opened the wooden

doors, the warmth from the fireplaces competing with the cold air swirling through the valley. He shut the door behind him and leaned against it. He wanted her to trust him. His unconventional proposal was not how he had ever planned on wooing a woman, but she had accepted. He had to wonder though if she had accepted because she wanted to give them a chance, or he just a means to an end. In just a few days' time, he had grown very attached to her. He was right nervous that in the light of day, she would regret her decision.

Knocking on her door, he waited. *Would she welcome me or send me far away?*

"Come in."

Her soft and hesitant voice sent awareness along his spine. She had already nudged her way into his heart with no effort on her part.

He peered around the door, giving her a chance to send him away if she didn't want him there, and left the door open for propriety's sake. Although they were married, they weren't really married in the true sense of the word.

"Did the doctor give you a measure of comfort?" he asked, becoming self-conscious within moments of seeing her. A thick trickle of sweat gathered between his shoulder blades and under his arms.

She was snuggled under the thick blankets with her hair pulled over one shoulder. "Yes. He told me everything looks to be healing."

"How are you feeling?" he asked.

Her eyes twinkled. "I slept the whole night, which is surely awful because the baby was likely hungry."

"Elizabeth watched over her. She has a youngin only a few months old and has plenty to share, or at least that was what she told me."

"I feel bad putting her in that position."

"Don't you worry none. She will help in any way she can," James side.

"Still, now that I'm rested, I can take care of her." The twinkle in her eyes disappeared. "Where is she?"

"The baby?"

She nodded.

"She's in the nursery with the other children."

"I'd like to see her," she said.

"Of course." Shame reddened his face.

Rose moved the blankets and got out of bed, the worn shirt hanging right above her knees. She strode across the room and went behind the dressing screen. Chastising himself for where his thoughts were going, he had to remember she just had a baby and as the doctor had kindly reminded him, he needed to keep his thoughts at bay.

A few minutes later, she emerged, dressed in a brown skirt and white shirtwaist. "I'm ready."

Entering the second-floor nursery, they found her little girl asleep in a wooden cradle. Elizabeth's son, Jimmy, was nestled in a second one with the nanny in a chair next to them, reading a book. Smiling, she placed it on the table.

"Ma'am, your little one is such a sweetheart. She's been sleeping peacefully. Would you like a moment alone with her?" The nanny was an older woman with white gray hair and a warm and friendly smile.

"Yes, please."

"If you need me, I'll be right outside."

Rose picked up her baby from the cradle and the nanny left them alone. She sat in the rocking chair, the baby in her arms. She ran her fingers across the baby's pink cheek, to her tiny hands and feet as though examining her to make sure nothing had changed.

James leaned against the door frame. After a few minutes, he said, "Have you decided on a name?"

"You're reading my mind," she said, smiling. Being with her daughter had improved her mood significantly. "I was thinking she warranted one. Calling her my little girl or my baby doesn't seem to do her justice."

"Anything come to mind?"

"Maybe I should name her after my mother?"

"What was her name?" He folded his arms.

"Sarah."

"That's a beautiful name. I think it suits her." James stepped inside the room and knelt in front of them. He ran a finger along the baby's fist. "Do you like it?" He raised his eyes to look at her.

"I think I do," she said.

"Well, that settles it then. You've named our baby girl."

Startled, Rose's eyes flew to his.

"Did I say something wrong?"

"You called her *our* baby girl."

"I know it's much to consider, but I'd like to call her my own."

She bored her eyes into his with an intensity that he felt to his toes. *Have I overstepped? Moved too soon?* In his eagerness, he had assumed she would immediately agree. "Are you not comfortable with that?"

"No, it's not that." She hesitated, fluttering her eyelids as she gazed at Sarah. "Everything has moved so fast. I'm having a hard time grasping it all."

He put a hand on her knee. "It can wait. You

think on it for a bit." His voice was low and soft before he stood and moved away.

Sarah stirred. Rose bounced her for a few minutes and whispered in her ear until she settled into slumber. She checked her nappy and then placed her in the cradle before they left the room.

The nanny met them in the hall, hearing them.

"Everything all right, ma'am?" the nanny asked.

"Yes. Will you call for me if there are any problems?"

"Of course, but don't you worry none, she'll be taken care of." The nanny's eyes were kind and James knew the children would be well cared for as Elizabeth wouldn't put them in anyone's care with whom she didn't trust.

"Thank you," Rose murmured.

James led her down the hall.

"I don't know what I would've done without your help," she said.

He was uncomfortable with the praise as he hadn't done more than anyone else would have done in the same situation, but he was grateful he had been there because if he hadn't, he would've never met Rose and that made him the happiest he had ever been. "Are you hungry?"

"Famished," she said.

"Then let's get you something to fill your belly," he said with a wide grin.

Chapter 10

Hours later, the women and children gathered in the large room at the rear of the house. Tommy and Elizabeth's little girl, Vicky, made quick work of becoming friends and had played for hours. When it became clear the children were due for naps, Rose went to put both her children down when Tommy threw a tantrum.

He was ill-tempered and even the nanny was startled with his screams. Rose had been embarrassed but tried her best to calm him with the promise of a story. He had been excited about being a big brother, but now that Sarah was here, his frustration with Rose tending to the baby was obvious. He was fussy and angry, and it took everything in her to get him to take a nap. Once he had finally closed his eyes, she wandered down the stairs and through the halls, peering into the rooms. The ranch house was bigger than anywhere she had ever lived, but there was no movement. All was quiet, as though everyone had disappeared to the far reaches of the ranch.

Rose eventually found James relaxed in front of the fireplace in the parlor, focused on the flames, and unaware she had stepped inside. He appeared contemplative, his broad shoulders snug against the armchair, his chiseled jaw highlighted from the light of the fire. She hated to interrupt.

Turning to leave, James said, "Please don't go." He spun in the chair. His hair was mussed, and he had dark circles under his eyes.

"I hate to interrupt. You looked deep in thought, and I didn't want to bother you."

"You're not a bother. Please sit." He waved to the chair next to him. "It's warm near the fire."

Rose hesitated. She wasn't entirely comfortable in his presence. "If you're sure?"

"I am. It'd be nice to have you here," he said.

There was something in the glance he gave her that she blushed before sitting. She adjusted her skirt, smoothing the brown folds as though flattening the wrinkles was of the utmost importance. It was a way to avoid looking him in the eye.

"Are Tommy and Sarah down for their naps?" he asked.

She raised her eyes to look at him, but his gaze had drifted away, giving her a moment to collect herself. Clearly, he had noticed her fidgeting.

"Yes." Her voice cracked, and she coughed. "Tommy fussed. He was tired but eventually fell asleep. The nanny's keeping an eye on them."

He didn't say a word, just looked at her.

"I'm not used to having someone watch over my children."

"I'm sure it can be unsettling, but you don't

have to leave them with her if you'd be more comfortable keeping them with you."

She didn't want to appear ungrateful because it was a luxury that was much appreciated. "I'll keep that in mind."

He shifted again, bending his arm at the elbow, scratching his fingers at the dark stubble on his chin. He was relaxed, extending his long legs, and crossing his feet at the ankles. He was comfortable and at home. Perhaps one day she would have the same comfort in his presence that he felt in hers.

"I talked with Ben, and he thought we could meet with his lawyer soon."

"About?" Rose didn't understand why they would do that. *Was their marriage not valid?*

He bent his legs and shifted to face her. "Making sure Charles can't lay any claim to Tommy and Sarah."

"Oh," she said. He had mentioned this earlier, but she still wasn't sure how she felt about it. Joseph was their father, not James.

"I don't want to rush you, but we need to see

what the law says to protect you and them. Are they my children now that we are married? Can Charles take them from us?"

Everything had moved so fast. She had married James to protect them, but she still worried she had made a mistake. *If their marriage didn't work, would James be their legal father?* She hadn't even considered the implications of marrying a man she barely knew. Confused, she knew nothing of James's past nor what he wanted for his future. She couldn't have imagined he had wanted a ready-made family when Charles had demanded she hand over her children. She didn't think any man would want to step into the mess of her life.

"Do I have time to consider what this means?" Her words were soft, quiet, almost a whisper.

"We don't have time to wait." James' voice was harsh. "There's no telling what your brother-in-law might do."

What should I do? She didn't want to make the wrong decision, but had she already done that by not considering what would happen if she married another man, even if he was the far better choice.

"Think on it for a few days. The lawyer can't get here 'til after the new year. He'll be able to tell us what will happen and if Charles has any claim."

"I will."

"Our living situation." He paused, as though trying to judge her reaction. "Ben offered us his parent's old homestead. They lived in it when they first settled here. He said it's not in the best of shape, but we could live there until I can earn enough to buy us our own spread. I can work here on the ranch until then."

She hadn't even considered where they would live. James was trying his best to make things agreeable and be a provider, but she didn't know if she was ready to have a proper marriage. She had to remember he promised it was up to her what their relationship would be. Would he keep that promise once they were far away from his family?

He sensed her hesitation. "Ben said that when the snow melts, it has a nice large meadow in front. Also has a wooden fence surrounding it for both Tommy and Sarah to play in, to keep them safe. There's even a spot in the back for a decent sized garden, if you'd like to have one. Would you like to see it?"

Do I want to see it? Slowly raising her eyes to his, she saw hope and an expectation for something she wasn't sure she was prepared to give. She sighed. She didn't want to disappoint him. "Yes."

"How about we go for a ride sometime next week and I'll show it to you? It might not be habitable, but if it is, we could likely move as soon as you're healed enough."

"It would be enjoyable to see the ranch." She hadn't been able to appreciate the view when they had arrived, her fatigue overwhelming, so it would be nice to see where she would spend her new life.

He smiled. "I even thought it might be nice to

call it Thundering Meadows, if'n that's agreeable with you after we see it, of course."

"Thundering Meadows has a pleasant ring to it, but we should see it first. Make sure it fits." She smiled. "You don't think Ben and Elizabeth will mind, do you?"

"Nah, I think they'd like it. Almost like a homage to Ben's parents who settled the ranch."

"I haven't met them. Do they live close by?"

"No. They passed years ago."

Rose frowned. She hadn't wanted to be insensitive. "I'm sorry, I didn't mean…"

"No apologies needed. You wouldn't have known." He squeezed her hand in comfort. "When we go to the cabin, I'll make note of any repairs as well."

"I have a little money, if that'd help."

"I'm not taking your money," he snapped.

Not understanding why he would refuse it, she said, "You won't be taking it. We're married now, so what I have is yours." Even Joseph had taken what little money she had brought into the marriage. It hadn't bothered her as he had always provided what she needed, so it didn't make sense to her why James angry at her for offering it. He was her husband, even if it was in name only.

He stood and walked over to the window, pulling open the drapes. "I want you to keep it for yourself. I'll make what we need. If'n you ever decide you need to leave, I want you to have it. I don't want you to be in the same predicament you were in when Joseph passed."

"That's ridiculous." Stubborn man. She wasn't naïve. If he had to rely on his brother-in-law for a job and a place to live, then he clearly wasn't drowning in money. "If you need it, there's no reason for you not to make use of it."

"Let's see the cabin first before we decide." He dropped the drapes and avoided her gaze. "Excuse me for a moment. I'm needed in the barn." He walked out of the room, ending the conversation.

Rose was confused as to his sudden defensiveness, but from the stern look on his face, she would do well to leave it alone. At least for now.

Chapter 11

On Sunday, Elizabeth and Ben were busy with party preparations and welcoming friends for their annual New Year's Party. It would be the year 1900 and was a cause for celebration. Neighbors were arriving at the ranch and planned on staying for a few days. The main barn had been cleared of the animals and swept clean as a number of families would bed down there and others would stay in covered wagons. Large fire pits were scattered around the yard with piles of fresh, dried wood available for their neighbors' use. It was still winter and plenty cold outside, and they didn't want their friends and neighbors to freeze.

It was an exciting time, and they prayed the weather held. Everyone was looking forward to the food, drinks, music, and gathering of friends. Ben had even purchased fireworks for that evening and the young folks were eagerly awaiting the lighting of them.

Rose walked inside the warm kitchen where many women had gathered, laughing and smiling. Multiple conversations were happening in the large, bright room. Elizabeth caught her eye and waved her over to where she was talking to a woman with bright blue eyes.

"Rose, I'd like you to meet my good friend, Susan." Elizabeth wrapped her arm around Susan's waist and the two of them appeared as close as sisters.

"Hello," Rose said. "It's nice to meet you."

"Rose is James's new wife," Elizabeth said. "And she has two beautiful children."

Rose blushed. She wasn't sure how she felt

about being called James's wife. "Do you live close by, Susan?"

"Yes. My husband and I live in Helena," Susan said, smiling. "We moved there last year, and it was a blessing to be near Elizabeth again."

"How did you two become friends?"

Elizabeth grinned and glanced at Susan. "We met several years ago while I was living in Spring Creek, and when we discovered that Susan's husband wanted to move to Helena, we were plum tickled to be near one another again."

"Spring Creek?"

"Yes," Elizabeth said. She let go of Susan and stirred a pot of beans resting on the stove. "James and I hadn't seen one another in years and when I found him, he had bought a ranch near there. I met Susan at church, and we became friends, although why she gave me a chance after I couldn't thread a needle, I don't know."

Susan and Rose laughed at the image Elizabeth described.

"Susan kept me from running out of the

church the afternoon of my wedding." Elizabeth chuckled.

"I did," Susan said, looking at Elizabeth quizzically.

"I never told you, did I?" Elizabeth said.

Susan shook her head. "But I think you should tell me now, though." Her smile was wide and infectious and Rose could see why they were friends.

"You remember that day? I was scared senseless. If I didn't marry Ben, I would've been stuck with that mean old friend of my pa's. I didn't understand why Ben had offered to marry me and you were trying to comfort me. You were telling me that everyone thought Ben had swept me off my feet and I said, *'he isn't my Ben'* and you said, *'that's where you're wrong, my friend. He is now and forever after, your Ben.'* I'll never forget that moment." Elizabeth held Susan's hands between hers, tears in her eyes. "That was likely the only thing that got me down the aisle that day."

"Oh, Elizabeth," Susan said. "I never knew

that. Things were such a mess with what your pa was doing, and I thought Ben was such a hero for swooping in to keep you safe."

Rose was surprised. She had assumed that Elizabeth and Ben had a love match. They were quite affectionate with one another. She was curious to know what had happened, but now wasn't the time for any questions, especially since Rose certainly didn't know any of them well enough to do so.

Susan and Elizabeth gave each other a quick hug before pulling away but smiled comfortingly at one another. Rose almost felt like she was intruding on a moment between two good friends. Perhaps one day she could have a friendship as close as the two of them had.

Elizabeth swiped away her tears. "Look at me, going on and on about that. I'm sorry, Rose. You likely don't want to hear that. You should be resting. I don't want you to overdo it. You just had a baby."

"I appreciate your concern, but I spent all day in bed yesterday and honestly, I'm not sure I could stand another minute in one." She laughed. "I'd like to help, if you'd let me."

Elizabeth wiped her hands on her apron. "Well, we could certainly use the help in here, but you must promise me that if you feel faint or tired, you are to rest. James is likely going to have my head for even letting you in the kitchen."

Rose bristled a little at the implication that she couldn't take care of herself, but she was in Elizabeth's home and relying on her hospitality. Besides, she didn't want to cause any problems, so she agreed.

Elizabeth clapped her hands. "There's bread to cut and vegetables to chop, so take your pick."

Rose went to the sink and washed her hands. Grabbing an apron she saw hanging behind the door, she wrapped the ribbons around her waist and reached for a large knife to cut the thick loaves of warm bread that sat resting on the table.

"Did James tell you about the cabin?" Elizabeth asked.

The warm bread was making Rose's mouth water, but she had to focus on Elizabeth. "Yes, we are going to go look at it sometime this week."

"That place hasn't seen life in years and is likely a filthy mess, so be prepared."

"James said it has a meadow. He thought we could name it Thundering Meadows."

"Oh, I love that," Elizabeth said. "That would be the perfect name."

The door opened and a ranch hand brought in a huge platter of cooked ribs, brisket, and large steaming steaks. The steaks were still sizzling, and the aroma was delectable. She was likely to eat a feast when it was time.

"Ma'am," he said, looking at Elizabeth. "Where do you want these?"

"Susan, Rose, if you'll excuse me." She then waved to the ranch hand. "Follow me." They disappeared through the swinging door into the large dining room, where the food was being laid out for the partygoers.

Rose went back to cutting the bread while Susan grabbed the vegetables and began chopping them. They spent a relaxing time making small talk while getting the food prepared. When she had done all she could, Rose said her goodbyes. She checked in on the children who were safe with the nanny and then went to her room to wash for the festivities.

* * *

The main house was bursting at the seams with the guests that had arrived for the party. Adults mingled both inside and out, sipping wine, champagne, and a few bottles of distilled whiskey that were floating around for those who wanted something with more of a kick. They were eating the abundance of food covering the wide tables; cakes, cookies, pies, and tarts along with thick slabs of ribs, brisket, tender cuts of beef, roasted chickens, potatoes, beans, roasted vegetables, and breads of every variety. There was something for everyone. Children laughed and played while the adults smiled indulgently, almost as excited as they, although containing it better.

Rose held Sarah in her arms while keeping a close eye on Tommy. Children of all ages were available for Tommy to play with, and he was having the time of his life. She hadn't seen him this happy since before his father had passed, and it was a comfort to see him enjoying himself.

Rose covered a yawn with her free hand. It had been a long day, and she'd be glad when she could drop in bed. Clearly more tired than she realized, she was trying to put on a brave face so James wouldn't know how tired she really was.

As she meandered through the crowds of people, a few older ladies stopped to compliment her on Sarah. Then the questions began as to who she was and also to pry into her relationship with Elizabeth and Ben. They were well meaning, but it felt intrusive.

Just when she was starting to become flustered and overwhelmed and wasn't sure how to answer the questions, especially about her marriage to James, Elizabeth interrupted the two well-meaning older women who reminded her of her grannies.

"Ladies," Elizabeth said. "I hope you're having a wonderful time."

The two women nodded, their white, grey hair bobbing, their brightly colored clothing almost blinding but clearly of an older fashion.

"I'm so glad to hear that. If you'll excuse me, I need to take Rose with me. There's someone I need her to meet." Taking her by the arm, Elizabeth gracefully dragged her away to the other room.

Sighing with relief, Rose gasped. "Thank you, Elizabeth. I just couldn't…"

Elizabeth shook her head. "Libby and Margaret are sweethearts, but they will inundate you with questions. I hope you don't think it was rude of me to pull you away, but I thought you might need a minute."

"Yes, yes. It's a tad overwhelming."

"I completely understand. Why don't you sit somewhere and take a breath?" Glancing around, Elizabeth pointed out an empty armchair in the small parlor at the front of the house. Elizabeth gazed at Sarah and smiled, caressing Sarah's little hand with her fingers. "She really is beautiful, Rose. Now go sit before that chair is taken."

Thanking her, Rose scooted her way through the crowds before someone else snagged it. There weren't too many empty seats with the houseful of guests. Sitting, she sighed, relaxing her shoulders from the strain of being on her feet all day. She had likely overdone it, not that she'd willingly admit it, but it was clear Elizabeth had seen that she needed a moment.

Looking at her little one, her heart nearly burst at the love she felt for her and for Tommy. Sarah's eyes were closed and she pursed her sweet lips. Her long eyelashes framed her cheeks. Sarah had been content, but with all the noise, it was refreshing to sit in a quieter room.

Rosed rested against the soft cushions of the chair and closed her eyes for just a minute. Her mind went blank as she let slumber overtake. Sometime later, she was startled awake.

A booming voice yelled, "It's almost time!"

How long have I been asleep?

Rose peered through sleep heavy eyes at Sarah. Her round eyes were slightly open, and she rubbed her hands at her cheeks. Rose kissed her sweet forehead before smothering a wide yawn. She was plum tuckered.

James walked into the room, his gaze finding her, before he ambled to her side. Merriment and spirts had flushed his cheeks, and a red and blue checkered shirt covered his broad chest, emphasizing his muscular body. After a few good meals at Ben and Elizabeth's, he had filled out and didn't look as gaunt as he had when they first met. He grew handsomer with each day that passed.

"Are you going to come into the other room?" he asked. "It's a few minutes 'til midnight."

"Yes. I must've fallen asleep." She scooted to the edge of the chair and shook off her drowsiness.

"Are you feeling any pain?" His concern was evident.

"No." She covered yet another yawn. "I'm sleepy, that's all. Let's go join the others."

He helped her stand and with his hand on her waist, they found the nanny who carried Sarah up to the nursery. Then James led her to where most of the revelers were waiting to bring in the new year.

Within moments, happy cheering, loud music, and merrymaking surrounded them. It was a new year and 1900 had begun. Hugging and kissing abounded amongst those around them. Rose turned, and James pulled her into his arms, covering her lips in a searing kiss. Rose's toes tingled and fireworks exploded inside of her as she grasped the edges of his collar.

When he released her, she blushed and

stumbled, dropping her fingers across his chest before he grabbed them and held tight.

"Happy New Year, Rose."

"Happy New Year, James."

And what a new year it was.

Chapter 12

Later that week, James and Rose left the
children in Elizabeth's care, and they headed to
the cabin in a small black sleigh that had room
enough for the two of them. No new snow had
fallen since they had arrived, and the air was
crisp and fresh. The blue sky was clear, with a
few random white fluffy clouds hovering above
the snow-covered mountain peaks. The sun
glared off the snowbanks, and Rose was glad
she had worn a wide-brimmed bonnet to keep it
out of her eyes. Snuggled under thick quilts,
nestled next to James's side, she could forget for

a minute all that had happened and enjoy the lovely day.

The cabin wasn't large like the main house, but it appeared sturdy and at one time, well loved. It shouldn't take long for them to bring it back to its former life. A large brick fireplace was on the right and extended through to the second story loft. The roof and windows were still intact, but the front porch needed to be cleared of debris.

Rose followed James as he bounded up the stairs to the porch and then watched as he struggled to open the door. She giggled as he made a show of trying to get it open. It stuck, but it didn't take him long to push it open. She followed him inside, but then wished she hadn't as dust billowed around them. Sneezing, her eyes watered, but she pulled a handkerchief from her sleeve and held it to her nose to protect her from the worst of it.

Once the dirt and dust settled, she quickly glanced around. The cabin had a unique charm to it;

big windows, a large hearth in front of the fireplace, and plenty of storage for their belongings. It was bigger than the home she had shared with Joseph. A few pieces of forgotten furniture sat scattered throughout, but they were worn and needed to be replaced. Rose made a mental list of the cleaning supplies she'd need while James scribbled in a tiny journal, making notes of the repairs to be accomplished before they could move in.

While wandering around the cabin, Rose realized there were only two bedrooms. The loft was not safe for the children, so that left one for her and James.

James placed his hands lightly on her shoulders. "Is everything all right?"

His breath tickled her ear.

Should I say something?

He sensed her hesitation. "You can tell me, Rose." He gently squeezed her shoulders, as though giving her the courage to continue.

"It's..."

"What?" he pressed.

"Where will I sleep?"

"Why in the… Oh, our arrangement?" James dropped his hands. He moved around her and walked around the room, avoiding her gaze. "Well, you can have this room, the children can take the other bedroom, and I'll make a pallet up in the loft."

Relief surged through her. She hoped he'd keep his end of the bargain, but legally he was her husband, so he could insist on his husbandly rights if he so chose.

"Will that be acceptable?" His gaze finally reached hers.

She nodded. She feared if she spoke, she might burst into tears, and she could no longer hide how worried she had been.

"I think this'll work. Ben told me they have a few pieces of old furniture we can use until we can buy our own."

"Remember, you can use the money I have."

He tightened his hands into fists and then released. If she hadn't been watching, she might've missed it. "I told you before, it's yours. I'll earn what we need. It might take me time, but one day I'll provide for you and the children."

He maneuvered around her, being careful not to touch her, and left her standing alone, the front door slamming in its casing. She cringed as it hit the door frame.

She hadn't meant to offend him, but she still didn't see any reason he couldn't use what she had. When she had offered it a few days ago, he had the same reaction. He claimed he wanted her to have it in the event she decided she didn't want to stay married. She appreciated the sentiment, but they were married, maybe not the conventional marriage, and one not made on a foundation of love, but they had an understanding.

She was willing to keep her end of the bargain. Was he?

* * *

A few days later, Rose was going crazy with boredom. No one wanted her help and kept insisting she should rest. Deciding she had enough, she'd head for the cabin. It wouldn't clean itself and it would give her something to do, a way to be useful. She convinced one of the ranch hands to hitch up a wagon and with a bucket full of supplies, and Tommy at her side, they had a pleasant ride. She had left the baby with the nanny. James and Ben were busy discussing James's new role on the ranch, and she didn't want to bother them. She could handle this small chore on her own.

From what little Rose had learned, Ben used to be a ranch hand on James's ranch. That was where he had met Elizabeth. Now their roles had reversed, and Rose was unaware of James's feelings on the change. The one thing she couldn't ascertain was why James no longer owned his ranch or why he had been without work. James was being vague with the details and Rose, not wanting to pry, kept the questions to herself. She didn't feel she had the right to ask. They had only known one another for just over a week and in that time, he had delivered her baby, married her, and brought her to his brother-in-law's ranch. They hadn't spent any real time together and certainly knew nothing about one another.

Arriving at the cabin, Rose lifted her skirts and carefully climbed out of the wagon. She was still somewhat sore, but not enough so she couldn't work. She reached for Tommy and helped him scamper down. He insisted he was a big boy and could do it on his own, but she at least held his hand so if he fell, she could keep him from hurting himself. He jumped the last few inches and jerked her arm in his descent. She took a moment to catch her breath.

Excited for his new home, Tommy ran up the porch steps and noticed the new things around him. His eyes were wide, and he squealed in excitement, pointing out nicks in the banister, a squirrel he startled, and a big spider on the ground. His enthusiasm was infectious, and she smiled at his exuberance.

Rose pulled out a bucket full of supplies from the bed of the wagon, as well as toys for Tommy to play with. With her hands full, she went up the porch stairs and pushed open the door. It was chilly inside, but it wouldn't take long to work up a sweat, and she'd start a small fire to remove the chill. She had dressed Tommy warmly, and she had no doubt he'd stay that way while playing.

In a corner of the room, she placed a worn blanket on the dirty floor and settled Tommy and his toys on it. Knowing he could play for hours with his blocks, she left him to take stock of the fireplace. Lighting a match, she knelt and peered into its depths. Not seeing any major blockages, she made sure the flue was open, picked up dry wood from a pile on the hearth, and prepared a fire.

Within a few minutes, roaring flames reached up into the dark black fireplace. Standing, she put her hands on her hips and looked around the room, trying to decide where to start. There was no shortage of cleaning opportunities.

Two hours later, the main living area had been swept and mopped, the windows washed, and the walls had been wiped clean. She scrubbed the kitchen by taking years of dust and grime off every surface. She made a mental note of areas on the walls that needed to be fixed and a few wooden floorboards that could stand being replaced. James had probably noted them, but it couldn't hurt to let him know what she had found.

Checking on Tommy, she was happy to see he was busy entertaining himself. Bending, she gave him a quick hug and a biscuit to eat. He gave her a toothy smile. With one hand on the biscuit and one hand on his toys, he went back to playing.

She climbed up the ladder to the loft to clean that as well. It wouldn't do for James to sleep up there if it was uninhabitable. After clearing out the dust and cobwebs, she carefully climbed down from the loft into the children's room. It wasn't large, and she was trying to decide how much furniture they'd need when a wagon rumbled outside. Wondering who it was, she pressed a strand of hair behind her ear. It had fallen from behind the kerchief she had used to protect her hair. Wiping her hands on her apron, she pulled open the door and found James.

"What the hell are you doing out here?" He was furious. Deep, dark red streaks covered his face.

She was stunned. How dare he speak to her like that. Glancing behind her to make sure Tommy was still occupied, she stepped outside and closed the door behind her. She didn't want Tommy to hear them as anger soared through her.

"What does it look like?" Her tone was defiant.

"You just had a baby and could've been hurt or killed," he yelled.

"That's ridiculous. I'm not an invalid, nor should I be treated as such," she said.

He hesitated, as if he couldn't believe she had any backbone. Just because she had been totally reliant on him over the last week didn't mean she would be spoken to in that manner.

"Didn't expect me to cower in fear, did you?"

She wasn't sure where this flash of anger had come from, but perhaps it was because she was tired of being afraid and subjected to a man's whims. Having peace and safety had unleashed a tiger in her. Either that or she had plum lost her mind.

He dropped his shoulders and immediately retreated. "I shouldn't have spoken to you that way. I was worried when I got to the house and couldn't find you. No one knew where you'd gone."

"I had a ranch hand hitch up a wagon so I could start cleaning. I'm fine. You shouldn't have worried."

"If we'd known where you'd gone, then maybe we wouldn't have." He pursed his lips.

"I didn't intend to worry you, but I have to be useful."

"You just had a baby. You should rest, not work."

He worried too much and was smothering her. "I've rested plenty and feel much better. I can certainly pull my weight."

"You may feel better, but the doctor said you needed to rest," James insisted.

"Would you stop? I couldn't sit around twiddling my thumbs." She placed her hands on her hips and glared at him.

He was exasperated with her, but she wouldn't concern herself over it. She hated that everyone had worried, but she couldn't be unproductive, especially since James only married her to protect her from Charles. He hadn't wanted to take on a family, no matter what he said. All his plans had to have been derailed when he met her. She wouldn't be a burden to him, and cleaning their new home kept her mind off their uncertain future.

His piercing gaze felt as though he was searching for answers to unanswered questions before shrugging. He held out his hands. "How can I help?"

Reassured, she went inside and he followed. She grinned, averting her face from his. For some reason, she was pretty satisfied with herself. She had stood up to him, and she suffered no harm as a result.

James knelt in front of Tommy and helped him stack the blocks. He then patted Tommy's knee, and Tommy giggled, the sound sweet and beautiful. It was clear James and Tommy would get along fine, and she was right pleased that Tommy would have a strong male figure in his life. He certainly deserved it after losing his own pa so young.

Less than an hour later, they grinned at their efforts. The cabin was clean from top to bottom. They could move in once James completed the few repairs. Rose was happy and apprehensive at the same time. It would be nice to have her own home again, but they were strangers.

Would they be able to work together to make their marriage work? Or would their tenuous bond be snuffed out before it began?

Chapter 13

James and Rose moved into the cabin two weeks later and settled into a daily routine. James left each morning to work on the never-ending list of responsibilities on the ranch while Rose continued to recover from the birth. She woke when the baby stirred and was on the run all day with both children. James slept in the loft, so he was blissfully unaware of her exhaustion, and she certainly didn't complain as she didn't feel she had the right to.

As the days wore on, the stubbornness and strength she had displayed to James on the day she cleaned the cabin seemed to dissipate. She was alone with the children and her mind went against her. Between her lack of sleep and her fear of what Charles might do, she became short-tempered with Tommy. She didn't want to be that way, and she regretted every word that came out of her mouth when she responded to anything he did. It didn't help that Sarah was not sleeping and had become quite fussy as well, likely responding to Rose's deteriorating disposition.

Rose would be startled by innocent noises and was constantly looking out the window to make sure no one came down the drive other than James. They hadn't heard from Charles, but it didn't stop her from her constant worry. Charles was not one to be content with someone else's decision, and she was convinced he would return, and with a vengeance.

When the children were down for their naps, she would plan ways to fight Charles. She had learned at a young age she needed to protect herself because those who were important to her were eventually taken from her in unforeseen and tragic ways. First, her mother and father and then, her older brother.

James tried to ease her fears by meeting with Ben's lawyer, but it didn't help. The lawyer said the tender years doctrine would likely work in her favor. She didn't understand what that meant, but the lawyer patiently described that children were generally kept with their mothers in their first few years of life. This was typically only used in divorce proceedings but should apply to their situation as well. She wanted to trust the lawyer, but she knew Charles better than they did. He wouldn't let anyone stop him from getting what he wanted.

She also didn't want to forget Joseph. Her children were born in love and by replacing him with James, she feared she was she doing a disservice to him. He had done nothing to justify that. He had loved her and Tommy and had been excited about the baby's birth.

These thoughts tumbled through her mind like a wheel running downhill with nothing in its way and never stopping. Between the guilt of replacing her late husband, Joseph, with her new husband, James, the fatigue of caring for both children, and the fear of Charles's actions, she became a shell of herself. She could see it happening but didn't have the strength to stop it.

Rose woke every morning at dawn to prepare James a hot meal before he left for the day. He ate his mid-day meal at the bunkhouse with the other ranch hands, but each evening a hot meal sat waiting for him, regardless of the hour. She ensured Tommy and Sarah were fed and in bed before he arrived to give him peace and quiet after a long, hard day working.

Scrubbing the house from top to bottom a couple times a week, she tried to keep Tommy entertained, fed Sarah at two-hour intervals, and did endless baby laundry. Dark circles formed under her eyes and her clothing hung limp on her. She lost the baby weight but continued to lose more. She had always been petite, but she became haggard with the lack of food and sleep.

She didn't think much of the changes in her body and the thoughts roaring through her mind, but perhaps she should have. As January moved into February, Rose began to feel the effects of her nonstop activities. She fell asleep at the table while feeding the baby and had little energy. Things fell apart around her, and she didn't want to do anything except sleep.

* * *

One evening in mid-February, James came home after a long day of checking the ranch's fences and found Tommy running wild through the house. Sarah screamed in her cradle, and there was no sign of Rose. The chaos surprised him. He stopped Tommy in his quest to wreak havoc and picked up Sarah, holding her next to his shoulder. She was wet and clearly hungry.

What is going on? Where is Rose?

He changed Sarah's nappy, found a bottle to

feed her, and gave a hungry Tommy a cookie. With the children's immediate needs satisfied, he started looking for his wife.

Looking at Tommy, he asked, "Where's your momma?"

Tommy gazed at him, stuck his thumb in his mouth, and shrugged as if to say, "I don't know."

Uneasy, James peered into the two bedrooms and into the loft, but she wasn't anywhere inside the house. She wouldn't have left the children unattended. His apprehension grew as he remembered what had occurred years ago when Elizabeth had been kidnapped by a deranged man, intent on hurting her. James had been behind bars and hadn't been able to help. He couldn't bear it if someone else in his care was hurt because he hadn't been there.

He feared Charles had finally come for Rose, sneaked onto the ranch unbeknownst to them and taken her. As he looked around, there didn't appear to be any signs of a struggle, so it couldn't be that. She had to be here somewhere.

With Sarah tucked into the crook of his arm,

he stepped out onto the back porch and found her. She sat on an old wooden rocking chair, a blanket wrapped around her slim frame, and she had buried her face in her hands. Her shoulders shook and heartbreaking sobs poured from her. He stepped inside, put Sarah in her crib, and went outside to Rose. Kneeling, he placed his hands on her knees, not wanting to alarm her.

"Rose, what's wrong?"

The confusion and fear in her eyes broke his heart. The desolation almost undid him. He believed they had made progress, although now he had doubts. He would come home every night and she would have a smile on her face and dinner on the table, although they spoke little. He wanted to comfort her, but feared she would reject him. The last thing he wanted was for her to be unhappy.

She wiped her eyes with a corner of the blanket. "I hate that you found me like this."

"It's all right."

Rose tried to stand, but James kept his hands on her knees and gently urged her to stay.

"Please let me help. Can you tell me what's bothering you?"

She shoved him away. "I should get inside. I left the children for too long, and I'm sure they're hungry. Sarah needs to be changed. I haven't started dinner, the laundry has piled up, and the house is a cluttered mess. I didn't mean for you to come home to this. I'll go inside and take care of everything," she said in a rush.

"Rose, stop," he said. "I'll take care of Tommy and Sarah. Why don't you sit out here and enjoy the break in the weather? I'll call you when dinner is on the table."

"No, no. You can't do that. I just needed a few minutes to catch my breath."

"No arguing. Let me do this for you."

Patting her hands, James stood. She wasn't confiding in him, and he couldn't blame her. They had been married for almost two months, but they didn't have any meaningful conversations. They were like two strangers living in a boarding house, being cordial and polite but discussing nothing about their pasts, let alone anything about their hopes, dreams, and desires. He had been so determined to do right by her and showing Ben he wasn't the man he was before, that he had ignored the woman who he'd pledged to protect.

"Stay here, watch the sunset. I'll take care of the children."

She wrapped her arms around her knees and stared into the dark trees. She was distraught and looking so alone that it brought forth disturbing memories he had long forgotten. When his sister Elizabeth was born, their ma had gone through a terrible time. He remembered how tired and how distracted she had been. She would cry at every little thing and forget to feed them. She was distracted with stilted movements and vacant eyes.

He would come home from school and find Elizabeth crying inconsolably in her cradle, covered in a wet nappy, and his ma curled on the bed oblivious to everything around her. He would care for both his ma and his baby sister while Elizabeth's pa spent his time in brothels and saloons, drinking away what little money they had. He had only been eleven when Elizabeth was born and during that time, he had grown up fast, taking on the responsibilities that should have been done by the man of the house.

Elizabeth's pa had been a hard man. He treated his ma no better than he did the cattle on their failing homestead. Every evening, the man would come home, immediately pick up a bottle, and drink himself into oblivion, and those were on the nights he came home. When he wasn't drowning his woes in a bottle, he'd be found at the nearest saloon or holed up in the drunk tank at the local jail.

His ma had tried to make her husband happy, but between his surly attitude and her lack of energy, things deteriorated rapidly. Scared and confused, James hadn't understood and tried to care for her the best way he knew how, but now he wondered if his ma and Rose suffered from the same affliction. With time, his ma had found her strength and went back to her normal self, but for months after Elizabeth's birth, she had been someone he hadn't recognized and he had worried he would never see the ma he loved ever again.

Rose was showing the same behaviors, and he had failed to recognize them until now.

Have I failed Rose as much as I failed my ma?

Chapter 14

After the children were clean, fed, and put to bed, James wiped away the crumbs on the table and thought about what might have brought them to this moment. He had let his own selfish desires dictate what he did. He might have been trying to care for his new family and proving to Ben he could be reliable, but he had failed to ensure Rose had everything she needed and that she was happy. Failing his mother, then his sister when he left all those years ago, still haunted him. *Will I ever learn?*

He never considered she might be overwhelmed, that she might regret the decision she made to marry him. He hadn't tried to ask her how her day was, what she enjoyed doing, and asked nothing about her past. He didn't offer to help her with the children or any of the household chores. She had lost her husband, was running scared from a horrible man, had given birth to a baby, and had married a stranger. It was no wonder she had reached her breaking point.

With their meal on the table, he lit a couple of candles and threw more logs on the fire. He wanted the evening to be special, not because he had any romantic notions, but because he wanted to show her, he cared. He didn't want her to believe she had made a mistake.

He was keeping his imprisonment from her and was anxious about what she would do if she discovered his past. By offering Rose a home for her and her children, he hoped he would be one step closer to becoming better than what he had been.

Elizabeth believed it was his duty and responsibility to tell Rose, and the longer he waited without mentioning it might increase the chances she would never forgive him. He wondered if Elizabeth was right. There were days he believed he had made the right decision. He paid his debt to society. Rose never asked questions, so he didn't see a reason to share that part of his life, but had he given her the opportunity to ask?

Going outside, he found Rose still curled in the chair, fast asleep. He hated to wake her, but the temperatures were dropping, and she needed to eat. She had lost a remarkable amount of weight and the significance of that weighed heavily on him. She was wasting away. He had been ignoring it instead of facing it. He needed to fix this now before it raged out of control.

With his hand on her shoulder, he shook her awake. She fluttered her eyes open, and it took her a moment to focus. She shifted and started apologizing. He placed his finger on her lips and silenced her. Surprised, she stopped. He couldn't believe what he had done. He hadn't touched her since New Year's and for a moment, he thought he had gone too far, but she didn't pull away.

He slowly removed his finger. Staring at her pink lips, he had an overwhelming urge to kiss her. He kept dreaming of the one they shared on New Year's and yearned to do it again, but knew it was far too soon.

Gulping down his uneasiness, he said, "Food's on the table. Come inside. Eat something."

"The children?" She uncurled her legs from the chair.

He tried not to stare but was finding it difficult. She was attractive and his blood hummed under his skin.

"James?"

"What?" He had lost focus. "Oh, they've eaten and are already abed."

"I didn't mean to fall asleep. I should've been inside helping."

"You're exhausted. I was happy to do it. It was the least I could do," he said.

"But—"

"No buts," James said. "Let's go inside. We can talk there."

Holding his hand out, he hoped she wouldn't reject what little comfort he tried to offer. Seconds passed before she placed her hand in his. It fit perfectly. She stood within a hair's breadth of him. He was desperate to pull her into his arms. She looked forlorn and alone. Not wanting to be rejected, he refrained.

Tugging her gently, he led her inside where it was warm.

She appeared to be coming out of her stupor, but her sluggish movements concerned him. "You cleaned and cooked?" She pulled her hand from his and ran her fingers across the table, looking at the warm food he had prepared.

"Yes. I hope you like it. I'm not much of a cook but can rustle up some food. Elizabeth never starved while we were together."

"Thank you for doing this."

James sat in the chair across from her. Dishing up eggs, he piled them high on her plate before handing it to her. One of the other things he had failed to do was provide her with enough foodstuffs. There wasn't much left on the shelves or in the cold cellar. He was ashamed. If he was to be the man of this house, then he needed to act as such. He had made sure Elizabeth had plenty while he had his ranch, so he didn't understand why had he failed to do the same for Rose and her children.

Taking the plate from him, she picked up her fork and moved the eggs around the plate, not really eating.

He moved a platter of warm bread closer to her, but she didn't seem to notice. He wanted to say something but was afraid if he did, she would get angry or reject his good intentions.

She lifted her eyes and saw him staring at her. "What?"

"Is something wrong with the food?" He waved toward her plate.

"No, why?"

"You haven't eaten."

"I have." She glared at him with her dark

green eyes as she shoved a forkful of eggs into her mouth as if to prove him wrong.

Once again, he had miscalculated. He shouldn't have said anything, but he was grateful he had angered her enough to eat. He could handle her anger but couldn't deal with her wasting away from lack of food.

* * *

The following day, Rose woke feeling slightly better, but still not as well as she'd like. Stretching her arms high above her head, she enjoyed the moment before it hit her—she hadn't woken during the night to feed Sarah. Aghast, she threw off the blankets and frantically looked for her slippers.

There was no way Sarah would've gone all night without a feeding. She found her slippers and shoved her now cold feet inside of them. She grabbed her wrapper and scurried to the cradle settled near the fireplace in her bedroom.

It was empty.

Her heart was in her throat and tears filled her eyes. *Where is my baby?* Devastation slammed into her. Charles must've found her and taken Sarah.

She yanked open the door and stopped in shock. James sat in the rocking chair, his back to her, the fire crackling before him. Sarah was nestled in his arms, fast asleep. Tommy played on the floor next to him.

She blinked to keep the tears at bay. Rose was a horrible mother. She hadn't been able to do anything right for days. James arrived and within a couple of hours, had everything under control.

Rose didn't know how she could she take care of her children. She was inadequate and overwhelmed. All she wanted to do was sleep. She hadn't felt this way after Tommy's birth, but now she felt helpless. She didn't understand what was happening to her.

Taking a deep breath, she touched his shoulder. He turned his head and placed his free hand on hers and smiled. What a gorgeous smile he had. She was married to a handsome man and seeing him like this made her heart tug.

"How do you feel?" he asked.

Determined to keep her feelings to herself, she lied. "Much better, thank you. I shouldn't have slept for so long. You're late for work."

"I sent word I'd be late. Ben'll understand."

"Still, I'm not sure what came over me."

He stood without waking Sarah and with his free hand, he brushed his knuckles across Rose's cheek, letting it slowly drop to where her neck met her shoulder.

"You needed the rest, and I wish I would've noticed how overwhelming things had become. I should've been looking out for you and gotten you help."

The hair on her neck crackled and defensiveness curled through her.

"I'm not overwhelmed." She let another lie slip past her lips. "I just haven't been sleeping well."

He placed a finger on her lips, stopping her from continuing. Angry, she pulled away from him. She wouldn't be soothed by a gentle touch, even from him.

"I think we both know it's more than that." Sarah stirred, and he shifted her until she quieted. "I've been ignoring what's been happening in my home."

"Everything's fine. I'm fine. I'm much better after getting a good night's sleep. You can go. I've got it handled." She reached for Sarah, but James stepped back, putting distance between them.

"I don't think so. I sent Elizabeth a note asking for help. She suggested you and the children come to the main house for a few days. There'll be plenty of help for you there."

Red, hot fury was circling through her. She glared at him. "I don't need to do that. I can take care of my own children."

"I don't agree. You've lost more weight than you should have, you aren't sleeping, and you don't have any energy. You need help and you're going to get it."

How dare he decide what I need.

"I've made up my mind. One of the ranch hands brought us a wagon. Go pack a bag for a few days. I've already gathered Tommy and Sarah's things."

It was then Rose noticed the bags sitting next to the front door. She wanted to argue with him. She wanted to stomp her feet in frustration, but she didn't have the energy to even do that. He was right. She needed help, but she wasn't willing to admit it to him or to anyone else. She couldn't let anyone know how she wanted to crawl inside a hole and never come out. That scared her more than she realized.

She slumped her shoulders, turned, and left James with her children. Failure pressed down on her so heavy it was a wonder she didn't stumble under the weight.

* * *

An hour later, James pulled the horses to a stop and set the brake in front of the main house where Elizabeth met them. She would know how to fix this, but he didn't know if Rose accept it. She had sat beside him, stiff and unyielding on the ride from the cabin. She didn't look at him and answered his questions with one or two words, not elaborating, and anger oozing from her like a festering wound.

He knew Rose was unhappy as he had been harsh, but he believed it was necessary. He couldn't help her and watch the children while he was working. Having more women to help Rose was the best thing for her. He didn't understand what was happening, but leaving her alone in the cabin was not the answer.

He jumped to the ground and reached to help her. She glared at him and waved him away.

"I don't need your help," she growled, anger and pain flashing from her eyes.

Ignoring her, he placed his hands around her very tiny waist and lifted her out of the wagon. As soon as her feet hit the ground, she moved around him, not saying a word. He reached into the bed of the wagon and pulled an excited Tommy into his arms. He pushed to be let down and then ran up the steps to Elizabeth and eagerly pulled on her skirts to get her attention. Her grin was infectious, and her eyes twinkled. She knelt to his eye level.

"Good morning, Tommy."

"Mornin'. Can I play with…" he looked up at Rose for help with her name.

"Vicky," Rose replied.

"Can I play with Vicky?" Excitement and anticipation burst from his eyes.

"Of course. Go inside. She's waiting for you."

Tommy ran for the front door but halted when Rose called out to him. "Tommy, no running please and be good for momma."

"Yes, Momma," he said over his shoulder as he hurried into the house, the door slamming behind him.

"I'll talk to him about the slamming doors. I hope he doesn't do any damage."

Elizabeth patted Rose on the arm. "No need to be concerned. He's excited. Vicky's always slamming doors, running through the house, having fun. A house is made to play in, to have fun. There isn't anything he can do that Vicky hasn't already done."

"I'm not sure about that as he is awfully rambunctious, but thank you," Rose murmured.

"No need to thank me. Now, let's get you inside and settled." Placing her arm around Rose's waist, Elizabeth led her inside. Elizabeth turned to look at James with questions in her eyes.

His note hadn't explained what had happened. It was up to him to tell Elizabeth that Rose was having a difficult time after the birth, as he didn't expect Rose would confide in her.

Chapter 15

April 1900

Rose moved the blankets, grabbed her wrapper, and looked in the cradle. Sarah slept soundly, her tiny butt sticking straight up in the air, and she nestled her pink cheek against her small hand. The last few weeks had been rough, but after spending time at Elizabeth's, she was feeling more like herself. The fog she had been living under had been lifting, although she still didn't understand what had come over her. Elizabeth called it the birthing blues, but she had never heard of it herself and wasn't sure what to make of it.

Elizabeth and Ben's sisters, Anne and Katy, welcomed her with open arms and had given Rose the love and support she hadn't realized she had been missing. Anne and Katy regaled her with stories about their four brothers, Ben, Michael, Luke, and Stanley. It was clear they loved their brothers with the utmost devotion and enjoyed teasing them when they visited. They also entertained Tommy, fed her fattening foods, and held Sarah when Rose was her most tired. They provided it without question and with an abundance of love.

Ever since Joseph's death, she had been lonely, scared, and unsure of herself. She wondered if that might have contributed to her feelings of inadequacy and despair after Sarah's birth. Elizabeth insisted some woman experienced it and it was perfectly normal what she was going through. Trying to put her trust in others was difficult for Rose, but it didn't take long for Elizabeth to break down her defenses and become someone with whom she could trust. Elizabeth was the sister she never had.

Thankfully, the strange feelings were receding. She was waking happy most days and didn't dread climbing out of bed. There were still days where she wanted to stay holed up in her room with the drapes closed, but they were becoming less and less. Getting enough sleep and having someone care for the children gave her time to herself. James had been right, as much as it pained her to admit, but because of his insistence on dragging her to Elizabeth's, she was slowly pushing away the feelings of anxiety and discomfort she felt after Sarah's birth.

Looking at her little girl, she marveled at how perfect she was. Both her children were a blessing, and she was so grateful they were in her life. She so wished Joseph could be here to see his little girl. He had wanted another child after the birth of Tommy, but now he'd never see her, know her, or love her. Tears formed, but she brushed them away. He wouldn't want her to be unhappy.

A knock sounded at the door. She tightened the sash on her wrapper and opened the door softly. Sarah had slept through the night and Rose wanted to savor the quiet for as long as it lasted. Once she woke, her demands to be fed would override everything else and her day would become hectic.

It was Elizabeth with a tray of food. Rose couldn't believe her good fortune in having such a wonderful sister-in-law. Someone had been looking out for her by putting James on the same train as she was on Christmas Eve.

Whispering, Elizabeth asked, "How'd you sleep last night? I didn't hear Sarah cry." She put the tray of food on the table near the fire.

Speaking quietly, Rose said, "She slept the whole night. I didn't stir."

"I'm so glad to hear that. As much as we love our little ones, it's such a relief when they sleep through the night." Elizabeth pointed to the tray. "I brought you a bite to eat as the morning meal was disappearing fast." She laughed softly, an engaging smile on her lips. There was no reason for Rose not be happy around someone as lovely as Elizabeth.

"You didn't have to do this. I could've joined the family."

"Nonsense. It was the least I could do. Besides, if I hadn't, there might not have been anything left. The men were awfully hungry this morning. Of course, it might've had something to do with Sophia making her pancakes with huckleberry syrup. They're delicious." She put her hands on her waist. "I didn't want you to miss these. She doesn't make them often, but when she does, they don't stay on the table for very long."

"Thank you for thinking of me. I'm being quite pampered."

Elizabeth laughed. "No one is pampered around here. Do you want me to take Sarah while you eat?"

"No. She's sleeping peacefully."

"If you change your mind, let me know. She's a precious little thing," Elizabeth said, touching her arm with light fingertips.

"Thank you."

Elizabeth left, leaving Rose to eat the warm food. She went to the table and got a whiff of the fluffy, golden-brown pancakes, and hunger rumbled through her belly. She slathered on warm butter and poured the thick purplish pink huckleberry syrup over the top. The syrup oozed over and dripped along the sides.

Cutting into the pancakes, Rose took a large bite and groaned with delight. They were delicious, positively decadent. A few minutes later, she finished eating the pancakes and was scraping the last drops from her plate when Sarah stirred. She emitted a small squeak. Rose sighed. She was awake and in need of a nappy change. Time to be a momma.

Rose picked up the now squalling Sarah, who was soaked through. Her face was red with anger and streaked with crocodile tears. She raised her fists in disapproval and kicked her legs in frustration. She had lost a sock and her foot was cold.

Rose couldn't help but chuckle at the

expressions crossing Sarah's face. She wondered what Sarah would be like once she was older and could express herself with words. Rose imagined it'd be an adventure, and she couldn't wait to watch it unfold.

She wondered if Sarah would be more like her pa, or if she would take after her. Perhaps she would be a combination of them both. Tommy had her hair, but he was a smaller version of Joseph with his soft heart and exuberance. She only prayed she could help him grow into a man just like her Joseph.

Once Sarah was in a dry nappy, Rose dressed her in clean, warm clothes, and settled into the rocking chair nestled next to the window. She liked to look outside at the snow covering the ground, the sun as it brightened the red on the barn, and even the cattle lowing when the men herded them to the corrals near the house. Shrugging her wrapper off her shoulders, she unbuttoned her nightgown and pulled her breast free. Sarah latched on and settled in for a good feeding.

She closed her eyes and let her mind wander while Sarah ate. The door clicked open. Rose wondered if Elizabeth had forgotten something.

She didn't open her eyes and said, "Elizabeth?"

Silence greeted her. Opening her eyes, Rose gasped. James stood gazing at her with such a look of longing it pierced her to her core. Grabbing a blanket, she draped it across her bared breasts. James was her husband, but he hadn't seen her in such a state other than when he delivered Sarah. Embarrassment flooded her cheeks. She shouldn't be uncomfortable, but they didn't have a traditional marriage. She didn't know how or what they were to each other.

"Forgive me. I didn't mean to interrupt." James' face was red, but he didn't avert his eyes. They stared a hole right through her.

"It's all right. I was feeding Sarah."

He rubbed his forehead. "I would've knocked, but Elizabeth said Sarah was sleeping. I didn't want to wake her."

Sarah moved and she released her mouth

from Rose's breast. Lifting the blanket, Rose switched her to the other side. Very hungry this morning, Sarah wasn't willing to wait and pulled at her. She was a voracious eater, but the tugs were comforting, albeit uncomfortable, when she pulled a little too tight.

Arranging the blanket, Rose tried to calm her racing heart. James watched unabashedly, and her stomach clenched at what it meant. Feeding her child was natural. He was her husband, and with time, he was bound to want a normal relationship. He had told her in the beginning he didn't expect it and would never presume, but Rose was realistic. It wasn't fair for her to keep James from her bed, but she wasn't ready for their relationship to progress to that level and wasn't sure when she would be.

Rose gazed at him, searching his eyes with hers, looking for what she wasn't sure.

He swallowed, his Adam's apple unmistakable as it bobbed up and down. He took a long moment before speaking. "I wanted to see how you were feeling and to ask if you'd like to go to Helena on Saturday?"

"Helena?"

"Yes, I thought it might be nice if we went to dinner and a play. Ben tells me there's a nice theater there. He mentioned Elizabeth enjoys going, so I thought you might fancy it."

"What about the children?"

"Elizabeth said Anne and Katy would keep an eye on them."

"Elizabeth won't be here?"

"No. She and Ben'll come with us. They haven't had a night out in some time and the weather's been decent, so we thought it might be a merry trip."

She smiled. "I'd like that." It would be nice to see a play. She hadn't been to one in years, not before she had married Joseph.

James smiled at her.

"How late will we be?" Rose asked.

"We thought we'd stay at a hotel in town. This way, we don't have to try to return after nightfall."

Rose was at a loss for words. A hotel room would require staying together in the same bed. She couldn't ask him to get a second room as that would be a supreme waste of money, but she didn't know if she was ready to share one.

As if sensing her hesitation and knowing exactly what was behind it, he said, "I'll sleep on the floor. That way, you aren't uncomfortable."

"I appreciate that, but I can't expect you to do that."

He chuckled wryly. "I've slept in worse places. The floor would be a step up from some of 'em. No need to worry about me none."

"I don't know." What if she was being selfish by expecting him to continue to keep his distance.

"I'd like to take you to Helena. If you'd let me." His eyes pleaded with her to agree.

Rose acquiesced and nodded.

Grinning, his face brightened with his smile and a dimple was showcased in his cheek. He was quite endearing. He clapped his hands. "Great. I'll let you and Elizabeth work out the details. We'll leave first thing Saturday morning."

* * *

Saturday morning dawned bright and clear. A vibrant blue sky greeted them, and no clouds were in sight. Clean air and the warm sun tickled their skin. Spring was right around the corner and before long, there'd be melting snow and blooming green buds.

Rose had never left her children before and was anxious, but Anne assured her that she and Katy had it well in hand. They had watched Elizabeth's children, Vicky and Jimmy, on numerous occasions and said they would have fun playing together. She grabbed her winter coat and worn carpetbag and met James outside. He took both their bags, put them under the seat of the buckboard where Elizabeth and Ben sat waiting for them. Then he helped Rose into the rear seats.

She wasn't wearing a bonnet, but the sun

was warm, so she shouldn't get too cold. James had other ideas as he pulled a thick wool blanket over their legs and then a bright blue cap out of his pocket. He placed it on her head before she could stop him.

"James, I'm fine." She giggled as he tugged it over her ears, as if she were a toddler he was dressing.

"You may think so, but it's cold out here. You don't want to catch your death."

"But…" She reached to pull it off when he placed his hand on hers.

"No buts. You need to stay warm."

"My hair'll be a rabbit's nest once we arrive in Helena."

"You'll still be the most beautiful woman I've ever seen," he whispered, so only she could hear.

She blushed something fierce. His gleeful look was charming, so she could stand to keep her ears warm, and it didn't take long for her ears to thank her after they left the ranch. The wind nipped around them, and she would've been wishing she had worn something warmer if James hadn't come prepared.

As the buckboard rumbled along the bumpy road made worse by the holes every few feet, Rose made a mental note to thank James when they were alone, to let him know she appreciated his thoughtfulness.

It didn't take long before they arrived in Helena. The streets bustled with movement, and she gazed around in amazement, swiveling her head this way and that, so she wouldn't miss a moment. So much excitement, so many people. When they had arrived in Helena after Christmas, her exhaustion and pain had overridden any curiosity she might have had. Now, with no distractions, she could take in the sights and sounds.

Ben pulled the buckboard to a stop in front of a magnificent hotel. The Hotel Helena boasted five stories and was quite grand. The main entrance was encased in a light granite that sparkled in the sunlight, and Rose's reflection greeted her as she walked up the steps.

Porters in crisp black suits with red bow ties and smart little black caps bustled around, picking up luggage and leading well-dressed ladies and gentlemen up the wide stairway supported by intricately carved oak pillars. She scanned the antique oak lobby finishings, the details sophisticated. She itched to run her fingers across the wood engravings. The floor under their feet was a whitish grey marble that matched the mantel surrounding an enormous fireplace on the east side of the room. Even the walls and ceilings were a sight to behold with bright white soapstone. Everything gleamed under the sunlight pouring in from the large open windows.

Before she had a chance to consume the decadence surrounding them, Ben had checked them in at the main desk. The clerk handed their door keys to the porters, and the four of them followed the porters to the elevator that would take them to the fifth floor. Rose had never been in an elevator before and hesitated, but Ben and Elizabeth walked inside as if they had done this many times. Not wanting to look as though she were a fish out of water, she swallowed her trepidation and followed.

The gate clanged shut and the lobby of the hotel could be viewed through the wrought iron bars designed in a filigree fashion. The porters pulled a bar before the cage jerked and slowly ascended to the fifth floor. It was the top floor, and she was eager to see the view. Joseph never had the money that would've allowed them to make such a trip for one evening. Could they afford such opulence?

When the elevator shuddered to a stop, they stepped into an elaborately decorated hallway. The walls contained gilded paintings, and their feet sank into the plush rugs. One porter opened a door for Rose and James, while another led Ben and Elizabeth to a room across the hall.

James and Rose's room was luxurious, more elegant than Rose could have ever imagined. Bright light poured through the tall windows surrounded by velvet blue drapes; the edges covered in delicate tassels. Brass trimmings lined the fireplace on the east side of the room. Plush, light blue colored sofas and chairs framed the fireplace along with a small intimate table for two. Gas and incandescent fixtures hung from the walls in the room and would offer light in the evening. A door to the right opened into a room holding one bed, an enormous bed she would need a staircase to climb into. Billowy pillows and a thick white and baby blue coverlet looked inviting and sumptuous.

Placing their bags on the floor near the bed, the porter spoke with James for a few moments before James handed him a couple of coins. Rose looked out the windows. The view was as she had imagined it would be. Helena was no small town and was fairly bursting at the seams. She stood there, absorbing as much as she could before she sensed James's presence.

"Beautiful, isn't it?" He tickled her neck with his breath.

"Oh, it is. I can't believe how fabulous this room is. Do we have the money for this?"

"Probably not"—he chuckled—"but Ben

insisted on paying. He said it's his treat, and I wasn't to argue. Besides, Elizabeth pulled me aside and insisted Ben would be insulted if I fought him."

"This is more than I could've ever imagined," she said. "The people seem so small from up here, don't they?"

"I thought the same thing." He smiled. "Almost like little ants. I don't think I've ever been to a place so fancy. I'm afraid I might break something if I'm not careful."

"Me too," she said before giggling.

"Well, I don't want that. We won't go to places like this very often, so we might as well enjoy it while we can."

A knock interrupted them. It was Elizabeth and Ben.

"What do you think of your room?" Elizabeth had a bright smile and held her hands out.

Rose took Elizabeth's hands. "It's lovely. James and I are very grateful."

"We're happy to do it." Elizabeth squeezed her fingers and was fairly jumping out of her skin.

"I thought we could go shopping, if you'd like? Just the two of us. Are you up for that?"

"I didn't think you were fond of shopping," Rose said.

"Normally, I'm not, but I need a pair of new stockings, and I thought you'd enjoy it."

"I would, but I don't have the money to spend."

"Nonsense. We don't need money to shop. We can just look."

"In that case, I'd love to," Rose said, smiling at Elizabeth's enthusiasm.

"Let's freshen up and meet downstairs in an hour."

* * *

Elizabeth and Rose spent an exhausting but delightful afternoon visiting many shops along the primary thoroughfare of Helena. Many fine clothes, trinkets, and even furnishings captured Rose's attention. As much as she would've liked to have bought a few of the items, especially toys for Sarah and Tommy, she didn't want to spend any of the money she had on frivolities and couldn't in good conscience take money from James. Instead, she concentrated on enjoying the sights and smells. They were enough to make her smile with joy.

At one boutique, Elizabeth convinced her to try on pre-made dresses, skirts, and shirtwaists that were nicer than any clothing Rose had ever worn. Everything Rose had been given had been passed onto her from someone. Nothing she owned had been new. She wasn't complaining, for she had been grateful for everything she had ever been given, but to try on something new was satisfaction in and of itself. Elizabeth even convinced her to try on an evening gown.

She came out of the dressing room wearing a deep emerald silk gown. It had a high neck with a diamond cut out in the bodice and was very fashionable, according to Elizabeth. Fitted sleeves stopped right below her elbows. The silk fabric gathered on either side of her waist, draping gracefully to the floor. Embroidery along the front and down the side of the dress completed the delicate design where it wrapped around the short but very fashionable train.

Elizabeth clapped her hands enthusiastically when she saw her. "You look gorgeous. I love that color on you." She walked around Rose and smoothed out a wrinkle at her side. "It brings out the red in your hair."

"It is quite beautiful, isn't it?" She stood in front of the full-length mirrors. Her waist looked small and delicate. A part of her longed to buy the dress but knew it was an expenditure she could ill afford. Her money had to be spent on practical items, not an evening dress she'd never have an occasion to wear.

"You are stunning in it," Elizabeth said.

Rose blushed. "Are you going to try on anything?"

"Oh, I have plenty of gowns. Ben insists on outfitting me with new ones every year. I think he hopes the more he buys, the more likely I'll stop wearing my trousers." Elizabeth wandered to a gown made of red silk, caressing the dress with her fingers.

"Trousers?" Rose stared at Elizabeth in shock. She always seemed so ladylike.

"Yes," Elizabeth said, an infectious smile on her lips. "I'm scandalous, if you must know, or at least Ben thinks I am." She giggled. "He doesn't like it when I wear them but has learned I'll wear them if I feel like it, although I do try and respect his wishes and only wear them when I'm riding or when I'm working with the calves."

"You work on the ranch?"

"Yes, not as often as I'd like, but I've been known to get a little dirty at times."

"I would've never guessed that."

Elizabeth turned away from the red dress. "You should try them. You might like 'em."

Rose giggled and looked at the dress on her frame. "Maybe I will one day, but for now I better remove this dress before I decide I can't live without it. It truly is beautiful."

Slipping into the dressing room, she quickly donned her shirtwaist and skirt. She missed the luxuriousness of the silk as it slipped off her skin, but she shouldn't be wishing for something she could never have, but it had been delicious dreaming about it.

Once dressed, she found Elizabeth admiring a pair of silk stockings on display. They had rose and yellow flowers and green leaves embroidered on the top edge with a delicate pink ribbon to keep them in place. They were as decadent as the gown. In desperate need of new stockings, she longed to have them, but the reasonably priced cotton pairs were what she should consider, not the fancy silk stockings. Silk wasn't practical for life on a ranch.

They left the boutique after Elizabeth had purchased a pair of silk stockings. She told Rose that Ben had encouraged her to buy new ones and normally she wouldn't indulge, but just couldn't help herself. A part of Rose wished she could spend her money in any way she pleased. If she had, she would have bought those impractical ones for herself, but good sense prevailed, and she shook off her unrealistic desires.

As they swept inside the hotel, they met the men leaving the billiards room.

"Ladies." Ben wrapped his arm around Elizabeth's side and pulled her close. "Did you have a nice time?"

Smiling at him, Elizabeth said, "I did. I hope Rose did as well."

Rose grinned. "Your wife is a delight to shop with and made it very enjoyable."

"I agree with you," Ben said. "She certainly is delightful." Ben gazed at his wife with such love, it almost broke Rose's heart.

She wanted the same kind of love Ben and Elizabeth shared. She looked at James and wondered if the two of them could eventually find that same kind of love and commitment with one another.

"I imagine the both of you are famished. Shall we get something to eat before leaving for the theater?" Ben asked.

"Yes. I could use a bite to eat. How about you, Rose?" Elizabeth said.

"Yes, I'd like that. It'd also give me a chance to rest my weary feet," Rose said.

"You didn't overdo it, did you?" James asked, looking her over as though to assure himself no harm had come to her.

Turning to him, she placed her fingers on his arm and squeezed gently. He tensed.

"No, I feel wonderful. I just need to get off my feet for a quick moment. I can't wait to go to the theater," Rose said.

"Then," Ben said, "let's go to the dining room. The hotel clerk said they have tender juicy steaks and large russet potatoes that have been roasting all day. I can even smell fresh bread from here."

Chapter 16

After eating, they retreated to their rooms to freshen and change for the theater. James watched Rose walk into the bedroom of their suite. He was eager to see what she would think of her surprise and wondered if she would love it. Or she could think it was too presumptuous.

He discussed ideas with Elizabeth earlier in the week and she suggested something that sounded right perfect. It took a bit of maneuvering to ensure Rose wouldn't know what they were up to, but he was confident Elizabeth had been successful.

"Oh, my!" she exclaimed.

Rose then appeared at the door of the room, holding a green dress. Her expression was one of pure delight.

"James! Good gracious! What? How?" She looked at the dress, one hand holding it to her, while the other stroked the fabric, running her fingers along the delicate silk.

A zing went straight through him. He wished she'd touch him as reverently and maybe one day she would.

"Elizabeth helped me. Do you like it?" he asked.

She reached for his hand and squeezed before letting go. "I love it, but do we have the money for this?"

"Don't you worry none about that. I wanted you to have somethin' special."

"This is more than special. It's exquisite, beautiful, fabulous. I can't think of enough words to describe how I'm feeling. Thank you!" she said, tears brimming.

James frowned. "I didn't mean to upset you. Should I have not gotten—"

"Oh, no." She swiped at her face. "These are happy tears."

James was relieved. He wanted to make this night something they would remember. It wasn't much, but he was thrilled she liked it.

Unexpectedly, she threw her arms around his neck. Shocked, he stood there for a moment before he wrapped his arms around her waist and pulled her close. She fit perfectly, and he wanted to hold her for longer than he should.

She pulled back a moment later and blushed. "I shouldn't have done that."

"I'm glad you did." His voice was low, solemn.

Embarrassed, her face and neck flushed a deeper red and she scurried to the bedroom.

A moment later, she squealed with excitement. "There are stockings and new… Oh my."

She had found the new undergarments as well. He told Elizabeth to outfit her from head to toe. She had done that and more from the sounds of it. He owed Elizabeth and Ben, as they had provided most of the funds for both the trip and the gifts. He would have to work it off, but it was well worth the expense if he had given Rose even a small measure of pleasure.

* * *

Hours later, they returned to the hotel. Exhausted but jubilant, the four of them had enjoyed a musical at the Ming's Opera House. Rose had been engaging and outgoing all evening. James hadn't seen this side of her, and it was a joy to behold. They had a bit too much to drink, but it had been a night of celebration and so the wine and whiskey had flowed.

James loosened his necktie and shrugged out of his suit jacket. He had forgotten how restricting a suit was, but it had been worth it to see the appreciation in Rose's eyes when she had gotten a good look at him. The last time he had worn one had been at Elizabeth and Ben's wedding. He had sent her off to be married, to be safe from her pa before his world came tumbling down. He never thought he'd have the occasion to wear such finery again.

Rose chattered about what they had seen and how lovely the music was. He listened and couldn't contain his own enjoyment, not necessarily about the show but how much she had relished the evening's entertainment. Disappearing from his view, he heard the rustle of her skirts as they fell to the floor.

He wanted to kiss her, pull her into his arms, hoping to forget all he had done and paid for, but he had promised her their marriage was one in name only and he couldn't break his promise. The last thing he wanted was to shake her confidence and trust in him.

Looking out into the night sky, he tried to think of anything besides his wife in the room next door. All evening, he had been intrigued with her. The green in her dress had brought out the red in her hair and her eyes twinkled from the thrill of the theater. As she donned her nightgown, his imagination ran wild.

While working on Ben's ranch, he had

exhausted himself, pushing himself hard, so he'd be too tired to want her when he came home in the evening. Tonight, here, now, he couldn't do that. He wasn't tired and was very much in tune with it being just the two of them, alone in a fancy room, far from anything he could ever give her on his own. It was as though it was a dream, one he could control and push to an end he had been hoping for, but his dreams didn't come true. They hadn't before, and they certainly wouldn't now.

The night sky was clear, and the moon shone brightly, but he couldn't forget what she was doing. It had been a long time in the making. He hadn't been with a woman in over seven years, let alone someone who was his wife. She might only be married to him because of the safety of his name, but that didn't stop his feelings from developing in ways he hadn't been prepared for.

Before being imprisoned, he hadn't been with many women. On occasion, he would stop at a brothel and enjoy a woman's embrace, but even that had been rare. He had always wanted a wife and a family and didn't want to spend his life in the arms of soiled doves. When his crimes had caught up with him, he didn't believe he'd be able to fulfill his dream of having a family. Now he had one and couldn't imagine his life without them. He didn't want to ruin what they had, no matter how much he craved her touch.

"James?"

He turned. Her grace captivated him as she burned her big, green eyes into his soul. She stood in a pale, yellow wrapper, her hair hung around her shoulders in a tangle of curls, looking at him, waiting for him to say something. He wanted to sink his hands into those curls and make her his own, but he had to remember that wasn't what she wanted.

Swallowing hard, he said, "Yes?"

"Is there something on your mind?"

He stepped behind a sofa to put distance between them. He didn't want to alarm her. "No, no. I was lost in my thoughts. Did you need something?"

"No, I was just chattering on." Her smile was

tentative but still engaging. "I wasn't saying anything of importance."

"Everything you say is of import to me. I should've been listening." *Damnit,* he needed to be aware of his surroundings and quit wishing for things that wouldn't happen.

"That's very nice of you to say, but I know I can go on and on. Not one of my finer qualities, but I had such a fabulous time tonight. You were kind to get me the new gown. It couldn't have been a more perfect evening. I can't thank you enough for doing this. I had a fantastic time. Now listen to me. I'm doing it again."

She twiddled with the sash around her waist, while, as she put it, gone on and on, but he loved that she did. It felt as though she was finally coming out of the doldrums she'd been in following Sarah's birth.

He stepped from behind the sofa and reached for her hands, the skin smooth and soft under his. He squeezed them and before he could stop himself, he brought her petite body closer to him. With flushed cheeks, parted lips, and the pale skin showing above her neckline, he just couldn't help himself.

She continued to chatter with nervousness, but he had an overwhelming and sudden wish to kiss her. It was a mistake, but he just couldn't help himself. He let go of one of her hands and cupped her cheek, running his thumb across her flushed skin and down her delicate chin. Her eyes were wide, but she didn't stop him. Lifting her chin, he bent and covered her lips with his own.

He pulled back. James couldn't do this, not without knowing what was going through her mind. He wanted a proper wife, not one who felt forced, manipulated, or caught up in the moment.

Stepping away, he trailed his fingers along her arms until he dropped them away. He turned and put distance between them. He was a better man, or at least he wanted to be.

"James?" Her voice was soft.

Leaning up against the fireplace mantel, he gripped the sharp edge of the corner, letting it dig into his palm. He needed the pain to pull his mind from the delectable woman standing a few feet away. He took several deep, calming breaths, trying to still his beating heartbeat.

"Please give me a minute, Rose."

"Why?" she asked.

"You know why."

A whisper of movement circled around him when she rested her hand on the small of his back. She didn't move her fingers, just stayed there as though she were holding him up from falling.

"Rose." His voice was strangled.

Her fingers then moved in small circular movements. Not pressing, just spinning a delicate web around him.

"No," he said and stepped away from her touch. "You can't do this. We can't do this." He bowed his head, his heart breaking.

"Yes, we can." She reached for his hand and held it between both of hers. He tried to pull away, extending his arm, but she didn't let go. "Why are you punishing yourself?"

"I don't deserve you!" he shouted, once again trying to pull himself free from the physical and emotional hold she had on him. He was not worthy of this woman and one day she would know, too.

"Don't you think I know my own mind?"

"Of course I do, but with—"

"A lot has happened, and I want you, James Dodson. Can't you feel my heart beating?" She placed his hand against her heart, forcing him to turn toward her. She held his palm there, gazing at him with a look of desire.

How can I resist?

"Rose?"

"Yes, James. Yes."

Chapter 17

A knock woke James, and he smiled at the memories from their evening. Her seeming innocence, as well as her unwavering trust in him, made him fall for her even more. He could never understand how he had gotten so lucky when everything in his life up to this point had been nothing but drudgery and mistakes he could never make up for.

She had buried deep in his heart and if luck were on his side, perhaps this time next year he'd be holding his own little one. All the dreams that he never thought possible might actually come true.

He looked at her one more time. This amazing, passionate woman was his wife, in the full sense of the word. He was careful not to wake her and opened the door.

Ben stood outside. His face was grim.

James tensed. "Is something wrong?"

"Is Rose awake?" Ben avoided his gaze and didn't answer James' question.

Unease snaked up his spine. "No. She's still sleeping." James leaned against the door, dread tingling his neck.

"We need to return to the ranch as soon as possible." Ben's thumbs hung in the belt loops of his trousers.

"We'll gather our things and meet you out front in an hour."

Ben scratched behind his ear. "No, we shouldn't wait."

"Why don't you tell me what's going on?" James replied, his taut voice filled with frustration.

Breathing heavily, Ben sighed. "It's Tommy."

James's heart seized. Rose would never

forgive him if anything happened to her son. "What's wrong?"

"He's fallen sick, and it doesn't look promising. The doc's been out to the ranch and is worried he won't make it through the night."

A gasp, broken in with a tight sob, tore through the room. James whipped around and saw Rose, a crestfallen expression on her lovely face.

"What happened?" she asked, creasing her forehead.

James stepped aside to let Ben into the room. "I'm not rightly sure," Ben said. "He fell ill with a fever soon after we left. Anne and Katy thought it was a touch of the flu, so they put him to bed and kept a close eye on him. As the evening wore on, they got worried. They sent for the doc, and after he looked the tyke over, he sent Sam to get us."

Rose started to crumble, but James raced to her side, catching her as she fell.

"Sweetheart, we don't know how sick he is.

We'll get you to the ranch as soon as possible so you can be with him, all right?"

She raised her eyes and nodded, but the self-recriminations in them were his undoing. She was doubting their night together, as if that were the reason for Tommy's illness. Wiping her eyes, she pushed him away, stood, and regained her composure.

"We'll be down momentarily," she said, her voice barely above a whisper.

Nodding, Ben stepped into the hallway. "I'm sorry. This isn't how I wanted our trip to end."

* * *

Not much later, they met Ben and Elizabeth on the steps in front of the hotel. Ben had the buckboard waiting, and they left Helena behind. Rose berated herself on the way back to the ranch. This had to be her punishment for finding a small measure of happiness. She had indulged herself without a thought for her children.

Before Ben applied the brake, Rose had gathered her skirt and jumped down, twisting her ankle, but the ache was mild compared to the pain in her heart. She ran up the steps and went inside. She wasn't sure where her little boy was, but she was going to find him. Frantic, she ripped open doors, her movements erratic, almost unhinged in her desperation.

When she couldn't find him on the main floor, she ran to the stairs where Anne met her halfway up.

"Rose, you're here. We didn't expect you 'til later this afternoon." Anne's smile was forced as she knew the reason why they had rushed home.

"Tommy? Where is he?"

"He's upstairs in the nursery."

Anne's concerned eyes were almost her undoing, but Rose stayed on her feet. She picked up her skirts, pushed past her, and ran up the remaining stairs.

"Rose, wait," Anne cried, but Rose had only one thing on her mind and that was to get to Tommy.

Bursting through the nursery room door, Rose saw Tommy lying in the bed next to the window. His eyes were closed, his face was flushed, and he looked so small and frail. She emitted a small screech of horror. "My baby."

The doc held out his hands to stop her. "Ma'am, please. Let's talk outside where Tommy can't hear us."

He ushered her into the hallway and closed the door behind them. The soft click was the only sound in the quiet hallway. By this time, James and Elizabeth had arrived.

"Please, Doc, what's wrong with Tommy?" Her voice sounded high-pitched to her own ears. She was anxious and likely going to be reduced to a puddle of tears if the doc didn't tell her soon.

"Why don't you sit?" He put his hand on her arm to encourage her.

She wrenched her arm from his grasp. "I don't want to sit. What's wrong with my son?"

The doc hesitated, glancing at James as if asking for his aid. This further infuriated her. She didn't need the doctor looking to her husband, but as James came toward her, she gave in and sat with a heavy sigh on the chair at the end of the hallway. If that is what they wanted, she would sit.

The doc's hands rested behind his back, the vest buttons pulling as he paced in front of her. "Tommy's seriously sick, dangerously so. His fever's extremely high, his chest is congested, and pneumonia has settled in. With his young age, I'm uneasy if—"

"He was fine when we left. How could this happen?" She swallowed her tears. "What can we do?"

"It's hard to say. He could've had a mild cough for days and not shown any real symptoms but doesn't matter now. We need to work on reducing his fever and removing the mucus from his chest."

"How long…" Her voice broke. "How long 'til we know he's out of danger?"

The doc raised his pudgy hand to his face and rubbed his wide forehead. His ears were small and looked out of place, and his round body reminded her of a roly-poly. He had been kind when he had looked her over after Sarah's birth. She had to trust he knew what he was doing.

"Typically, it lasts anywhere from seven to ten days, but what worries me is his breathing."

"Is there something that can help, Doc?" James asked. He placed his hand on Rose's shoulder and squeezed gently, the comfort he was trying to give her not welcome, and she shrugged out of his grasp. He dropped his hand to his side, but he still stood near her, his presence was both a comfort and a distraction.

"There are new techniques where they use oxygen, but I've never heard of it being used on a patient so young."

"Has it worked?" Rose asked.

"In a few adults, there have been surprisingly positive results, but we aren't sure how much to use in children. We don't want to use too much, you understand?"

"Are there other treatments?" she asked.

"Yes, we can create a steam tent to help break up the mucus, give him cool baths to help with the fever, lots of warm broth, and pray. There are those doctors who consider bloodletting, but I'm not a supporter of that treatment," the doc said.

"What about this oxygen?" James asked.

"As I mentioned, I hesitate because of his age. I don't want to try it unless we find nothing else works."

"If you think it can help, what does it hurt?" James pressed.

"I worry because if given too much, it could cause added complications."

"What type of complications?"

The doc hesitated before answering. "He could stop breathing altogether, have seizures, his ear drums could rupture, to name a few difficulties with using it."

Rose's eyes grew wide with horror.

James knelt at her side, picked up her hand, and held it in his large palm. "Do you want to try it? I'll support whatever you decide."

She looked at him, confused. "I don't think so, at least not yet." She was shaken and distraught, and she was afraid she was doomed regardless of what decision she made. Her little boy was sick, and she couldn't fix it.

James stood, not letting go. "Let's try the oxygen as a last resort."

The doc relaxed with the suggestion and he and Elizabeth discussed what they needed, while Rose's own breathing intensified with fear.

The doc studied her, concerned. "Are you all right, ma'am?"

"Yes, yes," she said, although she clearly wasn't.

His eyes probed, but he asked. "Do you want to go see your son?" He held up his hand. "But remember, he doesn't understand what's happening, so try not to show you're scared. If he senses your distress, it'll only make it harder for him to breathe."

Nodding, Rose wiped away the tears and struggled to regain her composure. She needed to be strong. When ready, she stood. James put his arm around her waist, but she hardly noticed. Her only thoughts were for her son.

He would survive. He had to. She couldn't lose Tommy so soon after the death of his father. She had lost too many people in her life, and losing Tommy would damage her beyond repair.

Chapter 18

James opened the door to the nursery, the firelight flickering and casting an orange and yellow glow across Tommy and Rose. She was nestled at his side, resting her hand on his belly as though needing to feel him take each breath.

His heart tugged painfully. It had been two days and Tommy wasn't improving. She was scared, and so was James. The doc had explained to him just moments before how dire the situation was. If the congestion didn't ease, there was a chance he would suffocate.

Wanting to spare Rose the ominous words, James asked the doc not to tell her, at least not yet. He didn't want her to worry any more than she already was. She couldn't stand to have more dreadful news. After weeks of sadness, she had broken free of the baby blues, but this could set her back.

While in Helena, they had grown closer. Something he hoped they could build from, but now, with this, he wasn't sure anymore. She was retreating and shied from his touch. The blankness in her eyes scared him. They reminded him of his own ma and how she had looked at him when they decided he had to leave their ramshackle homestead.

His ma's eyes had been lifeless and held no spark of happiness or the joy she had well before she met Elizabeth's pa, George. Within months of marrying him, she had been resigned to her fate, and when things spiraled out of control a few years later, she had given James what little money she had squirreled away. She tightly held his hand, the money folded inside. She had pushed a lock of his hair behind his ear, kissed his cheek, and shooed him gone before George came home. The memories were painful and ones he didn't care to remember.

Grabbing the cot they had brought into the room the day before, he placed it next to Tommy's bed and brushed her shoulder with his fingertips. She raised her head and rubbed her eyes. She looked at James and then at Tommy to make sure he was still there, still breathing.

"Is Tommy…" Her quiet voice was reverent as though speaking in a soft voice would help his recovery.

"He's still with us. Nothing's changed. I'll put the cot here so you can be next to him."

"I shouldn't sleep. I just wanted to rest for a moment." She yawned, widened her mouth, and closed her eyes with drowsiness.

"I understand. You want to be here when he wakes and needs you."

Telling her she wouldn't be of any help to her son if she didn't get any rest seemed heartless. James knew he was riding a fine line where, if he made the wrong move, any trust they had built could disappear as fast as an icy wind on a warm spring day.

Instead, he said, "I'll sit while you take a quick nap on the cot and wake you if there's any change. I won't go anywhere, I promise. I'll be here the entire time."

He could see the turmoil she tried to reason through, but her exhaustion won, and she nodded, albeit reluctantly. She stood and almost fell from fatigue. Breaking her fall, he tried to help her, but she stopped him, brushing his hands away.

"No, don't. Just give me a moment, please."

What have I done to deserve this?

It hurt that she didn't want his help. He shouldn't have been surprised, but he was.

"You'll wake me?" she asked.

"Yes."

"Promise me," she insisted.

"I promise." He'd give her whatever she wanted. He just wished she understood that.

When he had set up the cot, she sat and removed her shoes.

"Do you want to change into something more comfortable?" he asked.

She stared at him, anger, hurt, and desolation in her eyes.

"No, I'll be fine." She curled on the cot, facing Tommy. With one hand under her cheek, she rested her other on Tommy's leg.

Touched by her compassion, James settled into the chair she vacated and watched over them both. Within a few minutes, Rose's eyes closed. She fell into a fitful slumber, startling herself every so often, reaching for her son.

As the night wore on, Tommy's breathing was labored, but he struggled no more than he had since they had returned to the ranch. Eventually, James himself couldn't fight his sleepiness and he too fell asleep. After spending six years sleeping with one eye open for fear of what might happen, James was a light sleeper and knew if Tommy stirred, he'd wake.

As the days wore on, Tommy's condition stabilized until the seventh night, when he took a turn for the worse. He gasped for breath, opening and closing his mouth like a fish pulled from the stream, begging for it to end. He quit eating and refused to drink anything she tried to give him. All Tommy wanted to do was sleep, and no matter how much cajoling Rose did, he wouldn't take it. He kept his mouth closed tight. Then his fever reached a dangerous high. The doc reluctantly sent for the oxygen and told James to prepare Rose for the worst.

Taking a break from the constant vigil, James pulled Rose out of the room and left Tommy in the capable hands of his sister. Elizabeth said she would find them if things changed. James led Rose to the dining room, where he forced her to sit and to eat. He would not let her leave until she put food in her belly.

She stared at him in stony silence as he prepared a plate of food. What he had to tell her was going to break her heart. She would need to have as much strength as she could muster over the next twenty-four hours, especially if the oxygen did not do as wished. It had become their last measure of hope, one neither he nor the doctor believed would save the little boy.

Placing the food in front of her, he waved for her to eat. She glared at him, as if to say, "how will you make me?" Prepared to force feed her, if necessary, he scowled right back. As if reading his mind, she picked up the fork and shoved a forkful into her mouth. Her angry eyes spoke volumes. She was furious.

Dark circles had formed under her eyes, and she had lost more weight, weight she could ill afford to lose. She was only leaving Tommy's side long enough to feed Sarah and if she didn't eat, it wouldn't be long before her milk would disappear. After watching her eat for a few minutes, he was satisfied enough to fill his own plate.

For a while, nothing but the sound of the forks hitting their plates and the occasional swallow of drink filled the silence. When James felt she had eaten enough, he relaxed in his chair.

Stubbornness and irritation flashed in her eyes. "What?"

"I'm glad you finally ate." He didn't react to her anger.

"You didn't give me much choice," she replied, disgust lining each word. She shoved away from the table and stood. "Now that I've eaten, your royal highness, can I go to my son?"

"We should talk. Please, sit."

"Tommy needs me. I'm going upstairs."

Realizing he had very little time to talk to her, he stopped her by blocking the doorway. She tried to move around him, but he grabbed her wrists.

Eyes flashing, daggers fairly flew from her eyes. "Let me go."

"There's something we need to discuss."

"It can wait. I'm going upstairs." She tried pulling away, but he held her tight.

He had to tell her. He had waited long enough. "No, you aren't. Not until I have my say."

She fought him, and realizing he had few options, he grabbed her around the waist and lifted her over his shoulder. She hit his back with her fists and tried to kick her legs, but he held them firm with one arm. He carried her through the hall to Ben's study. He needed a room where they could talk without interruption.

"Let me down!" she screeched.

He ignored her and continued to carry her to the sofa, where he released her. Jumping up, she tried to run for the door, but he stopped her, slamming the door behind them.

"What are you doing? Let me out of here!" she screamed.

"No. We can do this the hard way or the easy way. It's up to you. But you'll listen."

Panting and nearly falling apart from hysteria, he could see her emotions. She fisted her hands and heaved her chest. Taking a deep breath, she twirled around and plopped in a chair. Crossing her arms over her chest, she stared at him and didn't say a word. If things weren't so dire, he would chuckle at the display she made. Spitting mad but capitulating as though to tell him she'd do as he'd say, but she certainly wouldn't listen.

He paced before he blurted it out. "The doc's convinced Tommy won't make it."

As the words tumbled out of his mouth, he wished he could take back every word he just uttered. He could have done this gently, tactfully, but he said the one thing she was scared to death of. That her son would die.

"No," she cried. "Tommy has lasted this long. He will not die."

Then she cracked. Huge wracking sobs tore through her slight frame, and she shook uncontrollably. He reached her side and held her hands in his. She fought him, but he pulled her into his arms.

She wrapped her arms around his sides and pressed her face against his shoulder. She cried and cried for what seemed like hours. He held her close, murmuring words of comfort into her ear, trying with everything in him to give her the support she needed.

Eventually, her sobs subsided, and she sniffled into his shirt. She tried to pull away, but he wouldn't let her. While she needed to cry her heart out, he needed to hold her. Tommy may not have been *his* child, but in the few months they had been married, Tommy had carved a place in his heart. James didn't want to lose him anymore than Rose did.

James wiped a tear from her cheek, touching her softly and gently. He needed to further explain to her what the doc had said. "Tommy's condition is deteriorating. The doc sent for the oxygen, but he isn't hopeful. He isn't coughing up the mucus that's in his chest and if it doesn't clear soon, he could suffocate and there's nothing he can do to stop it."

"No." She pleaded with him to understand. "I refuse to believe Tommy will leave us. Sometimes you have to get worse before you can get better. If we pray hard enough and encourage him, he will pull through." She stood and paced in front of him.

"You need to be realistic. Tommy isn't getting

any better." James's voice was hard but filled with sorrow.

She stumbled, grabbing a chair to keep from falling.

"I don't care what you say," she said, her voice broken. "Tommy will make it through the night and nothing you can say'll change my mind."

"Be reasonable."

"I am. I think you're the one who's being unreasonable. If you give up, he *will* pass away, and I'll never forgive you. If you hadn't made me go to Helena, I would've been here. I could've prevented this."

"That's not fair," he said. "Going to Helena had nothing to do with it."

"A mother knows when her child is sick. I could've given him something, made sure he didn't go outside and catch a chill. But because you wanted to go to Helena, I left my children and as a result Tommy is… he…" She choked on her sobs.

"I didn't mean—"

Rose interrupted him. "Stop. I don't want to do this anymore. I'm going to see my son."

She ripped open the door before he could say a word, leaving him alone. He watched her go, a weight so heavy on his shoulders, it fairly knocked him to the floor. He hadn't expected her words. What little respect and joy they had built no longer existed. If Tommy didn't make it through the night, he was afraid what they had cultivated would never be there again.

Chapter 19

The night was long and painful for Tommy. After his hurtful words, Rose didn't want James anywhere near them and made it clear he wasn't welcome. He wanted to be there for her, but she refused to speak to him. He left her with the doctor, the same pain in his eyes she held in hers.

The doctor used the oxygen, and it seemed to help Tommy breathe better, but it didn't break up the mucus that had settled deep in his chest. Leaving Tommy in Rose and Elizabeth's capable hands, the doctor retreated to Ben's study to consult his medical journals to see if there was something he missed.

Elizabeth suggested they try the steam tent again. Tommy didn't want to. In fact, he didn't want to do anything, but Rose couldn't let her little boy give up. Tommy was Joseph's and if he was watching from heaven above, she didn't want him to believe she had let go when there might've been a smidgen of hope.

She picked up Tommy, his clammy body was hot and sweaty next to hers. He didn't fight her. If he fought, he still had energy, but if he didn't, shew as afraid that meant he was too far gone. She was going to fight for him. He could hold on to her and use her strength. Her sweet little boy was everything to her. He was her angel, her reason for living.

Leaving for the kitchen, she met Elizabeth where pots of boiling water and a steam tent were waiting. Stepping under the thick tent, Rose once again tried to encourage him to breathe and cough up the nasty mucus. They sat for hours with very little results until the wee hours of the morning, when Tommy began hacking deep, hard, gut-wrenching coughs. He cried but spit out large chunks of thick green mucus.

It was a sign of improvement. After an hour of the pain-filled coughing, he quieted, and his breathing returned to normal. Exhausted but exhilarated, both Rose and Elizabeth smiled with satisfaction. He wasn't out of the woods, but they were optimistic.

Rose moved the wet strands of hair from his face, carried him down the hall, and met James as he walked out of the parlor. He gently pulled Tommy from her arms. She wanted to argue, but she didn't have the energy. As she looked at the stairs and the daunting task of climbing them with Tommy in her arms, she was grateful for his help. She was still angry with him and his lack of faith, but she was content he was there to help. He stepped into her life when she least expected it but needed it greatly.

Urging her up the stairs, James followed, clearly protecting her in case she was to stumble. Stepping into the nursery, Rose pulled out a clean nightshirt for Tommy. The one he was wearing was drenched in sweat and stained from the mucus. He needed a bath, but it could come later. For now, getting him into clean, dry clothes was her priority.

She reached for Tommy, but James stopped her.

"Please, sit. You're exhausted and I'm surprised you're still standing. Let me change Tommy, please." He pleaded with her.

Rose capitulated and sat. Her feet ached and her limbs cried with fatigue. She had avoided sitting because she had been afraid she wouldn't be able to stand if she did.

She watched as James removed Tommy's soiled clothing. He picked up a cool washcloth from the basin next to the bed and washed his face, neck, and hands before pulling clean, warm clothing onto him.

Tommy smiled at James, a great big, wonderful smile. Relief flowed through her. Her little boy was going to be all right. They were through the worst of it. It would take a few more days for him to recover, but she saw a light in him that had been absent for days. Now it was back.

* * *

James placed Tommy on the floor with a few of his favorite blocks. He then made quick work of stripping his bed of the dirty linens and replacing them. Rose hadn't asked, but it was the least he could do. She had pushed herself to the point of exhaustion and had finally fallen fast asleep.

James was on edge. Over the past few days, Rose had refused to listen and wouldn't let anyone take care of Tommy without her being just a few feet away. Crouching in front of Tommy, he tucked away a lock of his hair. His big green eyes were heavy with sleep, but he smiled a toothy grin and reached for James, wrapping his tiny arms around his neck.

He had accepted James into his life with no question. The little boy may not have been the son of his blood, but he had become the son of his heart. His relief was overwhelming. If he had lost Tommy, he would have lost Rose. They were firmly entrenched in his heart and his life, and he was determined to keep them there.

He stood, holding Tommy in his arms, before taking him to bed. Tommy climbed under the blankets and reached for his teddy bear, which he hadn't done in days. James tucked him in, pulling the blankets snugly around him. Within moments, Tommy was fast asleep and breathing much easier.

Sighing, he stood, stretching his back before turning to find Rose. He didn't want to disturb her, but sleeping in the chair would not give her the rest she needed. She hadn't had a decent night's sleep in over a week. He was determined she was going to get one tonight.

He carefully picked her up, her body small in his arms. She stirred, but her eyes remained closed.

Elizabeth peered around the door. "How is she doing?"

He whispered, "She's exhausted. I think

knowing Tommy's on the road to recovery helped her relax."

Elizabeth led James to Rose's bedroom and pulled back the blankets. He nodded his thanks as he settled her onto the soft mattress, her hair a disarray of curls. He wanted to make her comfortable but wasn't sure if he should remove her clothing. He was her husband, but he wasn't willing to push the boundaries.

Elizabeth, seeing his hesitation, touched his arm. "Give me a few minutes and I'll help her into her nightgown."

"Thank you." He backed out of the room.

Ten minutes later, Elizabeth opened the door and gestured him in.

"She's sleeping peacefully." She squeezed his arm. "She woke up long enough to remove most of her clothing, but then fell right to sleep. I don't think she even realized I was helping her."

Elizabeth left them alone, closing the door quietly behind her. He leaned against the wooden door, unsure if he should approach or leave. It seemed like years since they had spent that evening together, and yet it had only been a little more than a week ago. He wanted to comfort her but was afraid it would be too much, too soon.

She turned, the quilt shifted, and exposed her long legs. An intense longing seized him, but it wasn't the time or the place. He approached and lifted the quilt, covering her. She fluttered her eyelids open and gazed at him.

Not wanting to frighten her, he stepped away, but she lifted her hand and held it out.

"Please don't leave," she murmured.

"You need your sleep." He couldn't resist placing his hand in hers.

She pulled him close until his legs struck the side of the bed.

"I need you more," she whispered.

Giving him the opening, he needed and craved, he pulled her into his arms.

Chapter 20

Rose woke with a start.

"Tommy." She abruptly sat up in bed, the blankets tangled around her legs, disoriented from sleep.

Where's my little boy? Did he fall sick again?

She had to find him. Swinging her legs over the side of the bed, she shivered. Memories of the night before came flooding back, including the fact that Tommy's fever and congestion had been relieved.

Rose had slept like a rock once she had fallen asleep. She looked over her shoulder and saw she was alone. They had agreed early on this was to be a marriage in name only, but she had broken that promise and had taken advantage of his kindness both while in Helena and again last night. She had hurt him with her words, but he still came to her willingly and lovingly. She didn't know what had she done to deserve him.

She contemplated her behavior and was ashamed of herself. She fought against those who loved her, but she couldn't seem to stop herself. Doing it with Joseph when they first were married, and now she was repeating it with James. Rose didn't know why did she do this. If she wanted to stay married to James, she had to stop blaming him for things that were not his fault. He hadn't made Tommy sick, and he certainly hadn't forced her to go to Helena. All that had happened was unfortunate, but the good news was Tommy had recovered. It was time for a new beginning.

An hour later, Rose left her room, hunger rumbling inside her stomach. Before she could fill her belly, she had to look in on her children.

Opening the nursery door, she peered inside and found an empty room.

Trying not to let fear guide her, it was all she could do not to tear through the house looking for Tommy. She went down the stairs, peering into each room, her heart beating fast inside her chest when she heard it. Giggles and laughter coming from the parlor. Wrenching open the door, her heart fairly burst from her skin. Tommy played happily on the floor with Vicky. He had bright eyes, pink skin, and was acting as though nothing untoward had occurred over the last week.

Sarah and Jimmy were in matching cradles nestled against the wide windows, their heads covered with knitted caps, cooing and kicking their legs and arms as they each held wooden toy rattles in their tiny hands. Sunshine shimmered through the glass onto their sweet faces. Elizabeth, Anne, and Katy were on matching sofas speaking quietly and startled at her intrusion.

"Rose, we were thinking we'd need to send a

ten-man band to wake you," Elizabeth said, mirth twinkling in her eyes. "Did you sleep well last night?"

Before she could answer, Tommy squealed, "Momma." Jumping up, he knocked over the stack of blocks and stumbled his way to her.

She scooped him up. He wrapped his chubby little arms around her neck and squeezed. She held him tight and enjoyed this moment of pure joy. He smelled like a ray of sunshine; the sickness having ravaged his tiny frame, but now he had no hint of fever. It had been a tumultuous few days, but it was now over.

Holding him too long, Tommy pushed at her shoulders. "Down, Momma."

She laughed and let him return to his blocks. Watching him toddle over to his friend and cousin made Rose's eyes fill, but they were tears of gratitude.

"I'm sorry, Elizabeth. I didn't mean to sleep so late. Thank you for watching after Tommy and Sarah."

Elizabeth waved the comment away, but a warm smile was on her face. "Think nothing of it," she said. "I was happy to do it."

The lump in her throat grew. She didn't know what to do with the help that was in never-ending supply in Elizabeth and Ben's home.

"Now come here." Elizabeth patted the seat next to her. "Sit and talk with us, although I'm sure you're hungry. Do you want me to send for something?"

"No, I'll grab a bite to eat later." The grumbles from her stomach were in stark protest to her words. She laughed and rested her hand against her belly. "It'll be nice to sit and visit."

Rose stayed until Sarah and Jimmy woke, wanting to be fed. After the children had been put down for naps, Rose went outside for a walk. She grabbed a ham biscuit, her coat, and a thick woolen scarf from the rack near the door. The sky was overcast, and the wind had a bite to it, but it was refreshing to be out of the house. She hadn't ventured outside since they had returned from Helena, and she needed the fresh air.

Breathing in deeply, she thanked God for her good fortune.

She meandered along the path, the snow-covered pine trees creating a winter wonderland. Perching on a fallen log, the coldness seeped into her thick stockings, but it was welcome as it reminded her life was precious.

Rose closed her eyes, said a small prayer, and promised to do better.

* * *

Later that evening, most of Ben and Elizabeth's family gathered for dinner. James was pleased to visit with Ben's brothers, Luke and Michael. He hadn't seen them since the New Year's celebration and even then, it had been brief with the hordes of people visiting and celebrating. Luke was sporting a black eye and when questioned, he brushed it off, but from the glint in Ben's eye, James knew Luke would likely be explaining it to his older brother later.

The last time he spent any real time with

them was before he had been imprisoned. He wondered if they'd hold a grudge over what happened, but they were as welcoming now as they were before he had found himself behind bars. He was lucky the Seymour brothers were a forgiving bunch. The only brother missing was Stanley. James had never met him and was looking forward to the day he would.

He watched the dynamics between the brothers and thanked his lucky stars that his sister had married into the family. They were loving and occasionally disagreed but forgave one another just as quick, never letting things simmer after what had happened to their parents and the subsequent disaster of Stanley's wife, Connie. James knew little of what had happened but could empathize with Stanley's grief over his part in the murder of their parents. Stanley might not have been the one to end their lives, but he had married the woman who had.

Dinner was a lively affair, especially since little Tommy had recovered. Tensions had eased and there was laughter and storytelling happening at each end of the table. Katy and Anne grinned from ear to ear as Michael regaled them with stories. He worked as a blacksmith in Helena and had tales of citified men who didn't know how to saddle a horse to cowpokes who swaggered along the dirt roads, acting as though they owned the world. Luke worked in the newspaper office as a typesetter and reporter and had his own fair share of shenanigans he wrote about and saw daily.

As soon as dinner ended, the men left for Ben's study. Ben poured them each a glass of whiskey while the rest of them settled into armchairs. Ben sat at the end of his desk with one knee propped on the edge. They each sipped their whisky before Ben got straight to the point. "What's going on?"

"Not sure where to start," Luke said. He took another swig of the whiskey before placing the tumbler on the table next to his chair. He braced his hands on his knees, avoiding their gazes before raising his eyes to stare at his older brother.

"I saw Connie the other night."

"What?" Ben slammed his whiskey onto the desk. The liquid sloshed over the sides, droplets hitting his hand. He waved Luke to continue.

Luke described what he had seen and where he had seen it. It also explained Luke's black eye.

"Are you sure it was her?" Ben asked.

"As sure as I can be after seven years," Luke said. "I didn't get close, but it sure looked like her."

"I can't believe she's in Helena," Michael said. "Why would she return? She's got to know we'd still be looking for her."

"Who knows what that woman thinks," Luke said. "I have to find her, but we can't let Stanley know until we do." He clenched his jaw and pursed his lips in frustration.

"No, we can't," muttered Michael. "He still hasn't recovered from Connie killing ma and pa and then trying to kill him. He blames himself and hasn't been the same since that night. I still can't get over her scheming, manipulation, and makes me wonder what else she's done that we know nothin' about."

James kept quiet. He didn't believe he had the right to interrupt, but he'd help in any way they needed. It was a small way to thank them for everything they had done for him and his sister. From what James had gleaned, Stanley struggled with guilt and had left home years ago, coming home only once or twice a year. Elizabeth had told him that when Stanley did come home, he didn't stay long. His guilt for bringing Connie into their lives and the havoc she had created during their brief, but tumultuous marriage kept him away.

"Have you tried to find her?" Ben asked as he shifted against the desk, the papers rustling under his hip.

"Of course, I have," Luke muttered, "but she disappeared before I could grab her. Working for Walter's newspaper has opened doors, but it's been hard to find any trace of her. Besides, we don't even know if Connie was her real name."

"There's got to be a way to find her," Ben

said. "My blood boils knowing she has stayed hidden for this long. Every time we think we have a solid lead, she disappears again."

"I've put out the word with the hopes someone has seen or heard of anyone with her description. If she's in Helena, I'll find her." Luke braced his hands against his knees, determination lacing every inch of his stiff body.

"We've got to catch her, or we may never have Stanley back with us," Ben muttered.

"We've been looking for her for seven years. What's a few more days?" Michael joked.

Ben glared at his younger brother.

"Sorry," Michael mumbled, his gaze downcast from the censure.

"I'll keep asking around," Luke said. "She's bound to make a mistake and when she does, we'll catch her."

"Do we know any more about her past before she married Stanley?" Ben asked.

"I don't recall her ever talking about it," Michael said. "She was always blathering on about clothes and how Stanley needed to do this and that with the ranch, trying to talk him into convincing Pa to go along with her grand plans."

"I never got to know her," Luke said. "She might've known I thought little of her. I wasn't exactly welcoming before or after Pa died. You remember how angry I was."

"And I don't know if it's wise to ask Stanley," Ben said. "He's still too volatile. I don't want him to be disappointed if we lose her again. He was able to dissolve the marriage without her consent, considering everything, but I don't think he'll ever move on until she's behind bars. She's still wanted by the law, and I'm sure she knows that."

"Maybe Anne or Katy remember something," Michael said. "Any little detail is bound to help."

"Perhaps. I'll ask them and see if anything comes to mind. In the meantime, Luke, you'll keep us informed?"

"Of course, I will. Why would you doubt me?" Luke asked, his tight voice growing with anger.

"I'm not doubting you. Did you speak to the Marshal in Helena?" Ben asked.

"No, not yet." Luke glared at his brother.

"When you get to Helena, let him know you might've seen her. I'm sure he'll be interested," Ben said. "He's the one who sent out the wanted posters all those years ago. I'm sure he'd be happy to resolve this mess as much as we would."

"Can I help?" James asked.

The tension was growing thick in the room and in an effort to alleviate the anger that was brewing just under the surface, James felt he needed to offer.

"No, I appreciate the sentiment, but until we can find her, not much can be done," Ben said.

"Considering my past, I know a thing or two about hiding from the law." James smiled wryly.

The humor wasn't lost on them, and they chuckled, all too aware of what James had done and the price he paid.

"I'm happy to help in any way I can. All of you did so much for me even when I didn't deserve it, so I'd like to return the favor," James said.

"No need for that. You're a part of the family. Payback ain't necessary," Ben said.

"Well, the offer's out there just the same."

Ben acknowledged the sentiment and their conversation turned to events on the ranch and to less serious topics, laughter and ribbing one another with love and affection. James had missed the camaraderie the brothers had brought to his life when they lived in Spring Creek. Without them, he wouldn't have been able to sleep with one eye closed in those prison walls if Ben hadn't stepped up and offered to protect Elizabeth from her pa.

With a bit of luck and hard work, Ben and Elizabeth had found happiness in a situation that hadn't warranted it. If he could help bring Connie to justice, he would do everything in his power to give them the same support they had given him when he hadn't deserved it.

Chapter 21

A few days later, James led his horse into the stall, latched the door, and leaned heavily against it. Removing his hat, he rubbed his hand across the nape of his neck. It had been a long and exhausting day, and he wasn't looking forward to going inside and behaving as though everything was all right in his world. The last couple of days had been exhausting both physically and emotionally. He was conflicted.

He couldn't look at Rose without wanting more. She had become very important to him, but he didn't know if she felt the same way. He wanted a wife, someone to share his life with, but she didn't know what she wanted. She only had to cast her gaze on him for his hands to sweat and his heart to beat as fast as a galloping horse. He was acting like a rowdy teenager with every glance. Since Tommy's fever and congestion had broken, he had been avoiding her. He didn't want to upset their tenuous connection.

As Tommy's health improved, his guilt over not telling her about his past haunted him. Their marriage was supposed to have been one in name only. No feelings were to interfere. They could have lived their lives separately but together. Then he ruined it by taking her into his arms. He had broken his promise. Now he didn't know what to do.

He should be happy they were building a life together. He'd have everything he had always wanted. A beautiful, vivacious wife and two children who had a firm hold on his heart.

Ben and Elizabeth had insisted he tell her the truth, but he had ignored their advice. He believed he knew better, that he was doing the right thing, but it was clear he had made a terrible decision and didn't know how to right that wrong.

He kept asking himself what she would've done if he had told her the truth from the beginning, but he hadn't and now he was so ashamed of himself he didn't even want to be in his own company. He thought he learned his lesson after spending six long years in jail. He wanted to become someone his family could be proud of and had decided even before he left prison, he would live his life better. He ruined it by lying to the one person he shouldn't have.

His footsteps were heavy as he climbed onto the porch. Not wanting to go inside yet, he sat in one of the rocking chairs. Pushing with his feet, he rested against the curved wood and rocked. He ran his feet against the ground as thoughts raced through his mind. Thinking about what he should have done when he left his ma's care, what he should have done when Elizabeth had found him, and what he should have done when he met Rose for the first time. Instead, he made mistake after mistake, never seeming to learn from them.

The porch door opened, light from inside spilling out as Elizabeth appeared. She held a lantern in one hand and a knitted afghan in the other.

"James, is that you?" She squinted her eyes trying to see who was sitting outside.

He nodded, but she didn't move. It was dark, so she likely couldn't tell it was him. "Yes," he said.

"It's late. Is everything all right?" she asked. She sat in the chair next to him, placed the lantern on the table between them, and covered her legs with the knitted afghan.

James replied, "Yes, I just came from the south field. I wanted to take a moment and enjoy the night sky."

"You don't mind me sitting with you, do you?" The legs of her rocking chair squeaked on the wooden porch.

"Of course not. This is your home. You have every right to be here."

"That may be true, but if you want privacy, I can go inside and leave you alone with your thoughts."

"Nonsense, I enjoy your company." He reached over and squeezed her hand before letting go.

They stared at the sky, the stars sparkling and enjoyed the quiet, still night. The temperatures had dropped as the sun fell, but the porch protected them from the coldness of the breeze. It reminded him of a few nights they had spent together on their ranch in Spring Creek before his past had caught up with him. What he wouldn't give to have his ranch back and to show Rose he was capable of so much more. But he had purchased the ranch with stolen money, and he didn't know how to explain that without revealing what he had done. All his misdeeds were tied together in a tangled web of his own making, with no way out unless he upended everything.

After a few minutes, Elizabeth shifted in her seat and gazed at him, compassion filling her eyes. She hesitated, and he could see the questions she wanted to ask but didn't. Sighing, she turned to gaze at the dark blue sky.

"Is something wrong?" he asked.

"No. I just worry about you."

"You shouldn't." He didn't want to burden her with his problems, problems he had created with his selfishness.

"Are you sure about that?" she whispered.

"Why would you ask?"

Silence greeted him for a long moment before she murmured, "You've been avoiding Rose."

"I have not." His voice was defensive. She was right, but he wouldn't acknowledge it.

Her voice grew curt. "I beg to differ. The last few nights you haven't been home in time for dinner, and you work late, coming in long after we've gone to bed."

"There's much to get done. The ranch doesn't run itself."

"Is there?"

He hit the side of the chair. "Of course, there

is. You've lived here for years. Ben works just as hard, if not harder, than me."

"I know how hard Ben works." The wood of her chair creaked on the porch's wooden floor. "But he comes home for dinner, spends time with his children, and with me. Have you been doing the same?"

"I must pull my weight. Ben didn't have to give me a job, and I have a lot to make up for."

"We aren't expecting you to pay us back or to work yourself to death. You paid for your mistakes. Ben thinks highly of you and always has. He knew you tried to make a better life for yourself before you went away to prison. Besides, you protected me and, in my eyes, that makes up for quite a bit."

She reached over and squeezed his hand, trying to comfort him, but it was a cold comfort.

"I owe you both so much." He stopped, unsaid emotion closing his throat.

"I appreciate you wanting to work hard, but not at the price of your family."

"I must do this." He gulped hard, painfully, the words sticking.

"In your quest to do everything right, you're harming them."

Her words sent a sharp pain to his heart and a chill down his spine. "I'm not trying to."

"I know. You're feeling guilty for not telling Rose. You're afraid if she finds out the truth, she'll cut you out of her life."

He said nothing. She was right, so right.

"Tell her. She's kind and compassionate, and I believe she'll listen and won't hold your past against you, but"—she held up her hand—"the longer you keep this secret from her, the harder it'll be to tell her and the harder she'll take it when she hears the truth. The last thing you want is for her to discover your past from someone besides yourself."

Startled at what she said, he halted and looked hard at her. "You're not planning on telling her, are you?"

Anger flashed from her eyes. "Of course not. I would hope you know me better than that, but it doesn't mean she won't find out from someone else."

The porch door opened, and Ben stepped outside. "Elizabeth, what are you doing out here?"

"I'm coming, my love," she said.

Ben stood patiently in the doorframe, waiting and giving them time.

Elizabeth stood, gathering her afghan. She touched James's arm. "I love you. Consider what I said."

He dipped his head. "Goodnight."

"Sleep well," she said, her voice was low but full of love.

She stepped to her husband's side. He pulled her into his arms and murmured something in her ear. Elizabeth reached up and grazed his cheek before whispering something softly to him. He smiled tenderly, and they turned and left him alone on the porch.

James watched them go and wished he shared the same love with Rose that Elizabeth had with Ben. He was envious of their relationship and wanted the same.

Was Elizabeth right? Should I tell Rose everything? Would she forgive me?

He didn't know the answers and wasn't sure he wanted to take the chance.

* * *

James stared at the night sky long after Elizabeth and Ben went inside. When his lids were too heavy to keep open, he went up to his room. The morning would arrive sooner than he'd wish. While he could sit on a horse while half asleep, and he had done it often enough over the years, he preferred to be awake.

Nothing more embarrassing than falling off the saddle in front of the other cowhands and living down the ribbing that would surely come his way. There was no shortage of gaffes on a ranch with cowboys poking fun at one another. He didn't want to be the butt of any taunting because he fell off his horse from lack of sleep especially when the lack of sleep was fear over what his wife would do if she discovered his secrets.

After checking in on the children and finding them fast asleep, their soft snores a boon to his heart, he crossed the hall to his room. Stepping inside, he shrugged off his woolen coat. It was a far improvement from the threadbare one he had arrived with. Along with everything else, Ben had outfitted him with the warm clothing he needed for a working ranch. He was of no use to Ben if he caught a chill.

Hanging it on a hook behind the door, he moved to the fire to warm his hands. He bent to stoke the flames when movement caught his eye, and he was shocked to see Rose curled in the armchair. Her sweet countenance pulled him like a moth to a flame with her pink cheeks and plump lips. It was hard to resist her.

A thick quilt lay tangled around her waist and her yellow wrapper had fallen open, revealing a thin white cotton nightgown buttoned to the nape of her neck. A tray sat on the table next to her. She had brought food for him.

He still couldn't believe this magnificent woman was his wife, but he wasn't sure that would last. No matter what he did, there was always the chance she would leave him. James had no real hold on her. He had vowed to protect her so she wouldn't lose her children, but they had made no promises beyond that. She was too good, too pure to stay with a hardened criminal.

His path was doomed. He had to tell her and soon.

She stirred and stretched, fluttering her eyes open. She smiled, the smile so bright it fairly gleamed in the firelight. "James. You're home."

His gaze devoured every inch of her. She placed her stockinged feet on the floor and stood. Holding her hands out, she reached for him and tugged him close until he stood within an inch of her. She caressed his cheek. Her touch was delicate as she ran her fingers across his chin, his neck, and to his chest, where she placed her hand against his heart, beating wildly in his chest. It would likely burst into flames with a single breath.

Anticipation and desire thudded inside his blood. He couldn't let his feelings override his good sense. He had to put distance between them and tell her the truth.

He tried to step away, but she had other ideas and stopped him. She wrapped her arms around his neck and lifted on her toes. He inhaled, and her scent enveloped him like a wet spring morning, fresh, delicious, and intoxicating.

Rose placed her lips against his. It couldn't hurt to take one small, sweet taste and then he would let her go. A moment later when he raised his head, she looked at him dreamily and he thought to himself—one more night wouldn't hurt.

She was willing. He was willing. They shouldn't deny themselves. They could talk tomorrow, but tonight was a night for dreams to come true, not for dreams being shattered.

Chapter 22

Hours later, James woke with a start. Clanging prison doors, a wet, damp blanket, rats scurrying for crumbs dropped on the floor, and fists pounding into flesh roared through his mind like a mountain lion chasing its prey. Sweating and shaking, he had been back behind those metal bars where the sights and sounds of hell shook him to his very core with vicious men in every corner and nothing to lose. The nightmares would come when he'd least expect it and were hard to remember.

When he had been carted to prison six years

before, he had mistakenly believed it wouldn't be dangerous. His punishment had been just, after all. He thought he'd serve his time and be better for it. Little had he realized how tough the conditions were. The food was rotten most days, and if he got enough to fill his belly, it was a good day. The cells were dark and dank, moisture creeping through the cracks in the walls, leaving everything damp to the touch. It had been musty, and the air reeked of urine, rotten eggs, and horrendous smells he couldn't even identify. No fresh air and no privacy, a reminder of what he had done to earn the conditions he had been forced to survive.

All his choices had been taken away, and several cellmates had been downright evil. The crimes they committed were far beyond what James could even imagine, even in his worst nightmares. Fortunately, he had been quick on his feet and with a few quick punches in dark corners, most left him alone except for those first couple of months when the real thugs of the prison tried to prove their dominance. He learned early on to avoid eye contact and to keep to himself. It didn't prevent a few late-night beatings, but since he didn't rat out the perpetrators and didn't antagonize them, they soon let him be. He wasn't enough of a challenge and didn't cause problems, so they moved on to easier prey.

It still didn't take away the loneliness and despair he had felt most nights as he huddled in his cot, freezing in the winter and sweating like a roasting pig in the hot summer months. He didn't want to relive those memories, but they would swamp his thoughts when he least expected them and would pull him to the anger and self-deprecation he experienced for six long years.

Rose stirred and snuggled against him. Touching one of her silky curls, it grounded him and returned him to a happier time and helped him forget the misery, but sweat covered him from his nightmares. He didn't want her to worry, so he gently pulled away and went to the window, looking outside the glass panes. It was frigid in the room, making his skin shrivel, but he needed to experience the pain, to remind him how quickly everything could be ripped away.

Any man would be lucky to have her. She wouldn't have any trouble finding someone far more deserving of her affections and would be the man she needed. They wouldn't have a seedy past such as his. Her children would thrive under the care of someone who hadn't robbed stagecoaches for years.

Rose woke with an enormous smile on her face. She had feelings she never had before, not even with her late husband. Joseph had been reserved and quiet. Their life had been safe but complacent, even boring at times. As much as she had loved Joseph, their marriage had been built on a quiet, deep love. He had given her everything she needed and had been her best friend. She had imagined living the rest of her life with him and had been heartbroken when he passed away.

When she first met Joseph, she had been young and still reeling from her brother's death. They had been each other's rock in the years after their parent's death and had depended on one another while stuck inside an orphanage that was not filled with love or compassion. It had been nothing more than a labor camp for young children, where they used them for their own nefarious needs. Working in the cotton mills, the older children tied yarn threads together after they broke. The youngest crawled under the machinery, picked up cotton and cleared any dust and debris that accumulated under them. Their small hands and bodies would get into places the adults couldn't reach and the accidents could be horrific. Children lost limbs that maimed them permanently, or would die in appalling ways.

They were forced to work long hours. Whatever money they might have earned went into the hands of those running the orphanage.

The children never saw a penny and instead were lucky if they received a hot meal when most days it was cold porridge and stale bread. Beatings were common, toys were scarce, clothing was worn, and tears were an everyday occurrence.

Her brother Nicky was her only source of comfort, and he guarded her as best he could, stepping in as her protector in the only way he knew how. Unfortunately, he hadn't been able to stop the matrons from beating her, both physically and emotionally. When he had finally gone too far, they had taken him from her in a shocking and hideous manner and the nightmares of that day had been painful to watch and were agonizing to remember.

After they had thrown Nicky's body into a pauper's grave, giving little care or regard for what he had meant to her, she had snuck into the matron's office late one evening and grabbed the money she had rightfully earned. It would've been considered stealing if she were caught and in the eyes of the law, she likely was, but she had earned that money and only took what she would've been given if they had been honest and forthright. She had run with only the clothes on her back and the memories of her brother as the blood poured from his chest, telling her she had to survive. His last words had been the only thing that kept her from collapsing in despair.

Somehow, she had found employment as a governess. The family had taken her in and had treated her kindly. Then one day while walking in the park with the children, she had quite literally run into Joseph. She had wobbled, her head spun, but he held her steady, his kind eyes looking her over to ensure he hadn't hurt her.

His quick smile had been what had first attracted her to him. He asked her questions and cared about her well-being. Joseph appeared in the church she attended, would meet her in the park on her days off, and would give her small gifts; a bunch of wildflowers from the meadow, a poem he had written, a bottle of lilac perfume, and ribbons for her hair. The gifts weren't expensive or exciting, but no one had showered her with affection for years and she enjoyed the attention. Before long, he convinced her to become his wife and she had agreed.

Joseph finished school within months of their marrying and then whisked her away to his hometown of Smelter, Wyoming. He had been proud to introduce her to his brother, Charles, but Rose had sensed from day one that Charles had no regard for her and barely tolerated his younger brother. Securing a bookkeeper position within the lumber company Charles worked for had been enough for Joseph, and he had lived his life ignoring the contempt of his brother and being her best friend.

When Tommy had been born, he had been thrilled, and then when she had told him she was pregnant with another, he had been ecstatic. He wanted a sizable family and determined they would have a large brood. She had been happy, but there had been something missing. She never could identify what it was. When Joseph had died, a part of her died along with him.

Then James stepped into her life and woke

something inside of her she couldn't put to words. She prayed there would be something more, and that it would be more than physical. She wanted love, affection, and something lasting that would never end. She was tired of losing everyone who was important to her.

Rose stretched her arms. She was alone and wished she wasn't, but after the night they had spent together, she wasn't too worried he wasn't next to her. She wanted to treasure these feelings for as long as possible, but as much as she wanted to, she needed to get up and feed Sarah. Her breasts were heavy with milk and ached for relief. She was becoming flighty and irresponsible whenever she found herself in James's arms.

Shaking off her thoughts, she dressed and walked quietly and quickly to the nursery. Going in, she stopped in wonder. Once again, James sat in the rocking chair, Sarah curled in one arm, with Tommy nestled in his other. He spoke softly, and they both looked at him in fascination. She couldn't believe Sarah wasn't screaming to be fed, but James gave something special to her children. It brought a tear to her eye and tugged at her heart.

This is what she hadn't known she wanted, but she had been lucky enough to find. She just had to convince James he wanted this, too.

Chapter 23

May 1900

They settled into a routine, a blissful, wonderful existence although if Rose were honest with herself, it felt as though James was holding something from her, but because the nights were exquisite, she was letting her fears override her good sense. She had finally found what she hadn't known she'd been looking for.

Her days were filled with caring for her children and learning more about her new sisters. They laughed, played games and discussed any number of topics, from the latest gossip on the surrounding ranches to new beaus for Katy and Anne. The three were becoming more than friends to Rose. She didn't have sisters and had always wanted someone to share secrets with, to laugh and cry with, and she had finally found a large and loving family.

Spring had blossomed around them, and the snow was melting fast. James discussed moving them to the small cabin. He wanted privacy. Rose understood, but she wanted to stay near Elizabeth. She enjoyed their talks, their walks, and their time with the children. Tommy loved having a playmate and there was no shortage of people to pick up a fussy baby if she was otherwise occupied, but they couldn't impose on Ben and Elizabeth's hospitality much longer.

When the day arrived that they were to return to the small cabin, Rose packed their belongings and took them to the foyer while James readied the horses and wagon. She had just dropped the bags on the floor when a sharp knock sounded at the door. Pushing away a flyaway hair, she placed her hands on her hips and straightened her back. She then opened it with a welcoming smile, but it disappeared in an instant as her worst nightmare materialized in front of her.

"Hello, my dear," Charles said. His creepy face was only inches away, his hot foul breath touching her bare skin. He swept his gaze over her and reached his meaty hands as if to pull her into her arms.

Yelping, she fairly jumped out of her skin. She retreated a few steps to get out of his reach. "What are you doing here?"

"I wanted to visit my niece and nephew. Shouldn't an uncle be able to see his family when he wants?"

"Not my family and not my children," she said with more force than she felt inside. Her knees were quaking under her skirt and fear slithered up her spine.

"Now, now. Don't be that way. We're family and families belong together."

"We aren't a family. I want nothing to do with you," she spat.

Something dark and dangerous flickered in

his eyes but was quickly shuttered. The corners of his lips lifted into a sinister smile that spoke of a foreboding that chilled her to her core.

He leaned against the door frame, relaxed as though he had all the time in the world. "That definitely isn't the way to talk to your brother."

"You aren't my brother. Leave now."

"I'm not going anywhere." He shifted, seeming to grow larger and more intense in front of her very eyes. "You should invite me in, if you know what's good for you."

Before she could stop him, he shoved the door from her fingertips. The door slammed against the small table behind it, sending the vase of flowers crashing to the floor. Her skin crawled like ants from an anthill swarming all over her as he slid around her into the house.

"Well, well. You certainly have come up in the world now, haven't you?" He circled slowly, running his fingers against the gilded painting on the wall, sweeping his eyes along the plush rugs, various photographs, and knickknacks on small tables.

He glanced down and saw the bags on the floor. "Planning a trip?"

Rose stood stunned as Charles peered into each of the rooms off the main foyer, smacking his lips as though he were chewing on a sour apple. He had no qualms about exploring the home he now stood in. The savage calculation in his eyes petrified her. He was now more dangerous than before. She had defied him, and he was out for revenge.

Charles was a shrewd and dangerous man who thought only of himself and what he could get from others. He was ruthless in his pursuit. She didn't want what he offered and without Joseph's protection, she had been prey to his unwanted attentions.

Elizabeth came bouncing down the stairs, Vicky and Tommy trailing behind her.

"Rose, was someone at the door?"

Elizabeth hadn't seen Charles. He had sauntered into the parlor and had made himself comfortable on a sofa. His filthy boots were extended in front of him. He had draped his arm across the wooden back, trailing his fingers trailing the woodwork as though he was right where he belonged.

Rose couldn't speak. She was flustered and frightened. Elizabeth's words were swirling around her like a tornado straight out of the sky.

"Rose? Rose?" Elizabeth asked, her smile fading. Turning to the children, she told them to go to the kitchen to get a cookie from Sophia.

Rose watched this from a thick, murky fog. She had to say something, but the words wouldn't form on her lips. She didn't know what to say or how to say it.

Elizabeth took her hands and clasped them tight.

"Speak to me. Tell me what's wrong."

Finding the strength to force out the words, Rose said, "He's here. He found me." Tears pooled and fell down her cheeks.

"Who found you? What are you talking about?"

"My..." She had difficulty swallowing the

lump in her throat. "My brother-in-law... Ch... Charles."

"What? Oh, no," Elizabeth replied. "Where is he?"

She had told Elizabeth one day a few weeks ago a bit of what Charles had promised if she hadn't complied, so she well knew what threat Charles posed to her.

Rose pulled her hands from Elizabeth's and pointed to the parlor. Elizabeth whipped around. He stared at them, darting his tongue out and licking his lips in anticipation. It was as if he believed they were a piece of delicious cake he was getting ready to devour.

Rose was horrified. He looked at Elizabeth with as much disrespect as he had shown her. Rose was appalled and embarrassed. She had brought this man into Elizabeth's home.

Elizabeth grabbed Rose's hands and led her into Ben's study. She stared at Rose with concern.

"Sit. I'll take care of our visitor," Elizabeth said.

Rose grabbed her sleeve. "No. You shouldn't have to do that. I can handle him. Just give me a minute." She took a deep breath and braced her hands against the wooden table. "I have to compose myself."

Elizabeth shook her head. "You're in no shape to deal with that man. If you won't sit, go find James while I *entertain* our guest."

"You can't be alone with him. I don't know what he'll do."

"Don't worry about me. I can handle him. He wouldn't be crazy enough to do a thing to me while in my home with my husband and the ranch hands a scream away. I don't know the man, but I doubt he's that stupid. Now go find James or Ben and send them in here."

Rose ran down the hall and out the back door, frantically searching for the men. Tears streamed down her cheeks and she shook uncontrollably. She shouldn't have left Elizabeth alone with him.

Elizabeth had opened her home and her heart, and Rose would be heartbroken if anything dreadful happened to her new sister.

Rushing into the barn, Rose didn't see a soul, and her fear was becoming debilitating. She didn't know what she would do if she couldn't find the men. She glanced into the stalls as she ran through the main aisle. As she reached the rear of the barn, the door creaked open and James and Ben walked in, smiling and ribbing one another.

"James!"

Rose hurtled into his arms.

"What's wrong? Has something happened to the children?" He was as steady as a cliff of rocks that had stood tall and proud for centuries.

Her knees buckled, but he was there. He could help. Gripping his forearms, she squeezed and stuttered, "He's here. He found me. Elizabeth's with him."

"What?" James said.

"Who?" Ben said.

They spoke at the same time.

Taking a breath, she said, "My brother-in-law, Charles."

James said, "Get inside with Elizabeth now. She can't be left alone with that man."

Ben opened his mouth to say more but saw the look in James's eyes and ran out of the barn and to the house.

James pulled her into his arms and whispered, "He can't hurt you anymore. There's nothing he can do."

She trembled in fear. "You don't know that. He wants to see my children."

"You don't have to do anything you don't want. You're married to me now. There's nothing he can do."

She wanted to believe James but was afraid her newfound security was gone, and nothing would ever be the same again. Charles had found her once again and this time she didn't think he was going to disappear willingly and assuredly, not without a fight.

She didn't know if she had the strength to fight someone ruthless again. It had taken all her strength to escape the orphanage with her body and mind no more damaged than it had been. She thought she had found safety when Joseph stepped into her life and brought her the happiness she had craved. Little did she realize she had stepped into another firestorm that was as vicious and angry as the one she had left behind ten years before.

Chapter 24

Hours later, James tucked Rose into bed, pulling the thick blankets over her delicate shoulders. It wasn't cold, but she shivered uncontrollably from terror. She had finally fallen asleep after being inconsolable, long after Charles had left.

He smoothed the curls from her face before kissing her pale forehead. Charles was gone, but his cockiness and assurance that he'd acquire his nephew and niece was disturbing. He hadn't been overtly rude, but he had made it obvious he believed his brother's children would be under his care before long.

"I'll see you in court," Charles said, his voice

haughty. "I've got myself a lawyer but wanted to give my dear Rose a chance to hand the children over without a fight."

"Never," Rose yelled.

James held her back for fear she would try to attack the man who was threatening her.

"I'm rightly disappointed in you, Rose. Joseph would've been so disappointed in your behavior and seems a shame you didn't do what you'd promised. No wonder the judge'll have no issue in giving me the children when I explain your erratic and uncontrollable behavior."

"Why are you doing this?" she cried.

His face contorted into a rage like nothing James had ever seen. Spittle flew from his mouth as words poured from his lips. "Because, you harlot, Joseph could've done so much better than you. You came waltzin' in his life, swinging your hips and swaying him with your highfalutin ways, taking his money, taking my money and if you think your children are going to get a penny..." he abruptly stopped, seeming to be aware of what he had said.

He straightened his coat and had doffed his hat like he was a gentleman. "I'll take my leave." He strolled to the front door, his yellow teeth gleaming in the sunlight. "My lawyer'll be in touch. Have a nice day. I'll be speakin' with you soon."

After he had left, they tried to assure Rose he had no legal standing, but she had been grief-stricken and frightened half to death. She told them she needed to leave with Tommy and Sarah, where Charles couldn't find her. Stumbling over her words, she talked in circles about where she could go and where she could hide. She kept mumbling that if she did it once, she could do it again. She had been so distraught, James had been frightened she would do something she would regret.

With love and patience, Elizabeth talked some sense into Rose and convinced her they should continue the conversation in the morning. Rose needed sleep and after a good night's rest, they'd decide their plan of attack.

Seeming to relax after that, they ate a small

dinner before James led Rose to her room. James wasn't altogether sure she would sleep well, but at least she'd closed her eyes.

Touching her cheek one last time, James turned the lamp down low so if she woke, she wouldn't be in the dark. He then found Ben and Elizabeth talking quietly in the study. They looked up and shared a glance when he walked into the room.

"Ben, Elizabeth, I didn't mean to interrupt."

"You didn't," Ben said. "Come inside and have a seat. Do you want a drink?" Ben stood and opened the liquor cabinet.

"Thanks. I could use one."

Chuckling wryly, Ben poured them both a healthy dose from a whiskey decanter. Handing James the glass, Ben sat on the arm of Elizabeth's chair, draping his arm across her shoulders.

James walked to the window and took a healthy swallow. Pulling open the drapes, he looked out into the night sky.

"Did she fall asleep?" Elizabeth asked.

Turning to face them, James replied, "Yes, finally. Although I'm not sure she's going to sleep well."

"It's to be expected," Elizabeth said, rustling her skirts as she pulled her legs onto the sofa.

"I don't know how to calm her fears."

"The poor thing." Elizabeth reached for Ben's hand and squeezed as though seeking his comfort.

"She shouldn't be worried now that she's married to you," Ben said.

"I think she knows she's safe, but she believes he *could* and *will* get her children. It isn't rational, but until they're mine, the worry'll always be there."

Ben shifted on the arm of Elizabeth's chair. "I sent word to our lawyer. He should be here soon. Then we can ease her fears and discuss what we can do."

"I think that'd be helpful. I should've followed up with him weeks ago, but I'd gotten distracted and thought little of it."

"None of us did," Elizabeth said.

* * *

"I truly believe you have nothing to be concerned with, Mrs. Dodson. You've remarried, and as I described weeks ago, I can't see a judge removing them from your care. If you'd been negligent and couldn't provide for them, then we might have something to worry about, but that doesn't apply to you. But to give you comfort, I'll check with the courts."

Rose mumbled her thanks, but it was clear to James she wasn't convinced that Ben's lawyer, Mr. Parker, could stop Charles from gaining her children.

"Thank you, Mr. Parker. I appreciate you coming and discussing this with us," James said, shaking the lawyer's hand.

"It has been my pleasure. I'm sorry Mrs. Dodson was so frightened yesterday by her former brother-in-law. It sounds like he's just bluster. I wouldn't worry too much about it, but if you'd like to make it more legal, I can certainly request that a judge grants legal custody to you both."

"Yes. How soon can we do this?" James asked.

"I'll file the paperwork as soon as I get back to Helena. It should be done within the week."

"How long 'til it's legal?" James said.

"Depends on the court but shouldn't be more than a few weeks as long as nothing concerns the judge."

James nodded. He'd like to have this settled as soon as possible, not only for Rose's sake, but for his own as well.

Gathering his hat and briefcase, Mr. Parker stood. Ben opened the study door. "Thanks for coming out so quickly. I'll walk you out. I've some ranch business to discuss with you before you leave."

"Certainly, Mr. Seymour." He smiled at the women. "Mrs. Seymour, it's been a pleasure. Mrs. Dodson, try not to worry. These things always sort themselves out. You've nothing to fear."

Mr. Parker followed Ben out the door. Their voices faded as they walked down the hall.

James looked at Rose. "It sounds as if everything's going to be fine. Mr. Parker seems confident everything'll be fine."

She stared at him, alarm still in her eyes. "I hope you're right. I have this sickening feeling this isn't over, a sense of foreboding, if you will. If he's able to convince the judge that Tommy and Sarah belong with him, I don't know what I would do or how I could bear it."

"I won't let it happen. I promise." He knelt in front of her, holding her hands, and running his thumbs across the soft palms. He leaned in and kissed her brow.

"They're your children and belong only with you."

Chapter 25

June 1900

When they didn't hear from Charles or Mr. Parker, James believed all was well, but Rose wasn't convinced. Something was wrong, seriously wrong, but finally Mr. Parker sent word. The judge wanted to see them, and Rose's terror grew. She tried to hide it but knew she was unsuccessful.

They would leave the children with Anne and Katy, and Ben and Elizabeth would go with them to Helena. They would leave early the next morning.

Rose clucked over her children, tucking them into bed, and ensuring they had no fevers, coughs, or any other ailments, as she wasn't about to leave them if there was any chance they would fall sick again.

Retreating to her room, she removed her clothes and pulled on an old cotton nightgown. James left to get a glass of water and to give her a moment. He was nervous and apprehensive around her, and she hated it.

She wanted to believe tomorrow would be a success and the judge would tell them that James was their father. There was a part of her that knew Charles would ruin it for them. She never got a moment's peace. Something always ruined what little happiness she found. From the moment she had lost her parents and then her older brother, she had known she was doomed.

She had considered every possibility and what she would do if things didn't go their way. She would defy the judge's orders if it came down to it. James did his best to reassure her, but she wasn't comforted. Charles always got what he wanted. He had with Joseph, and he would with her, of that she had no doubt. She had mistakenly believed she could evade his clutches. He told her she would pay, and it appeared he was carrying through with his threats.

Curling onto her side, the blankets were heavy on her. She stared out the window and to the bright twinkling stars shining like beacons to her aching heart. Nightmares plucked at her through the long night, her children screaming with fear, and seeing the malicious grin on Charles's face as he yanked them from her arms.

* * *

The buckboard rolled to a stop in front of the courthouse. The ride had been quiet, pensive. No one spoke, as though saying a word would bring them rotten luck. James helped Elizabeth and Rose down while Ben took the buckboard and horses to the livery. He would meet them inside the courthouse when he was done.

James placed his hands on Elizabeth and Rose's backs and led them up the wide stone stairs of the courthouse. Their movements were unhurried, as though the slower they went, the less likely things would not go their way. James's muscles tensed, and his heart beat erratically. It wasn't jail, but it was too much of a reminder of his past and what could happen inside. Taking a deep breath, he tried to calm his heart, as he didn't want Rose to suspect he was nervous.

Mr. Parker stood inside the front doors. Instead of greeting them with a smile, his lips were pulled into a grimace.

"Is Mr. Seymour with you?" he asked, without any of the usual pleasantries.

James's spine straightened. Something was wrong and he wanted to ask, but hesitated. He didn't want Rose to worry any more than she already had. "Yes. He'll be here soon. He wanted to leave the horses and buckboard at the livery."

"Hmm," Mr. Parker murmured, running his hand across his suit jacket, straightening it.

"Is something amiss?" James asked.

"I don't rightly know," Mr. Parker said. "I'll explain everything once Mr. Seymour joins us."

Gesturing toward a bench against the wall, he encouraged Elizabeth and Rose to have a seat. A bit later, Ben joined them.

"Hope you haven't been waiting too long. It took longer than I'd expected," Ben said.

"Understandable, Mr. Seymour. Why don't we go find a quiet room and talk before we're due in court."

They found an empty room on the second floor. Mr. Parker pulled the door closed behind them and placed his brown leather briefcase onto the large table. He sighed and avoided everyone's gaze.

"What's going on, Mr. Parker?" Ben said.

"I wish I knew," Mr. Parker said. "My clerk overheard something concerning this morning."

"What is it?" James said.

He looked at James and then at Rose. "Your brother-in-law's here. He's claiming you're both unfit and he can prove it. This is why the judge insisted you were to be here today."

Rose gasped and dropped into a chair.

"We knew he'd present a problem, so not sure I understand," James muttered. What had gone wrong?

"I'm surprised he's been able to speak to the judge. There must be a relevant reason for him to have gotten this far. The problem is, I don't know what it is. Do any of you know?"

They all shook their heads, but James's heart stopped. There was no way Charles could have discovered his past, but if he was the reason for this, it would break Rose's heart and the tenuous bond they had might be broken forever. Sweat beaded across his neck and down his back. Taking a deep breath, he shuddered. He considered telling the lawyer but before he could reason through his thoughts, the decision was taken from him.

Mr. Parker sighed again. "No point in dwelling on what we don't know. Let's go on into the courtroom and find out what he's claiming."

"Can he convince the judge that he should have the children?" James asked.

"I don't think so. The two of you are married, and he was only Mrs. Dodson's brother-in-law. He wasn't their father, so there shouldn't be anything we need to be concerned about, but I wanted you to be prepared. There's no telling what he's up to."

Rose tried to stand, but dropped into her seat, shaking from fear. James took her hand and squeezed it.

"Everything's gonna be fine. He's just trying to scare you. Don't let him, as I'm positive everything'll work out."

She tried to smile but failed. Helping her to stand, he wrapped his arm around her waist and followed Mr. Parker down the hall and up a flight of stairs. Mr. Parker told them to wait while he opened the massive courtroom doors to inquire if it was their turn. Murmuring to someone inside, Mr. Parker nodded.

"It's time."

* * *

The size and stateliness of the courtroom was intimidating. Rose was small and inconsequential in such a place. Benches lined half of the room and a dark wooden wall stood waist high that separated the audience from the lawyers. Both the American flag and the seal of Montana hung behind the judge's bench.

Rose worried she would say or do something wrong that would jeopardize the safety of her children. She kept telling herself Charles couldn't gain custody of them, but she couldn't stop the doubts that crept in like a long snake, wrapping itself around every inch of her brain, squeezing, pulsating until any positive thought was squashed.

Taking a deep breath to calm her queasy stomach, she followed Mr. Parker to the front of the room, James close behind. His presence was both a reassurance and a hinderance. She wasn't as fragile as he believed, although she had given him plenty of reasons to be cautious over her well-being during the past few months, but she would be strong today. She had to be for her children.

Mr. Parker set his briefcase on a table and pointed to the seats where she and James were to sit. She set her handbag on the table, untied her bonnet and removed it, and patted her hair. She wanted to look presentable, even if she didn't feel the same inside.

James squeezed her shoulders before sitting next to her. He placed his hands on top of hers, and she was grateful for the comfort he offered.

Just as the bailiff opened his mouth to speak, the doors slammed open. Everyone turned to see who had caused the commotion. Charles came strolling inside, a harried older gentleman trailing behind him. They sat to the left of Rose and James, behind the short wall. Making their presence known, tension crackled like a lightning storm brewing, ready to strike at any time.

The bailiff quieted the room and ordered everyone to stand as the judge entered. He was an older man with white hair and beard, and his stern expression spoke of a harsh countenance.

His black robes billowed around him as he sat behind the tall wall. He banged the gavel and everyone quieted.

Rose watched the events unfold, but it was as if she were in a fog floating above, watching from a distance. The judge spoke and Mr. Parker responded, but she couldn't get a good look. The mist was thick and heavy. Her breath was shallow, and she broke into a cold sweat.

She couldn't hear what the judge or Mr. Parker were saying. No words penetrated through the fog, but something horrible was about to unfold. Charles and the older man stood and made their way to the podium, where he produced a document from his coat pocket and handed it with fanfare to the bailiff. The judge looked it over and asked James to come forward.

She didn't understand why the judge was questioning James. What was on the paper Charles gave to the judge? Thoughts tumbled over and over while a loud ringing grew with intensity in her ears as every second passed.

With a significant force of will, she pulled herself out of the fog and her senses sharpened as the words finally penetrated.

James was a criminal. He had robbed stagecoaches and had been behind bars.

She was married to an outlaw.

Oh, what have I done?

How could she have married someone who had done unimaginable things. She didn't understand why had James kept this secret from her. Unanswered questions pushed and fought for an explanation. She wanted to stand and scream.

When the judge dismissed James, Ben and Elizabeth were asked to come forward, to speak on his behalf. They both knew and hadn't told her. They kept his secret, but they were his family, after all, not hers. She couldn't expect them to tell her of his past. Their loyalty was to James first and foremost. She and Elizabeth had grown close, as close as sisters, or so she thought, and even Elizabeth hadn't seen fit to tell her James's secret.

No one had.

The judge asked many questions, and before she could gather her thoughts, it was her turn. Mr. Parker nudged her and looked at her with concern. "Mrs. Dodson, are you all right?"

Nodding, she whispered, "I'm fine, Mr. Parker, but I didn't know."

"You didn't know about your husband's incarceration?" he said, harshly.

"No. We married quickly, and it wasn't a question I thought to ask," she said, emotion thick in her voice.

"Mr. Parker," the judge interrupted, and both Rose and Mr. Parker startled at his tone. "Is Mrs. Dodson ready to come forward? I've plenty to do and don't like to be kept waiting."

"I apologize, your honor. Mrs. Dodson is coming now."

Mr. Parker held out his hand to help her stand. She tried to stop the shaking in her knees, but it was a useless endeavor. They quaked under her skirts, the fabric rustling. She stepped up to the podium and gripped it painfully to keep herself from falling. She tried to prepare herself for the questions he was going to ask and prayed she could muster the strength to answer.

When done, she retreated to her seat, grateful her legs hadn't collapsed under her. The judge sifted through the paperwork in front of him and pursed his mouth in silence. His face was blank, but he made hmm'ing sounds. He tapped with a thin pencil, put it down, flipped through the pages again and again. The tension and anticipation in the room could have been cut with a large scythe. No one spoke a word for fear of retaliation.

When Rose was near to screaming, he said, "I'm going to think a bit about this unique situation. This will need careful consideration." He picked up the papers and shuffled them into a neat stack. "I'll inform my clerk when my decision's ready, but don't expect one soon. In the meantime, the children will stay with Mr. and Mrs. Dodson until such time as I make my final decision."

Charles jumped to his feet. "No!" he shouted.

"Those children are mine! They aren't staying with her for one day longer!"

"Mr. McGaven," the judge said, narrowing his eyes into thin slits. "Sit down. This is my courtroom. I've made my decision."

Ignoring his words, Charles clenched his hat between his hands. "They should come home with me until you decide their future," he snarled. "This ain't right."

"Enough! I do not have to explain myself. If you know what's good for you, you'll drop your complaints, or I'll have you thrown in jail."

Charles's lawyer grabbed his arm and spoke furiously in his ear. Charles seethed with anger, his contempt palpable, but he snapped his mouth shut and stalked out of the courtroom, the door slamming behind him. His lawyer apologized to the judge before following in Charles's wake. The judge motioned to the bailiff, who then adjourned the court. The judge stood, his robe flapping behind him like a black hawk snapping away in the bright blue sky.

Rose sat stunned. She didn't understand

what had just happened. The judge wouldn't give them a final decision today. She needed to know now, for if she had to wait, then she felt certain Charles would win and she wasn't about to let that happen. She would leave with her children and go where no one could ever find her.

"Rose?" James swam in her vision, two or three of him before they finally merged into one. His eyes were sad, furrowing his brows as though he had something to be ashamed of.

She blinked her eyes. She had nothing to say.

"I think we need to talk so I can explain a few things."

Mr. Parker interrupted and said, "Not here. We must leave. You can talk outside."

Standing, Rose gathered her bonnet and handbag and walked stiffly behind Mr. Parker. James tried to touch her, but she shrugged away from him. She didn't want him to touch her.

He had lied to her. He hadn't told her about his past and now, because of him, she might lose her children.

Chapter 26

Rose sat in the hotel room alone, curled in a chair in front of the fireplace. They had finished in court later than expected, so it was decided they would stay in Helena for the night and would return in the morning. Another decision she had no control over for if she had, she would have gone to Thundering Mountain Ranch, gathered her children, and disappeared.

After refusing to talk with him, James let her be. Before he left, he said he'd give her the time she required, but they needed to discuss what happened.

She didn't want to talk with him or hear his excuses.

James had lied to her.

Her entire world had crumbled around her *again*, and she needed time to think. Mr. Parker didn't believe the judge would give the children to Charles, but Rose wasn't willing to take that chance.

She stood, stuffed her few belongings into her bag, and left the room. Finding the staircase used by the staff, she scurried out the rear of the hotel. Once she reached the livery, she procured a small carriage and horse and left town. She would go to the ranch, hold Tommy and Sarah close, and leave for the nearest train station in the opposite direction.

As she left Helena behind, her tenuous control broke and tears fell from her cheeks, dripping on her collar. She cried for what might have been. Rose had fooled herself into believing she and James had a future together. She had married a man who had done unthinkable things that led to his imprisonment. She didn't think any judge would allow James to keep precious little children when Charles had never been in trouble with the law.

She had to do what was necessary to protect them, even at the sake of her own happiness.

As she led the horse around the bend, a horse galloped behind her. Pulling on the reins to lead her horse and carriage out of the way, the horse and rider drew alongside her. The man bent and reached for the bridle. Startled, Rose fought for control, but he brought them to an abrupt stop. She fell to the floor of the carriage, the impact burning her knees. A moment later, the man yanked her out of the carriage.

Kicking and screaming, she hit him with her fists in a desperate attempt to escape. What had she gotten herself into now?

"Rose! Rose!" He grabbed her wrists and held them tight.

She looked up and into James's eyes. Furious, but relieved it wasn't a nefarious creature, she yanked her arms away. Her bonnet had fallen, and she was likely a teary-eyed mess.

"What are you doing here? Why did you do that?" she yelled.

James's eyes widened. "What am I doing here?" he roared. "What are you doing leaving without telling anyone where you were going?"

"I don't need to explain myself to you," she said.

"Oh, I think you do, Rose Dodson."

"Don't call me that," she growled. Anger was pulsating inside her like a rabid raccoon, wild, snarling, and out of control.

"Call you what?" he asked, looking puzzled. "Your name?"

"It won't be for long," she snapped.

"And what do you mean by that?" His tone was low, angry.

"You lied to me."

James was furious with her, but there was pain in his eyes. He was in the wrong, not her, and besides, she didn't care.

"I didn't lie to you."

"Yes, you did. You didn't tell me about your

past." Everything was falling apart around her, right before her very eyes.

"I didn't think it was relevant."

"Relevant! You didn't think it was relevant to let your wife know you'd been in jail? That you'd been a criminal?"

"You didn't ask." His voice had grown soft, but belligerent at the same time.

"Why would I ask you that?"

"You married a stranger. You should've asked if you were so concerned about what I did before I met you. I would've told you and I was going to. I just didn't know when or how."

"How about the night we married?"

"Would you have married me, if you'd known?"

She didn't know. The choice had been taken from her.

"If I'd told you, you would've run from me so fast, my head would've spun." He stepped away from her, hanging his shoulders in shame. "I wouldn't have blamed you. I made my share of mistakes, but I wanted to do better. I am doing better."

"You had plenty of opportunities to tell me, but you didn't. Instead, I had to find out there, in the courtroom, in front of the judge. I'm going to lose my children because of you."

"You won't lose your children. I won't let it happen."

"You can't stop it if the judge decides Charles should have them. So, I decided"—she pushed her finger into his chest—"that I had to stop it from happening."

"What are you planning on doing?"

"I'm going to get my children and take the next train out of here. I'll disappear with them, to a place where Charles will never find me."

"You can't disappear. He found you once. He could find you again. A woman traveling alone with two children can't make it far and will be easy to follow. If you run, the judge may certainly take them. You need to stop and think this through." He held out his hand to touch her, but she recoiled from him. He dropped his hand like a limb from a dead tree with no life left inside.

"I can't. I won't let him take them." Her voice broke as the pain ripped through her.

He was right, but she needed to hide, to protect them the best way she knew how.

James again reached for her, but she swatted at him.

"Don't touch me!" she screeched, but this time he didn't stop and pulled her into his arms.

Fighting him, she pounded at his chest, great gulping sobs tearing through her. She gripped his shirt and buried her face into his neck as the fear, frustration, and anger at her helplessness weighed her down.

James held her, rocked her as she cried until the last of the tears fell away. Taking a breath, she attempted to pull away, but he wouldn't let go.

He whispered into her ear, "You can't run. We won't lose Tommy or Sarah, I promise."

* * *

James took Rose back to the hotel. It might have been better if they had continued to the ranch, but he didn't believe she was in any condition to see Tommy or Sarah. They needed their mother to be strong. Right now, she was far from strong.

She sat, stiff and straight in the carriage, curling away from him as though his touch was horrifying. She refused to talk, refused to look at him. His stomach was tied in knots. He had to persuade her everything was going to be all right, but he wasn't convinced it would be. He couldn't imagine losing Tommy and Sarah, and if they did, she would never forgive him.

When they reached the hotel, Rose left the carriage before he could stop her.

"Rose."

She stopped. He wanted her to look at him. James needed to tell her how much she meant to him, but it was clear now wasn't the time. She wouldn't hear what he had to say, no matter how hard he tried.

"I'll return the horses and carriage and be back soon."

When he said nothing more, she stalked up the steps into the hotel. He blew out a breath of frustration. He had been warned by both Ben and Elizabeth on numerous occasions, but thought he knew better. Little did he realize Charles would unearth the details of his past and try to use it against them in court.

This was the last way he had wanted Rose to learn the truth about him. He wasn't sure if he could ever repair the damage. They had been growing close, but now a huge divide had ripped them apart, a divide large enough he wasn't sure he could bridge.

James rested in the front parlor of their hotel room. He considered going into the bedroom, but was uncertain of her reaction. After the horses and carriage were returned to the livery, he found the bedroom door of their suite shut tight. He was walking on precarious ground and had to be extra careful of his next steps.

Ben and Elizabeth came by asking if they wanted to get a bite to eat, but James declined. He told them Rose was exhausted and didn't feel up to an evening out.

"How is she doing?" Elizabeth asked.

James hesitated. He didn't want to lie to her, but didn't want to tell her the truth, either. "She's angry, but with time, I'm sure we'll work our way through it." He just wasn't convinced they would.

"Is there anything we can do?" She placed her hand on his arm.

He patted it before pulling away. He hadn't earned her sympathy. James had put himself in this mess, so it was up to him to figure a way out of it.

"Nah," he said. "I appreciate your concern, but I imagine giving her time will do wonders."

"Please, let her know we are here for you both."

After wishing them a good night, he closed the door and leaned heavily against it.

Totally unprepared for what Charles exposed, James didn't know what to say or do to fix this.

He should have listened to his gut when Mr. Parker asked them if there was anything in their past he should know about, but once again, he had thought only of himself. He should have spoken up then, confessed his sins so she wouldn't have been blindsided by the truth of his past.

When Charles's lawyer had exposed him, he saw his future roar out of the courtroom like a wild, dangerous dust storm picking up everything in its path and pushing it to where no one could ever find it again.

He didn't think she'd ever forgive him. The judge *had* left the children with them while he considered his decision, so James had to believe it was a good sign. If the judge had been concerned, he surely wouldn't have left them in his care.

But she was right. He had lied by omission and deceived her. There was no reason she should forgive him for the mistakes he had made then and now.

He pushed away from the wall and rapped

his knuckles on the hard wood of the closed door. Silence greeted him. She had likely fallen asleep angry. Seconds passed and there was no movement. He dropped his shoulders in despair. He didn't want to wait, for he feared the longer she went without talking to him, the harder it would become.

As he stepped away, the knob turned, and the door slowly opened. Her eyes were red rimmed from crying. The whole world was resting squarely on her shoulders. It was his fault.

The words he needed to speak were stuck in his throat.

"What do you want?" she asked, not a bit of warmth in her tone.

Gathering his courage, he said, "I should explain."

"Do we have to do it now?" she muttered.

"No, we don't, but I'm afraid if I don't explain soon, you won't ever understand."

"What is there to explain?" She looked at him, her eyes devoid of emotion. "You've had many opportunities to tell me, but you never did."

He gulped at the truth to her words.

"I don't know what to think. My children are not safe from Charles, and I'm left with virtually no choices, just like I was when Joseph died. Except this is worse because at least then I knew what Charles wanted, what he expected. But with you, what I thought I knew about you has been totally shattered." With every word she spoke, his heart splintered into a million pieces.

"Please give me a chance," he whispered.

"No, I can't do this right now."

Despair rippled through him

"I want to sleep alone tonight," she murmured.

Pain, like nothing he had ever experienced, pierced through him. "I understand." It was deep and tearing him apart. "I'll sleep out here. If you need anything, anything at all, please let me know."

She nodded and closed the door softly

behind her, but to him the click was loud and jarring.

He had ruined the best thing in his long and pathetic life.

Chapter 27

Rose was pale and uttered little on their way to the ranch. Ben and Elizabeth tried to fill the silence, but the tension was tight and all-consuming. James worried the edge Rose was desperately hanging onto would crumble beneath her.

Reaching the ranch, Rose hurried inside. James watched her go and was desperate to follow. Instead, once Ben and Elizabeth alighted the buckboard, he led the horses into the barn. As he unhitched them, the barn door opened, and Ben joined him.

"How are you doing?"

Not looking at him, James said, "I'm fine."

"It's unfortunate what's happened. Give her time. She'll realize you had good intentions."

"I don't know," he said, leading each horse into its stall, the dry hay crunching under his feet. "I messed up, and I don't think she'll ever forgive me."

Ben grimaced. "Once she considers everything, I'm sure she'll understand. You didn't mean to deceive her and frankly, you're her husband, for better or for worse."

"That may be true, but I entered our marriage falsely. I should've been up front and honest with her and if I didn't tell her when we got married, I had ample opportunities to tell her after."

"We all make mistakes." Ben leaned against the stall and patted the horse's muzzle. "You owned up to your deeds and paid a price for them. She shouldn't hold that against you."

"I don't think she'll do that." He picked up a brush and ran it down the horse's rump, avoiding Ben's gaze. "What I do believe is she can't or won't be able to forgive me for lying to her."

* * *

As the days drifted by, Rose withdrew from everyone around her. Her days were spent in the nursery rocking chair, staring at the walls and only moving when Sarah cried. She picked at her food, pushing it around her plate without eating it, and didn't sleep well. Dark circles formed under her eyes. She was retreating faster than she had after Sarah's birth, but the despair was all-consuming.

Each day crawled by with no word from the lawyer. After struggling for a few days, she approached Elizabeth late one afternoon. They were both in the large sunny room at the rear of the house. Vicky and Tommy were sitting on the floor playing and Elizabeth had a book in one hand, flipping through the pages. Rose had finished feeding Sarah, and not wanting to put her down, held her close. The little girl gave her a small measure of comfort.

"Elizabeth," she said. "Do you have a moment?"

A smile brightened Elizabeth's face. "Certainly."

Sarah stirred but didn't wake. Gazing at her daughter's face for a moment, Rose gathered her courage.

"Would it be all right if I moved back to the small cabin?"

"Of course," Elizabeth said. "You and James are welcome to stay there for as long as you'd like. I should've realized you two would need time alone."

"No. I don't think you understand."

Elizabeth looked at her, questions burning in her eyes.

"I'd like to move there with Sarah and Tommy so I can think without having…" She gulped and gathered her resolve. "Without having James near me. I know he's your brother, and I hate to put you in this position, but the time apart will be good for both of us."

Elizabeth's gaze sharpened, but compassion filled her eyes. "If you're sure that's what you truly want?"

"It is. It won't be for very long. Maybe a week. We haven't heard from Mr. Parker, and it'll give me time to figure out how I feel and what I want to do."

"Have you talked with James about this?"

"No, not yet. I'll tell him tonight."

"When would you leave?" Elizabeth placed the book on the table next to her.

"In the morning if Ben will let a ranch hand take us to the cabin." She adjusted the blanket around Sarah, tugging it more firmly around her.

"You don't want James to take you and the children?"

"No, it's best if we say our goodbyes here." If he came with her, she wouldn't be able to convince him she needed to be alone.

"I'll talk with Ben, and someone'll take you in the morning."

* * *

The next morning, Rose picked up the children's bags and made her way down the stairs and out the front door. Elizabeth had arranged everything and told her they would send plenty of food and firewood as well. The cabin had been vacant since February, and she didn't know if any foodstuffs remained.

The wagon sat waiting for her and she placed the bags in the bed. She needed to get Sarah and Tommy, and then she'd be ready to leave. She looked around for the ranch hand but didn't see him. He was likely in the barn and would return momentarily.

Not wanting to keep him waiting, she hurried inside. Gathering Sarah into her arms, she found Tommy playing with Vicky.

"Tommy, it's time to go."

"No," he grumbled. "I'm playin' with Vicky." He picked up his toy train and moved it around the floor, not looking at Rose and instead continued to play.

"Sweetheart, we discussed this last night. We're going to our home. Aren't you excited about taking a ride?"

"No." He then plopped on his backside and stuffed his thumb in his mouth.

"Tommy, we need to leave. I don't want to keep them waiting." Her patience was wearing thin. He had been cranky and out of sorts all morning.

"Don't wanna," he mumbled, his thumb still firmly stuck in his mouth. "Stay here. Play with Vicky." A petulant and whiny tone to his voice. It was time for his nap, and she should have planned better.

"Please, Tommy. You'll see Vicky soon."

He shook his head and refused to stand. Placing Sarah gently on the floor, Rose went to pick him up when Tommy arched his back and started fighting her.

"Nooooo!" he screamed, flaying his tiny fists this way and that.

Startled, Rose let go, and he scampered away. He raced behind a chair against the wall to hide from her. She tried to pull him from behind it, but he fought and wouldn't let her grab him. Frustrated, she pulled the chair away from the wall and picked him up. He swatted and hollered, "No! No! No!"

"Tommy," James said, his voice stern.

Rose whipped around. She had hoped to avoid James this morning, but he clearly had other plans.

Tommy's eyes raised and his tears dried as he looked at the man standing behind her.

"Rose," he said, "let me take him while you get Sarah. I'll bring him out to the wagon."

Surprised he offered to help her since they fought the night before and she was leaving against his wishes, she let James get Tommy and picked up a now fussy Sarah. Rose placed Sarah against her chest to comfort her.

James left with Tommy, and she could hear him talking sternly, yet with a gentleness that tore into her heart. She wouldn't let that sway her. No matter James's objections, going to the cabin alone was the best for now.

When she stepped outside, James was sitting on the wagon seat with Tommy nestled beside him.

"What are you doing?" she stammered.

"I'm taking you to the cabin." He refused to look at her and instead stared straight ahead.

This wasn't what she wanted. "Elizabeth told me one of the ranch hands would take us."

"One of the ranch hands *is* taking you." He gripped the reins, pulling them taut, causing the horses to paw the ground.

"We talked about this last night."

"I don't want to fight in front of the children. Please don't argue with me." He was clearly not budging. "I won't try to talk you out of this or do anything you don't want. I just need to make sure you're safe and have everything you need."

Sighing, Rose didn't know what else to do. She didn't want to quarrel with him yet again, so she handed Sarah up to his waiting arms and climbed next to him. Once settled, she took Sarah back into her arms. James released the brake and urged the horses forward.

A tense few moments later, they arrived at the small cabin. Jumping down, James placed Tommy on the ground, then reached for Rose.

With her hands full of Sarah, she couldn't stop him from grabbing her waist and lifting her out of the wagon. He placed her gently on the ground, but his hands lingered. He gazed at her, and the heat of his eyes burned into her, but she avoided looking at him. After a long moment, he retreated, and the warmth disappeared, leaving her forlorn and lonely.

She reached for her bags when James took them from her. He didn't say a word but made his way up the stairs and into the cabin. Following him, she put Sarah in the cradle and grabbed a log from the pile lying next to the hearth to start a fire. She grabbed the matches, but once again, James did what he wanted. He removed the matches from her hand and brushed her aside.

"I'll do this. Get the children settled."

Rose's frustration grew. She hadn't asked him to bring her here, and she certainly didn't need his help. Opening Tommy's bag, she pulled out a blanket and toys and handed them to him. She told him to play in the corner.

She turned to James and said, "Can I talk to you outside?"

Crouched next to the fire, he hesitated before standing. He brushed his hands on his trousers and nodded. They stepped outside, and Rose closed the door.

Folding her arms across her chest, she raised her eyes and tried to calm the fierce beating of her heart. "You need to leave."

"What? Why?" he said.

"I don't need your help, and I'd like you to leave."

"Did I do something?" His gaze begged for her forgiveness.

"Yes, you did," she replied. "I didn't ask you to bring me here. In fact, I told you last night I didn't want you to."

"You're my wife, and those are my children. I think I have every right to make sure you're safe."

"Not yet, they aren't, and you gave that up when you lied to me."

Exasperated, he stiffened, and she could tell

he was trying to control his temper. Red flared up his neck and he clenched his fists. "How long are you going to punish me?"

"I'm not. I asked you to stay away last night, and you ignored me. You don't listen and won't leave me be."

The hurt flashed again in his eyes before disappearing behind a mask of indifference. "I'll stay away, but we should talk, and the sooner the better. You can't avoid me forever, Rose."

She hated that she was hurting him, but she needed time to think. When she was ready, she would talk to him, but not a moment before.

Chapter 28

July 1900

James worked from sunup to sundown. He didn't eat with the family and only ate with the ranch hands on occasion. By working hard, he could stop thinking of Rose and the mess he made of their marriage.

He couldn't rely on Ben and Elizabeth's help forever, so he was trying to save every penny he earned. He'd considered working again with horses. It was what he had done before he went to prison and it had always been his dream, but he had no idea if Rose would support it or even if she would stay married to him.

Will she ever forgive me? Will I ever be worthy of her?

Rose didn't come up to the main house, and the only time anyone saw her was when they went to the cabin. Whenever Elizabeth visited, she only shared that Rose was doing fine and the children were thriving. He desperately wanted to see her, but she made it clear he wasn't welcome. She was only supposed to stay for a week, but that week had turned into another and then another.

As the heat of summer boiled around them, James withdrew. He lost weight and was brusque to those around him. No one wanted to work with him and stayed clear of him and his brutal comments and unrelenting pace.

James knew Elizabeth was concerned, but Rose had made her position known. Until she was ready to speak with him, he had to stay away. Elizabeth tried to tell him if he continued this way, it would only intensify the hurt and anger, but he wouldn't budge.

Elizabeth even relayed how difficult it had been for her and Ben to resolve their differences when they were first married. They had almost let their stubbornness ruin their relationship. Elizabeth believed if James and Rose would hash out their grievances, it would go a long way in mending the rift that had grown between them. But as he told Elizabeth, Rose dictated their next steps, not him. Until she was ready to speak with him, he had to abide by her wishes.

Then the lawyer sent word. The judge was ready with his decision. He wanted to see them in court in three days and they were to bring the children with them.

* * *

Elizabeth had visited Rose two days before to tell her the judge wanted to see them and to be prepared to leave that morning. What she hadn't expected was for James to be standing at her door. She hadn't seen him since the day he had dropped her and the children off weeks ago.

When she saw him standing in front of her, her breath caught in her throat. She had forgotten how handsome he was, how he made her heart race, but he didn't look well. He had lost weight and looked as though he was carrying a large log on his shoulders, the weight pushing him to the ground.

Avoiding her gaze, he picked up her packed bags and carried them to the wagon. Returning a few minutes later, he asked, "Are you ready to go?"

Nodding, the pain of the tension between them cutting her deep. "Yes."

"Where's Tommy?" he asked.

"He's playing in his room."

James walked past her, and Rose's fingers rose to touch him, but she stopped. She had lost the right to touch him when she banished him from her life. Spending time alone in the cabin had been tough and painful, but it had given her the time to consider everything that had happened and what she wanted going forward. She had to stay strong until she knew what the outcome would be. If the judge ruled in her favor, then she would see if there was anything left of their relationship, but until then, her one and only concern had to be her children.

A moment later, he held a chattering Tommy in his arms. Thrilled to see him, Tommy told him about the stick he had found in the meadow, the squirrels fighting over a nut, the big spider he saw the other day, and a million other things a little boy would be eager to talk to his pa about.

His pa.

If the judge ruled in their favor, then James would be his pa, now and forevermore. Tommy and Sarah needed a pa, but did she need a husband?

Chapter 29

Rose's palms were soaked in sweat and her legs wobbled under her skirts as she walked into the courtroom, James beside her. Elizabeth and Ben held the children and settled in the back of the room, as ordered by the judge. Tommy giggled and jabbered to Ben telling him the same things he had told James earlier that day. Knowing her children were happy, in that moment, was the only thing keeping Rose from collapsing in trepidation. She tried to contain it but was fighting a losing battle. The judge would decide her future today, and she feared it would be in Charles's favor.

Not wanting the judge to believe there was any contention between the two of them, she and James both tried to act as if they were a loving couple. Sitting next to Mr. Parker, they conferred for a few minutes when Charles waltzed into the courtroom, strutting like a peacock, proudly displaying his feathers before he and his lawyer found a seat. Confidence oozing from him in spades, he had no fear he would get exactly what he had come for.

A few moments later, the judge appeared and brought the court to session. He discussed the difficulty in deciding the proper course of action. It was unusual. A brother-in-law trying to gain custody of his late brother's children when his widow was again married, and how James's criminal past should be considered before allowing two young children into his charge.

The judge's words floated above Rose, and she sat once again in a fog. It was easier that way. She had to swallow multiple times to keep acid from spilling from her mouth and onto the wooden table in front of her. James placed his palms over her shaking hands. His touch was gentle and caring. She raised her lashes to look at him and he smiled at her. His gaze was a calming influence, taking her from a place of fear to a semblance of peace.

"The custody of the children, Tommy Joseph and Sarah Marie McGaven, will stay with their natural mother, Rose Dodson and her husband, James Dodson."

Charles stood and slammed his fist against the wooden wall separating the lawyers from those sitting on the benches.

"No," he yelled. "I won't stand for this. Those children are mine, and you're a fool for not doing as I say."

As Charles continued to rant and holler angry words toward the judge, Rose sat stunned. She hadn't lost her children. She had won. They had won.

"I aim to take them." Charles threw back his chair and stepped toward the aisle as though he were going for the judge to harm him. The bailiff intervened and stopped him from advancing farther. His pudgy lawyer pulled at his sleeve, trying to get him to calm down, but Charles pushed him away, his anger roaring fiercely through the room like an angry mountain lion prepared to eat his prey.

The judge said, "Enough, Mr. McGaven. My decision is final."

"No, that ain't right," Charles demanded. "He's an outlaw, a degenerate. My brother's children need a better home, a safe home where I can raise 'em right. There's no way that man"—he pointed to James in a threatening manner—"is a suitable influence on my niece and nephew. Not to mention she's a two-bit hussy."

James hissed with anger, his face boiling red. Rose placed her hand on his arm to prevent him from charging Charles and throwing him to the ground. Charles could no longer hurt her. She did not care what he called her.

"I've made my decision. You can sit and be quiet, or I'll have you removed."

Charles pulled away from the bailiff and stared at Rose with fury. "This ain't over, Rose. I'll get those children. Mark my words." He stormed out of the courtroom, the door slamming behind him. His lawyer shuffled out of the courtroom, muttering apologies as he ran after him.

The judge frowned. "Mr. and Mrs. Dodson, please be wary of Mr. McGaven. I urge you to make peace with the man. He wants to be a part of their life. You don't have to allow him access, but for the sake of your family, it might be wise not to shut him out."

He made a few notations on the papers in front of him and handed them to the bailiff.

"Mr. Parker, please have that filed with the clerk." He then stared hard at James. "Mr. Dodson, I realize you've made mistakes, but it appears you've owned up to them, served your time, and are attempting to make the best of your future. I hope I haven't been amiss, but I believe you'll make a good father to those children and will provide for them. With the support of your family, you should do well. We are adjourned." He pounded his gavel once, stood, and disappeared behind a large wooden door.

Ben and Elizabeth joined them, smiling. Tommy jumped into James's arms and wrapped his tiny arms around his neck, squealing with delight. He hadn't understood what happened, but when James asked him if it was all right if he became his pa, Tommy yelled, "My pa."

They laughed and James moved a lock of Tommy's red hair from his forehead, a look of sweet love on his face before Tommy insisted on being put on the ground, his little hand firmly entrenched in James's hand.

The bailiff ushered them out of the courtroom, their celebration needing to be done elsewhere.

After profuse thanks for his help, Mr. Parker left them, a smile on his face, swinging his briefcase at his side. His good deeds were done for the day. She wanted to thank him, but the words were stuck in her throat.

"We should celebrate," Ben said.

James and Elizabeth agreed, their grins on full display, not noticing Rose was quiet.

As they left the courthouse, it was decided they would stay the night once again in Helena. After they reached their room, Rose relaxed for the first time in weeks. Removing her bonnet with one hand, she dropped it on the table next to the sofa.

Not looking at James, she went to the bedroom and said over her shoulder, "Sarah needs to be fed. Can you keep an eye on Tommy?"

She didn't wait for his response and closed the door. She sat in the chair next to the window and Sarah latched onto her breast almost immediately. Rose stared at the bustling activity outside. Carriages, buckboards, and freight wagons clambered along the dirt roads. Women with elaborate hats and parasols in their hands strolled along the pavers lining the edges of the road, lifting their skirts when stepping off the edges. Men doffed their hats, stepped out of the way, smiling, and carrying on with their day.

Life continued and hadn't stopped. Now she had a decision to make.

* * *

An hour later, Rose emerged from the bedroom, a sleeping Sarah in her arms. James's heart ached with a longing so deep and fierce it was a surprise he didn't fall dead at her feet. He once again marveled at the beauty of his wife. Her hair was a wave of reddish blonde curls, begging him to run his hands through them. He wanted to hold her close, but knew if he didn't tread carefully, he would never again get the opportunity.

Rose looked at him and started to speak but then stopped as if unsure of what to say. She flitted her eyes around the room, looking everywhere but at him. He held his breath and prayed she would she finally allow him to tell her about his past.

"I think we need to talk," she said.

Surprised, James's breath whooshed out of him like a tornado that had crashed out of the sky. "I agree, but I don't want the children to hear."

"Do you suppose Elizabeth and Ben would watch them for an hour?"

He jumped to his feet. "I'm sure they won't mind."

James rushed out of their room and down the hall. He knocked on Ben and Elizabeth's door a little more forcefully than he should have, but he was anxious and nervous. This was the first overture she had made, and he didn't want her to change her mind.

Ben pulled open the door. "Is everything all right?"

"Yes." James ran a hand through his hair. "I'm sorry if I'm disturbing you, but would you and Elizabeth watch the children for an hour? Rose and I need to talk, and it would be a tad distracting having them underfoot."

"Bring 'em here. We'd be happy to,"

Elizabeth said. She appeared behind Ben soon after the door opened.

James thanked them and hustled to their room, where he took Sarah from Rose's arms and held Tommy's hand in the other.

"I'll be right back. Don't go nowhere."

Chapter 30

"I'm sure you have lots of questions." James was as nervous as a cat on a hot tar roof. His hands shook, and his heart was fairly bursting out of his chest. There was no place to hide, and he had to tell her everything, no matter how hard it might be. "If you'd let me, I'd like to tell you about my past and what led me to the decisions I made. Why I ended up in jail." He ran his fingers through his hair. "You can ask me whatever you'd like, and I'll answer in the most honest way I know."

James had scurried back after dropping Sarah and Tommy with Ben and Elizabeth and had paced in front of the fireplace, likely wearing holes in the thick rugs under his feet, trying to decide where to start. Sensing her discomfort, he dived in and prayed she'd understand.

"Ma and Pa moved to the Dakotas when I was but a babe. Pa tried to make a good living and worked hard, but when I was nigh on ten years of age, he got sick with the fever and passed away. Ma, not having much in the way of money and having no way to feed me, met a man named George Winslow who offered to marry her. He claimed he wanted a wife, and she needed a provider. What he wanted was my Pa's spread and had to take the woman to get it." James walked toward the flames of the fire, needing to stare at something steady and calm. That time was painful, and he hated to remember. "They had my sister Elizabeth soon after, but George was a drunk and over the years he gambled what little money they had. I wasn't his son, and he made that clear. He started to hit me and if Ma interfered, he'd turn his rage on her. She didn't want me to go, but we thought it best if I did. I was near fifteen when I left with a few dollars she had squirreled away, the rifle my pa gave me right before he passed, and the few clothes I owned in a worn knapsack."

He had been too young to know what his future held, but old enough to know staying was only hurting his ma. He wanted to protect her and if that was the only way he could do it, then he'd willingly leave.

"I tried to do what I could to find food. I looked for work, but no one wanted to hire a boy, as I was scrawny and looked much younger than I was. There were days I was so hungry, I could feel a hole burning in my gut. I stole from farmers, but I told myself I'd pay 'em back. I kept a small journal detailing what I took and from whom. When I could do a small chore, such as muck out the stalls or feed the horses, I would do it to ease my guilt. I knew what I was doing was wrong, but not starving is a powerful motivator." He paused, remembering the moment he met Thomas. "One day, I stole from the wrong person, or perhaps he was the right person." He chuckled softly. "I suppose it depends on your perspective if he was or wasn't."

Thomas treated him as his own. Taught him everything he knew, and that was where things had gone wrong. James had never examined their relationship, but he wondered if it would've been better for him if he had never met Thomas. Maybe he wouldn't have gone from pilfering for food to stealing cash and gold, holding people at gunpoint, and at times striking blows, but he'd never know. He had made his choice and would have to live with those fateful decisions for the rest of his life.

"Thomas was kind to me. He'd been robbing stagecoaches and brought me under his wing. As time went on and we never got caught, I justified my actions. I can't imagine what my ma thought about my actions from heaven above. I don't think I could look her in the eye if she were here today. She'd be awfully disappointed in me." He paused, emotion growing thick in his throat. He was ashamed of himself, but he forced himself to continue. "The last job I did was mere days after Elizabeth had found me after years of us being apart. Her eyes had been full of hope that I'd protect her from her pa. It made me want to make a proper home for her. I had saved enough to buy a ranch in Spring Creek and was attempting to be on the right side of the law, and that's where Ben and Elizabeth met."

Those few months in Spring Creek were some of his happiest memories. He had the ranch he always wanted, and Elizabeth had been with him, safe from harm, at least for a time.

"Things fell apart when her pa found us. George demanded Elizabeth marry an old friend of his. He was a vile man and Elizabeth was scared to death of him. Somehow, George discovered my past and threatened to expose me to the Marshal if she didn't marry this man. Ben and I had become friends and, being the decent man he was, he intervened. He didn't know what I had done, but offered to marry Elizabeth so she wouldn't have to marry the man her pa had chosen for her. In the end, George still turned me over to the law."

James could have tried to fight the accusations and made it seem like a senile old man was making up stories. He wondered if he could have convinced the Marshal he had been lying. However, if he had truly wanted to start over, he had to own up to his mistakes. He didn't want Elizabeth to lie for him, and she knew he had robbed stagecoaches. After all, she had watched him do his last job and had even taken part by bashing a snooping Ben over the head.

"The only positive thing out of the mess was Elizabeth was far from his clutches."

James watched Rose as she tried to absorb everything he was telling her, but she showed nothing. She had curled her hands in her lap and had tucked her feet under her skirt. She was the picture of a lady, a beautiful lady whom he would lose if she couldn't find it in her heart to forgive him. "Once caught, I confessed. I didn't want Elizabeth to suffer any more or to be implicated in any of my selfish decisions. She'd been through too much, more than I've told you tonight."

"What happened to her?" The first words she had spoken since coming to him earlier.

He didn't know if it was a crack in her resolve or an opening to a new start. "That's her story to tell. Just know that once she gave Ben a chance, they built a future together. He cared for her when I couldn't."

Then the questions poured from her like a well pump after a long drought. "How long were you in prison?"

"Six years."

She gasped, covering her hand with her mouth. He wasn't sure if she was hiding her disgust or anguish.

Her hand dropped to her neck as though cradling a babe. "Did you kill anyone?"

"No, never." He couldn't have lived with himself if he had.

"Did you hurt anyone?"

He cringed, but he promised he would be honest. "There were times when I wasn't gentle and there were likely broken bones or blood as a result, but nothing, at least that I can remember, where someone couldn't have recovered from any injuries I would've inflicted."

"Why did you hide it from me?"

The question he dreaded but had to answer. "I'd just been released when I met you. I was headed to Elizabeth's for Christmas when fate intervened. There were moments when I wanted to tell you, but I thought I knew better. I didn't want to take the chance you'd hate me and run as far from me as you could get." He hung his head in shame.

"Why did you help me and offer to marry me on the train?"

"I'd done little in my life that was good, and I saw it as an opportunity to make amends." He had fallen for this amazingly strong woman faster than anyone before and hadn't wanted to let her step out of his life. He had stood in the passenger car praying night after night there would be a way to keep her.

Then, when her brother-in-law had stepped

into the passenger car, James had been given a chance to grasp a dream he believed had been out of reach. He feared he had taken advantage of her in her time of need but justified it by believing she needed him as much as he needed her.

She grew silent, and it stretched between them, long and painful.

Feeling uncomfortable with the growing awkwardness, he said, "I was wrong to keep this from you, and you'll never know how much I regret that decision. I love Tommy and Sarah with everything in me and want to make this work between us. Can you ever forgive me?"

She said nothing for a minute before speaking. "I don't know. Can I have time to think about what you've told me?"

Have I said too much or too little? "Do you want me to get the children?"

"No, not yet." She clenched her hands in her lap, her eyes faced the floor, and avoided his gaze.

"I'll leave you in peace. Can you consider one thing?"

"What?" She raised her eyes that were filled with the pain he had put there.

"I know we didn't marry because we were in love. You didn't know me and took a chance. I'll be forever grateful and honored you let me be a part of your world. You've given me more happiness than I've ever had in most my life." He swallowed. He hadn't realized until that moment how much he loved her and couldn't leave without telling her, no matter what she decided. Kneeling at her feet, he picked up her cold, clammy hands in his. She didn't pull away. Pouring everything he was feeling into three simple words, he said, "I love you." And prayed he hadn't ruined what remained of their fragile relationship.

* * *

James had stunned her silent. She had not expected him to tell her he loved her. After his declaration, he left the room, leaving her in peace as she had asked. She analyzed everything he said, and her anger disappeared like a flame on a single white candle snuffed out between two fingers. She had been unfair to him and hadn't given him a chance to tell her the truth. When they met, he went out of his way to help her, a stranger on a train with a young boy at her side, and a baby begging to be delivered.

Other men might have found a way out of the dire situation. In fact, her Joseph had been of no help when she delivered Tommy. He had been a nervous wreck, stuttering and sweating when the labor pains had clamped tight around her belly. Relieved when the midwife had arrived, Joseph couldn't get out of the room fast enough and only returned when she and the baby were presentable, and their bedroom had been put back to rights. He couldn't handle the sight of blood and it would've likely ended badly if he had been the one there for Sarah's birth.

He had been so unlike James, who had taken stock of the situation and did what needed to be done without a second thought and without complaint. In her anger, she had ignored what James had done for her before that horrible day in the courtroom. And even as those events unfolded, he had owned up to his actions, explained his past to the judge, and made it clear he would be the best father in the world to her two precious children. He had never given her a reason to believe he would be anything but kind, loving, compassionate, and patient.

Why am I being so contrary?

He was willing to give them a second chance. *Am I?*

Her decision made, she grabbed her cloak and hastened to the lobby. It was late and few people were milling around. Losing her nerve, she gave the room one last glance when the main doors opened, and James stepped through. The wind blew in behind him, scattering newspapers on the small tables and fluttering the leaves of the plants sitting in large planters next to the doors. He came to an abrupt halt when his eyes met hers. The air between them crackling with electricity, it fairly singed her fingertips.

"James."

"Rose."

They both chuckled, forced ones, but chuckles, nonetheless. Silence brewed between them.

Not wanting to lose him, she moved close to his side. What she had to say didn't need to be heard by those still in the lobby. "I owe you an apology."

Startled, he said, "You've nothing to apologize for."

"I do. I was horribly wrong to judge you. I should've let you tell me why you'd made the choices you made. My behavior's been inexcusable." She gripped her cloak painfully around her neck. "We didn't start this relationship as a love match, and I knew that. I shouldn't have expected you to tell me about your past when I didn't divulge mine to you. That was unfair."

"I should've been honest with you." His voice broke.

"Stop, please." She released her grip and held out her hand. "This was my fault, and I... I want you to know how sorry I am." She paused, gulped, and blurted it out, "I'm in love with you too."

Did I just say that? Am I in love with him?

Her senses sharpened. His musky woodsy scent and the tangy citrus of the orange he had eaten earlier gathered around her like a warm blanket. He came into focus. His woolen coat was wrapped snug around his broad chest. He held his hands behind his back, and he looked at her through his piercing brown eyes. It was as though he could see deep in her soul. The man standing in front of her was everything she could have ever wanted. The choices he had made in his past had nothing to do with the choices he had made from the moment they met.

She hoped she wasn't too late.

Rose gripped her hands together, the skin turning white from the pressure. Her skirt lifted from the wind that blew in as another couple walked inside the hotel. The couple's eyes drifted toward them as they walked to the front desk, clearly interested in what was happening between her and James, but too polite to stop and watch.

James swallowed and a slew of different expressions crossed his face, but she couldn't identify them. She wanted to touch him. She wanted him to forgive her.

He stepped hesitantly forward, placing his hand on top of hers. "I love you, Rose."

Relief swept through her, and she turned her lips upward in to a wide smile. Happy tears brimmed in her eyes. He pulled her close and wrapped his powerful arms around her, right there in the hotel lobby where God, the porters, and the desk clerk stood watching them. He shuddered and his wet tears dropped into her hair.

She lifted her head and gazed at him, touching her fingers to his cheek. He looked deep into her eyes, asking for permission. She nodded. The movement slight but enough that he knew she was giving him the approval to move forward. He placed his lips against hers for a sweet kiss that sent a zing straight to her toes.

"We have much to work through, but we can do it," she murmured.

"I agree. Can you forgive me?" He gently brushed his fingers against her ear.

"There's nothing to forgive. No more apologies, no more recriminations. Let's start over." She grabbed his hand and led him upstairs.

Chapter 31

Rose and James talked late into the night, long after Tommy and Sarah had fallen asleep. They had retrieved them from Elizabeth and Ben and brought them back to their room, both sleepy and entirely ready to be put down for the night. They made a pallet on the floor for Tommy and pulled out a drawer from the wardrobe, padding it with thick blankets to keep Sarah safe from rolling around. Once the children were asleep, they were honest with one another for the first time. They kept nothing hidden and discussed what had brought them to today and what they wanted for tomorrow.

When James asked about her family, she hadn't wanted to remember, but the compassion in his eyes, and the fact that he had bared his soul, gave her the strength to recount those difficult years. The pain of her parents' passing and the horrible way they had been taken was not something she relished telling, but he understood and he didn't push. Instead, he held her hand, his warm palm comforting and offering empathy for her pain.

It had been a warm spring day when she and her brother had ridden the mule their father had purchased for the five-mile trek to and from the one-room schoolhouse in Geneva, Illinois. They had been laughing and playing their normal guessing game when they had arrived home. Nicky had noticed first that something was amiss. Their milk cow had been wandering outside of the barn, their pa's horses were gone, and the front door of their white two-story clapboard house was wide open. The only sounds were of the cow mooing and the barn door swishing in the wind from not being latched properly.

Nicky had stopped laughing and told her to stay on the mule until he came and got her. The tension in Nicky's voice caused her eyes to widen. He rarely got stern with her, so she did as he asked. Holding onto the mule's short prickly mane, she had sat fidgeting, not understanding what might be happening.

When Nicky screamed in terror, his sobs frightening her more than anything she had ever heard before, she slid from the mule's back and ran inside, forgetting his command to stay outside. She should have listened as the memory of the blood pooling under her parents' bodies and the splatter on the walls was a horrifying image that stayed with her during her waking hours and when she slept. The nightmares kept her up most nights for years.

James's eyes widened at the image she described. "What a horrible thing for you to have endured. How old were you?"

"About seven, I think. Too many things

happened after that for me to know for sure." She tried to smile, but it was difficult. "Having Tommy close made the pain easier until Joseph was killed. Everyone I've loved has been taken from me and so it has been easier to pretend I could do it on my own and that I didn't need anyone. I didn't want your help, and I felt cornered and out of options."

He grimaced at the implication, and she cringed at what it sounded like.

"I didn't mean I'm not grateful you came into my life, James."

He patted her hand before pulling away. "I understand." He didn't meet her gaze, closing down his emotions in front of her.

She knew in her gut he didn't understand, but she had to make him. She reached for his hands and held them in hers, not letting him pull away, and trying to find the words to express what was in her heart. "I've had a lot of loss in my life. Nicky was taken from me about ten years later, and when I met Joseph, I thought all would finally be well. He loved me and we had these plans, but then he too was taken from me. Once Joseph was gone, I told myself I couldn't love again. It was too painful. I thought I could be happy with just my children, but then you came into my life like a strong, stalwart tree."

He laughed, the sound hearty and deep, and she giggled alongside him.

"I know that sounds… well, not sure how that sounds exactly, but you comforted me, helped me when I needed it the most, and then offered your protection. I was angry and yes, I was hurt when I found out about your past, but I think I was angrier at myself for letting Charles hurt me and for letting him hurt us. I shouldn't have gotten angry with you. I should have listened and given you a chance to explain. I'll always regret making you suffer while I wallowed in my self-pity."

"You didn't…"

"Oh yes, I did," she said, interrupting him. She dropped his hands and then grazed her fingers across his cheek before she stepped to the window and looked out at the dark sky. "I left you and took the children to the cabin, knowing full well you loved them as much as I did."

"But..."

"No, you can't excuse my behavior. I was being selfish, but I can do better. I will do better." She stomped her foot and turned to face him, her hands on her hips, her heart racing. "I must do better. I want to make this work with you." Tears suddenly filled her eyes, and she blinked furiously to keep them at bay. "I can't keep believing that everyone I love is going to be taken from me."

The next thing she knew, James held her in his arms and smoothed back her curls. She tried to pull away, but he didn't let her.

"Please," he said. "Let me hold you."

She gripped the front of his shirt and then ran her fingers across the seams where the pearl buttons kept it closed. They stood this way for a long time, the clock ticking behind them, holding one another close. Then finally, James blew out his breath, pulled slightly away so he could take her hand and lead her to the sofa.

She opened her mouth to speak when he touched his finger to her lips.

"I love you, Rose, more than I ever thought I could love someone. We can't fix what has happened, but we can work together to improve the future, don't you agree?"

She looked deep into his brown eyes and saw forgiveness and love. Hope bloomed inside of her. She hadn't made a mistake in forgiving James. He had a past, but so did she. If she could trust him and, in his love, then maybe, just maybe, she could forgive herself.

Leaning forward, she placed a tender kiss on his lips. His hot breath mingled with hers. She wanted to linger, but instead pulled back. She didn't want to push too soon, too fast. She had hurt him.

"There's nothing to forgive, so whatever thoughts are going through your mind, you throw them away right now. We both have made mistakes, thought things we shouldn't have, and didn't listen to one another. So maybe we start over?"

She laughed. He had the uncanny ability to see deep inside her soul. "Yes, I'd like that."

He grinned, delight lighting his eyes. "How about we go to bed? I think we've talked enough for the night. It's getting late."

Nodding, she let him lead her to the bedroom where they lay cuddled in one another's arms. Just holding each other close, giving one another comfort before they both fell asleep, getting the first good night's rest either of them had had in weeks.

* * *

The next morning, they, along with the children, met Ben and Elizabeth in front of the hotel. Rose held James's hand, her smile full of joy, a stark difference to the day before.

Handing Sarah into James's waiting arms, Rose grasped Elizabeth's elbow and pulled her to the side. "Thank you for keeping the children for us last night."

"Am I right to believe that the two of you finally talked?" Elizabeth asked.

Rose smiled warmly. "I realized last night how much I love your brother, and I was so wrong to treat him the way I did."

Elizabeth's eyes widened at Rose's words. "You love him?"

"Yes, yes, I do," Rose said, a giddiness to her tone. "Can you forgive me?"

"There's nothing to forgive." Elizabeth squeezed Rose's hand in affection.

"Thank you for being my friend and for giving me the time to work through my feelings."

"You don't need to thank me," Elizabeth protested. "I did nothing."

"You gave me the opportunity to get to know your brother and for that, I'm forever grateful. It hasn't been easy, but we talked last night, and we want to start over, get to know one another proper like and see if we can make a life with one another."

Elizabeth beamed. "I'm so happy to hear that. You two are right for one another."

"With time, patience, and not having any more secrets, we have a chance. We both want it and now that James is legally Sarah and Tommy's father, well, that is reason enough to start over. Not to mention, your brother is one handsome man." As soon as the words came out of her mouth, she slapped a hand across her lips. She couldn't believe she had said that.

Elizabeth's eyes twinkled with mirth, but she didn't embarrass Rose. "What can I do to help?"

"You've done so much. I can't ask you to do more."

"Nonsense. I'm happy to help you with whatever you need."

Rose pulled at her bottom lip with her teeth. She didn't want to ask, but Elizabeth seemed willing. "Would you watch Tommy and Sarah for a few days? I think if James and I can go away, just the two of us, that maybe we can get to know one another better, this time without the secrets between us."

"Of course, I would. You don't have to ask. We're family."

Elizabeth pulled Rose into a hug and the joy in Rose's heart was fairly bursting. She had come too close to losing the man who could make her dreams come true, and she would do everything in her power not to make the same mistakes again.

Chapter 32

A week later, James and Rose left for the train station. James had suggested Spring Creek as a place for them to get away and to continue to work through their misunderstandings. He wanted to show her where he and Elizabeth had tried to start over as well as ask for the townsfolk's forgiveness. He never had the chance to tell those who had done so much for Elizabeth how sorry he was for deceiving them. It'd be hard to return, but it needed to be done if he truly wanted to make things right.

Rose was supportive and eager to see the town that had made such a difference for them all those years ago. The two of them spent hours each evening, after the children went to bed, discussing their future and getting to know one another.

When the train pulled into the station, James peered out the window and smiled. Spring Creek was a bustling town and had grown in the past six years. He shouldn't be surprised things had changed. Nothing ever stood still. James helped Rose down the metal steps and stood on the train platform, hesitant but resolved that returning to Spring Creek was the right thing to do.

The conductor pointed them to the porter, who was removing the bags from the cargo car, and they gathered their belongings before heading to the main street. James held both of their bags and rested his other hand against the small of Rose's back. He took every opportunity to touch her, to let her know he was going nowhere.

At first, no one gave them a second glance, but as they walked along the wooden pathway on the side of the road, a few heads turned, and people began to point and whisper. James tensed but kept a pleasant smile on his face. He was determined to make this work and their first stop was the Marshal's office.

Walking up the steps, James pulled open the door and followed Rose inside.

The Marshal faced away from the door, digging in a cabinet. "Be right with you," he said.

"Thank you, Marshal," James said.

The Marshal froze and slowly turned to face them.

A stone-cold look crossed his features. He sharpened his gaze. "You're the last person I expected to see." His tone was tense, reaching his hand for the pistol nestled on his hip.

"I'm not here to cause trouble." James carefully dropped their bags to the floor before holding his hands out to show he wasn't of any threat.

"Then what in the sam hill are you doin' here?" The Marshal's hand still hovered over his pistol. He was braced against the cabinet, a serious and intent gaze as he watched James's every move.

"I wanted to make amends to the people I hurt."

"Why'd you want to do that?" He narrowed his thick eyebrows, so they appeared to be one dark line, clearly not trusting a word out of James's mouth, which in retrospect was what he would've done if they'd been on opposite sides of the situation.

"To prove to my wife, I can own up to my mistakes." James reached for Rose's hand and squeezed it. She nestled up against him, offering comfort and support.

The Marshal finally looked at Rose as if realizing James wasn't alone. "Ma'am."

"Marshal," she said. "I hope our being here isn't an issue."

"No, unless he plans on robbing another stagecoach?" He cocked his head to James.

James wanted to laugh but feared it wouldn't go over so well. "No, sir," James said. "I meant what I said. I'm here to make amends, nothing else. I enjoyed living here, and I regret the choices I made."

The Marshal relaxed a bit, although his eyes never left James. He scratched behind his ear. "How long you planning on staying in town?"

"Just a few days. I want to show my wife, Rose, around and introduce her to the people who'd been kind to me and Elizabeth."

"And how is your sister doing?" The Marshal was clearly trying to be civil, but it was difficult for him.

"She's right fine." Not wanting to cause the Marshal any further grief, he would make this brief. "First apology needs to go to you for causing you so much trouble."

The Marshal was startled at the unexpected pronouncement but nodded in acknowledgement.

"Thank you for being kind to Elizabeth when I had made such a mess of things." He bent and picked up their bags. "We won't be keeping you, as I'm sure you have plenty holding you busy." James doffed his hat. "We'll be staying at the hotel if'n you feel the need to keep an eye on me."

"You served your time," the Marshal said. "I shouldn't have to watch you unless you decide to make it hard on yourself."

"Nah," James said. "I learned my lesson and won't ever do that again."

"I hope you're right, son."

James smiled. Now that he had gotten that over with, he could breathe easier. The rest of his apologies couldn't be any worse than that.

* * *

James and Rose secured a room at the new hotel at the far end of town. James wanted to take her to the ranch he had bought and lost, but it had grown late, and Rose was fighting to keep her eyes open.

"Would you care for something to eat?" James asked.

Rose smiled. "Yes, but could we stay in tonight?"

James took her hand and pulled her into his arms. "We can do that. Why don't I find us something warm to eat and bring it up here? You can freshen up while I'm gone."

"I don't want to be difficult. If it's too much, we can find a place to eat."

"No, it isn't too much. It's been a rough few weeks. I want you to rest." He held her for a moment before placing a gentle kiss on her forehead.

Thirty minutes later, he held had two steaming plates of food and a bottle of wine tucked under his arm. He knocked on the door, juggling the plates with care, not wanting to spill them. It took a moment before Rose opened the door, staying hidden from view. When she closed it, he got a good look at her, and heat rushed to his belly.

She was wearing a sheer nightgown, the light from the candles showing and hiding her petite frame at the same time. Her hair hung across her shoulders, and her feet were bare. As he stared at her, a deep red blush traveled up her chest and flushed her cheeks. James hadn't expected to find her waiting for him, and he wasn't sure how to proceed.

He forced his stiff legs to move. His eyes didn't waver from hers as he found the nearest table to drop the warm plates of food and bottle of wine. His hands were sweaty, and he wiped them on his trousers. The room wasn't overly warm, but a deep inferno had built inside of him.

"Hungry?" he asked.

"Yes, but not for food."

Chapter 33

A gentle knock sounded at the door. If she hadn't been half awake already, she might not have heard it. Rose opened her eyes and looked over at James. He lay on his side with an arm draped around her waist. His eyes were closed, and the stress lines that had lined his face for days were gone. A lock of his brown hair graced his forehead, and she itched to rub it through her fingers but instead scooted out from under him. She grabbed her wrap from the chair next to the bed and tucked her hair behind her ears.

A knock sounded again, this time louder. She hurried to the door, holding her wrapper closed at her neck, and opened it before the knocks woke him.

A tall, slim gentleman clad in a dark suit and string tie stood on the other side, his hat in his hand.

"Can I help you?" she asked.

"Sorry to bother you, ma'am. Is Mr. Dodson available?" His gaze was friendly.

"He's sleeping," she said. "I hate to wake him. Can I help you?"

"I heard he was in town and…"

"Doc, is that you?" James appeared behind her. He had pulled on a pair of trousers and was buttoning his shirt.

The doc grinned, his smile reaching from ear to ear. "I apologize for interrupting, but I ran into the Marshal, and he said you were here. I wanted to invite you to supper with me and the missus. Both of you," he said, looking at her, a question in his eyes.

"Doc, this here is my wife, Rose. Rose, this is Doc Wilson. He was right neighborly to me and Elizabeth when we lived here."

"And how is Elizabeth doing?" the doc asked.

"She's doing well. She and Ben have two little ones now."

"Janie is going to be thrilled to hear that. Well, I can see I woke you, so I'll get. Dinner's at six."

"We look forward to visiting with you both," James said.

"Ma'am." James reached for the door and closed it behind him. He dropped his smile, and he withered in front of her.

"What's wrong?"

"Nothing. Why would you ask?" James said.

"You appear sad but yet you were excited to see the doc."

"Oh, I am." He ran his hand through his hair, mussing it further but only making him more handsome in her eyes.

"What is it? You can tell me."

He pushed a stray hair from her cheek, resting his fingers on her neck. "Nothing to tell. I guess I just didn't expect anyone to want to see me after…" He bent his head to his chest, dropping his hand.

"After what happened?" she whispered.

He nodded. He went to the window and leaned against it. "No one should want to have a thing to do with me. I'm not sure what I expected coming back here, but I didn't expect anyone to be nice or welcoming."

"Maybe they've forgotten."

He choked out a laugh. "Oh, I doubt that. Between what happened to Elizabeth and then my quick downfall, it created quite the scandal and probably the most excitement they've had in years."

She hesitated for a moment. She didn't want to be insensitive, but she thought he was worrying about nothing considering the reception they had received thus far. "Not forgotten then, but maybe forgiveness."

"I don't expect their forgiveness, Rose. I certainly don't deserve it."

"You paid for your crimes."

"Did I?" he said, turning to look at her,

anguish in his eyes. "I confessed, but did I pay for the things I did? I hurt many people over the years. Sure, I killed no one, but I took something from them."

"You're being too hard on yourself."

"No. I'm not." He fished his hands next to his side, and fury made his face red.

She didn't move, just watched him closely.

He had clearly held this in for some time, and he needed to let it go. James was angry with himself. He heaved his chest as though he had run a mile in the sweltering sun, sweat glistening on his skin. "It was harder than I thought seeing the doc as it was a reminder of everything I had and all that I lost because of my stupid decisions. I'm not sure I should've brought you here."

She touched his arm, but he pulled away once again.

"I'm not a good man."

"Shh," she said. "We've been over this. You've been honest with me, and you've paid for your crimes. You'll not continue to berate yourself. No good will come of it. We've squandered the morning fooling around"—she blushed—"albeit a very delightful morning, but let's wash and you can show me your old ranch. Then we'll come back and have dinner with the doc and his wife. You might've made mistakes, but they don't want to hold them against you."

An hour later, they found the livery so James could rent them a horse and buggy. On their way out of town, several people waved. A few turned their backs, but those were few.

The warm wind rustled through the trees and fields of green grass. The horse shook his head at a few irritating flies, but the ride was relaxing. James pointed out a few homesteads here and there and what he remembered of the people that had once lived there. When they arrived, James stopped the buggy outside the wide arches of the ranch he had once called home.

"When I was arrested and sent to prison, the ranch was auctioned to the highest bidder to retrieve as much money as possible to repay what I'd stolen. I wish I could've kept it, but it only seemed right, although it wasn't as though I was given a choice when I couldn't give back the money I had stolen."

She placed her hand on his. "It appears to have gone to a good family. They've taken care of the place, or at least, it appears so." She gazed at the wooden fence, the well-cared for drive, and the sturdy house that sat at the end.

"Yes, it does."

Climbing out of the buggy, he lifted her on to the ground and pointed out the old barn that sat behind the house.

"I remember coming back from town right after we arrived. Ben comes sauntering out of the barn like he owns the place." James chuckled. "He asked Elizabeth if I was hiring and offered to work to show me what he could do to gain employment."

"So, that is how you met?"

"Yeah, he had been looking for work, and I needed the help. Although if you ask Elizabeth, she'd tell you otherwise. I was stubborn, though, and didn't think she could work as hard as a man. I was wrong, and she let me know it."

"She did?"

"Oh, yes, she did. Her pa treated her like a boy, and she could ride and shoot better than most men, but I didn't believe her for a time." He turned his gaze to the ranch. "Me and Ben fixed up the main house, repaired the walls, shored up the old fireplace, and replaced the roof. In fact, Ben fell off the roof and pert near scared Elizabeth to death one day." He chuckled. "She clucked over him like a mother hen, but he wouldn't hear anything of it. Then there was the time Elizabeth fell straight into a muddy puddle. I shouldn't have laughed, but it was right near hilarious to see her coated in the thick mud. Ben was kinder to her than I was, and at the time, they could barely stand one another. She didn't trust him, and Ben didn't think she was a lady with her strutting around in trousers."

Rose laughed. "She told me she loves to wear them."

"Yes, she does and would wear them around

the ranch. She'd wear skirts in town, but if given the chance, I think she'd likely wear 'em all the time."

"What freedom that must bring her."

He grinned. "I don't think she wears 'em as much now, likely cause Ben hated it although I don't think he'd tell her no, at least not now anyways."

"Then how did they… I mean, they seem so happy."

"Oh, they are now, but it took them time to get there." He smiled at the memories. "Ben and I were courtin' this woman in town and when she ran off with another man unbeknownst to us, it was about near the time that Elizabeth's pa had shown up demanding she marry his friend. Remember I told you about him?"

"Yes. He was a cruel man, wasn't he?" she asked.

James had told her that Elizabeth's pa tried marrying her to someone else, but then Ben had intervened and offered to marry her instead, but he hadn't told her much more.

"Yes, he was. Ben convinced Elizabeth's pa to let him marry Elizabeth, although it was at a price."

"A price?"

"Not sure I should tell you this, as it isn't something Elizabeth and Ben discuss, but Ben paid her pa to marry her. George basically sold her to the highest bidder."

"Oh my." Rose lifted her hands to her lips.

"Yep, it sure was a mighty mess, but it turned out all right in the end." James leaned against the fence and looked around. It was clear the memories were strong and precious to him.

Rose was glad he had shared this place with her, but it was now part of his history. The two of them could work on building their own future in an honest and worthwhile manner. No more secrets.

"It's getting late, so we best head on back," James said as he pushed away from the fence.

Stopping him, Rose pulled him to her for a soft kiss. He held onto her and buried his face in her neck. They stood quiet for a long while before climbing into the buggy and going back to town.

Stopping at the hotel, they washed the dirt and dust away. They might've been a few minutes late to the doc's place, as a few amorous kisses and passionate touches distracted them. They were like young newlyweds experiencing joy and fondness without tiny children begging for their attention.

They held hands, their fingers intertwined, their steps slow as they enjoyed the night air. Once they arrived, Rose was introduced once again to the doc and to his charming wife Janie.

They shared a lovely meal, where the doc was happy to catch James up with the people he had once lived among. James apologized to the doc for deceiving him and the doc was quick to tell him apologies weren't needed; it was all in the past.

When they left, James was more like himself, relaxed and carefree. She was glad the doc had invited them over for dinner. What James needed to realize was that although he had made mistakes, it was time to put them in the past where they belonged.

* * *

Sharp and vicious pounding on the door woke them early the next morning. James jumped out of bed and went to the door while Rose scrambled to grab her wrapper. James muttered under his breath as he yanked open the door and found the Marshal standing outside of it.

Why would the Marshal be here?

James had been with her the whole time they had been in Spring Creek, so there was no way he could be accused of any criminal behavior. It was possible he had done something else she was unaware of. Then she immediately chastised herself for thinking those kinds of thoughts. James had changed, and she knew better. The Marshal had to be there for an entirely different reason.

"Marshal," James said, his voice low, but

there was a sharp edge to it. "What can we do for you?"

"I hate to interrupt," the Marshal said, "but I got an urgent message here from Ben Seymour."

"Thank you," James said as he reached for the note.

Rose stood and tightened the sash. She watched as James opened the folded piece of paper. He widened his eyes.

"What is it?" Rose asked, an unspoken fear climbing her spine.

James glanced at her but didn't answer her question, instead focusing on the Marshal. "I appreciate you bringing this. Do you know when the next train leaves for Helena?"

"You've got an hour. If you hurry, you should be able to make it." The Marshal's hands rested above the pistols on his hips, his eyes were kinder than they'd been before. He was bringing them bad news.

"We'll try to make it."

"Why are we going to catch a train?" Rose asked, frustration lacing each word.

"Just a minute, Rose," James said, his voice curt.

She bristled with anger but wouldn't lose her temper in front of the Marshal. Whatever was in that message was not something he wanted to share with her just yet.

"Let me know if you need anything," the Marshal said.

"Thank you," James said.

The Marshal bent his hat at the brim. "Ma'am."

"Tell me what was in the message," she said once the door was closed.

"We need to be on the next train." James grabbed his bag from the floor and threw his clothes inside. His movements were curt, almost erratic.

"Why?"

"We just do."

"James Dodson, if you don't tell me what is going on, I'm going to scream." She placed her hands on her hips. Annoyance burning her face.

"Not now, Rose. Please, let's get our things.

I'll tell you on the train." He continued to avoid looking her in the eyes.

"I will not do as you ask until you tell me why he was here."

He sighed with resignation. "All right, but you have to promise not to get upset."

"I will promise no such thing," she said, anger and fear raising her voice.

"Rose…"

"Don't Rose me!" she yelled. "What is going on?"

"Please."

She stared at him, not moving. She would not budge until he told her what was in that message.

He ran his hand across his face. It was obvious he was nervous about something, and she needed to know what it was.

"I'm waiting," she said, tapping her bare foot on the hard floor.

"Fine," he said. "But you need to be sitting before I tell you."

Sensing he wouldn't tell her any information

until she did as she was told, she stalked to an armchair and sat. She crossed her arms and fury blazed inside her eyes. "Well, I'm sitting."

He paced back and forth in front of her for a long minute, the seconds ticking by.

"There was a fire on the ranch."

"How? Why? Is everyone all right?" It was as though she was being strung up on the gallows, the rope tight across her neck. Her breathing grew shallow with each second that slipped by.

"Everyone is fine, or at least I think so. Ben didn't write that anyone was hurt."

"If no one was hurt, why would we need to go back so soon?" She turned to the side, trying to understand. "Did something happen to Tommy and Sarah?"

He stared at her, not saying a word, and in that instant it was clear something had happened to her babies.

She leapt to her feet. "What happened?"

"Sit, Rose, please."

She ignored him. "What happened?"

"Tommy, Sarah, and Anne have disappeared."

"What do you mean, they've disappeared?" Ringing filled her ears, her voice sounded hollow, and a kaleidoscope of colors swirled around her.

Where are my babies?

"The message only said they've disappeared."

"What do you mean, *disappeared*? They can't be gone."

"I don't know. He said nothing more, just to return as soon as we could."

She stood and ran to the bedroom, found her bag, and threw her belongings into it as fast as she could. Tears streamed unchecked down her face, and she took in great gulping breaths. Her heartbeat increased as sweat poured along her neck and down her spine.

Suddenly, James's hands were on her shoulders, stopping her.

"Rose, calm down."

"I can't be calm." She shrugged out of his grasp.

She threw the last of her clothes into the bag and turned right into James's arms. He tried to hold her close, but she fought him, her movements filled with anger.

"Don't touch me!"

Anguish and pain filled his eyes, and her heart shattered into a million pieces. She dropped the bag at her feet and started to crumble, but he caught her before she fell. She gripped his arms, digging her fingers into the soft flesh, but he didn't let go. Instead, he sank to the ground with her, his strong arms constant as once again her world collapsed under her feet.

* * *

They finally reached Thundering Mountain Ranch after a long day of traveling. James had sent a telegram before their train left Spring Creek asking Ben to have someone waiting for them in Helena. James watched Rose out of the corner of his eye. She had been quiet but hadn't let him out of her sight. She relied on him as though he was the only thing keeping her standing.

As requested, a ranch hand was waiting and as the buckboard clattered along the dirt path, James saw the devastation from the fire spread out in front of them. He winced.

"Oh," Rose cried. "Tommy and Sarah, are they dead?"

"No," James said. "They're not. I'm sure Ben would've said something in his telegram."

They stopped in front of what survived of the main house. The rear was a smoldering pile of blackened wood, but the front remained standing as though the walls were being held up strictly by the will of God. The main barn was a shambled mess of burnt remains. Steam traveled from the pile of wood toward the bright blue sky, a stark contrast to the destruction that lay before them.

The front door opened, and Ben stepped outside to greet them. Smudges of dark black soot covered his face, dirt and grime covered his clothes, and he was grim.

"You made good time."

James's hands wrapped around Rose's waist and she gripped his shoulders as he lifted her out of the buckboard. She held onto him for a brief second before patting his arm. Elizabeth followed Ben onto the porch, looking just as bedraggled. Her hair was in a ratty braid, and her dress was filthy, a shoulder torn as she held a shawl tight around her.

Elizabeth held out her arms as Rose rushed into them, her sobs ripping James from the inside out.

"It's all right, Rose. We'll find them, I promise," Elizabeth said as soothingly as she could, considering the desolation surrounding them.

Ben shook James's hand, their hands gripped tight for a long moment before letting go.

"What happened?" James asked.

Ben gestured toward the house. "Let's go inside, and I'll explain what we know."

The smell of smoke was thick in what

remained of the house. Windows were open to air out the rooms, but nothing could hide the damage the fire had caused.

Reaching the front parlor, Ben ushered them inside. Elizabeth led Rose to a sofa and urged her to sit. A pot of tea rested on the table and Elizabeth poured Rose a cup before settling next to her. Elizabeth squeezed his wife's hand, but there was nothing reassuring about what lay ahead of them.

"I know it's early, but I need a drink. We've been up all night," Ben said. "Would you care for one?"

"No," James said. He was impatient to know what had happened, but it was obvious Ben and Elizabeth were exhausted, and he didn't need to be insensitive to their suffering. They had lost much as well. They'd tell them what happened soon enough, he was sure.

Ben tilted his head. James followed him to the liquor cabinet on the other side of the room, far from where the women could hear them. He poured himself a healthy dollop of whiskey into a tumbler before downing it in a few gulps. Wiping his mouth with the back of his hand, he sat the glass on the table. "It's been a long night. We just finished putting out the fires in the corrals moments before you arrived."

"Was anyone hurt?"

"A few scrapes and bruises, except for Sam. He was knocked unconscious. He's still out cold, so we haven't been able to question him."

"I hope he's all right."

"He's breathing and is a tough old man. He's been through worse. We're praying he pulls through."

"I wish we would've been here to help," James said.

"Nothing you could've done."

"Still, I wish I could've been here."

"I appreciate the sentiments. You and Rose needed the time away."

"But at what cost?"

Ben said nothing, as his eyes said all that needed to be said.

Waiting long enough, James asked the one thing he needed to know. "What happened to Anne and the children?"

Ben's face fell with sorrow and despair, and it took him a moment to speak. "I don't know. No one saw them leave."

"They didn't perish in the fire, did they?" James asked.

"No, thank heavens. We know that for sure. There were no remains," Ben said.

"Where could they have gone?"

"I wish I knew. Anne was watching all the children, but Jimmy and Vicky were all that we found."

"Did Vicky see anything?"

"No. I wish she had. She and Jimmy were sound asleep when the alarm was raised. When we didn't see Anne or the children, I ran inside to get them. Vicky had pulled Jimmy out of his crib and was trying to carry him down the hall. If she hadn't woken, I…" he stopped, emotion choking his throat. After a moment, he continued. "I got 'em out. When I questioned her, she said she and Jimmy had been alone when she woke. Thank goodness she was smart enough to get them as far as she had. The nursery is a charred disaster, but we found no remains and Vicky swears they were alone. She was scared because she hadn't seen her Aunty Anne, but since Tommy and Sarah were gone, she thought Anne had taken 'em. But we don't know where they are."

"You do think someone took them, don't you?" A rage like nothing he had ever felt before consumed him. What had happened to his children?

"It's the only thing that makes sense. Anne wouldn't have left Vicky and Jimmy alone. She wouldn't have willingly left any of the children. Not to mention someone attacked Sam."

"Who?"

"I don't know, James. No one saw a thing. We were too busy fighting the fires that exploded around us. The fire started in the barn, the brush around the corrals lit up like lightning had hit it, and then smoke and flames started pouring out of the house. It was all we could do to stop it from spreading farther than it did. Lucky for us, most of the ranch hands were coming in for their evening meal when the fires broke out."

"It sounds like a planned attack."

"We think so. Whoever did this knew exactly what they were doing and how to divert our attention." Ben poured himself another drink.

"Do you think Sam saw something?"

Ben leaned against the liquor cabinet, this time sipping the whiskey. "He put up quite the fight, so we're sure he saw something. What, we don't know yet." Ben's voice broke.

Sam was important to the family, and James prayed he'd survive.

James grimaced. "What am I supposed to tell Rose?" He kept his back to the women so Rose couldn't overhear him.

"I don't know. We're devastated they're gone. Katy's frantic. She and Anne are extremely close, and she insists Anne wouldn't have left of her own accord. The only thing we can figure is she went with whoever took the children to protect them."

"Could it have been Rose's brother-in-law, Charles?"

"That's what we believe, but we can't say for sure. I sent old Howie to Helena to see what he could discover about her brother-in-law, but he hasn't come back yet."

"Is he trustworthy?"

"He's been with us for as long as I can remember. Both him and Sam worked with my pa, so I trust him with my life."

James trusted Ben's judgment, but he had to do something. "I can't sit here and wait."

"Don't have much of a choice. We don't know who and don't know where to start. We can't find a trace of 'em anywhere. The ranch hands are out scouring the fields, roads, and surrounding ranches, looking for any trace of them, but no one has found a thing. They've vanished."

"I'm going outside for a minute," James said.

He left the room and went out front, closing the door softly behind him. What he wanted to do was slam it. No one knew what had happened or who had taken Tommy and Sarah and there was nothing he could do to fix it.

Chapter 34

Late August 1900

Rose sat in the small cabin, a warm heat emanating from the fireplace. The flames were blazing hot, and the cabin sweltered from the heat both inside and outside, but a chill ran across her skin grew when she thought of her missing children. She needed the heat to keep from completely withdrawing into herself.

She had been in the small cabin now for over a month and there was no word, no sign of Anne and her children. Gathering what she could salvage of their belongings the night they had returned from Spring Creek, she and James went to the small cabin. Not much had remained; her comb, a few items of clothing tucked into the back of the wardrobe, Tommy's blocks, a rattle Sarah had chewed on, but not much else.

Anne and the children had disappeared without a trace. Ben, James, and the ranch hands searched the valley far and wide, but it had been to no avail.

After those first few days of shedding the last drop of moisture from her, she had stopped crying and had become numb. Every day she sat wrapped in a blanket in front of the fire, watching the flames climb high and then burn low, just as her heart had done. As each day slipped by, her hopes had dwindled.

James's despair was as deep as her own and he felt responsible, but it wasn't his fault any more than it was hers. It was Charles's fault and if she could wrap her hands around his neck and squeeze the life out of him, she would have.

James spent the days helping Ben with the repairs while sending out telegrams and inquiring with the men who were looking for any trace of the children. He came home exhausted every night, fell into bed late with only a few words to her if she was even awake, and then left early every morning long before she crawled out of bed. They sought one another's comfort when the hard sun dipped behind the mountains each night, but barely spoke in the light of the day.

She ate little and picked at the food she prepared. Sometimes James would come from the main house with a basket of food Sophia sent with him. She assumed James told them she wasn't eating, and they tried to tempt her with foods that at any other time would have made her mouth water. Now it only made her gag, but she would force a bite or two to keep James from becoming too concerned over her well-being. She didn't want him to worry about her any more than he already had.

It was a late August morning when Rose felt

it. At first, she thought it was a hunger cramp and most days she ignored those, but today it was different. It felt different; it moved differently. It wasn't painful, but it was noticeable. She rested in bed, the window open, a cool breeze moving the drapes lazily around, sweeping across the floor and against the wall when it happened. A flutter, a movement so slight if she hadn't been still, she likely wouldn't have sensed it.

Her mind raced with the implications as she counted back, trying to remember when she had her last menses. It had been long before they had gone to Spring Creek and she scrambled to remember when. She realized she hadn't had her menses since Tommy had gotten sick in April. She had to be near on five months along or somewhere thereabouts and she hadn't even noticed. Moving her hand across her belly, it was clear her belly had rounded. Not near as round when she had been carrying Sarah, but round enough, she should have noticed by now.

She was with child, James's child. A new life, a new beginning. Nothing would replace Tommy and Sarah in her heart, but her arms longed to hold another little one, to comfort them, to sing songs to them and her heart slowly but surely filled with a joy she had believed had disappeared. The delight she had before Tommy and Sarah's disappearance had been sucked out of her, had left her dry, but something curled inside of her as a delicate and precious life grew within her once again.

Slowly, inch by inch, Rose began to care again. She got out of bed each morning, washed her face, and started eating. She wasn't doing it for herself. Rose was doing it for the new life growing inside of her.

* * *

James's breath was heavy as he lugged another burned piece of wood from the rubble and moved it away from where they would build the new barn. It was easier to work than to think about Tommy and Sarah, if they were safe, or if they would ever see them again.

Grabbing another piece of burnt wood, he dragged it across the open field. They were separating what could be salvaged and chopping it into kindling what was beyond saving. They wasted nothing on the ranch and although they had lost much in the fire, Ben had replaced the building materials without hurting the solvency of the ranch. Ben's pa had saved well, and Ben insisted they had enough. It wouldn't take long to rebuild, although with winter in a few months, they weren't wasting any time.

"James," Ben said, coming around the corner of the main house, a metal canteen held in one hand. "You've made quite a bit of progress. Care to take a break?"

James pulled out his kerchief and wiped his face before taking the canteen. He took a long swallow of the cool water.

"Sure, you're the boss." Anger was in his voice.

Ben sharpened his gaze as if trying to decide what James might've implied.

"That was rude and uncalled for," James said.

"When you have a moment, come on up to the house."

James nodded. "I'm almost done clearing the rest of the debris. I'll be up soon."

James knew he had been abrupt and had to stop. It wasn't fair to Ben or Elizabeth for him to be curt and unappreciative.

He drank another healthy swallow of water before going back to work. An hour later, he had removed what was left of the debris. New lumber was being delivered by the end of the week, so the burnt and ruined wood needed to be hauled away. Ben hadn't expected him to finish it on his own, but James felt the need to get as much done as he could. He needed the time to work out his anger and frustration and what better way to do it than by working hard. It kept his mind off his troubles and allowed him to be productive.

The sun fell behind the mountains. It was

stifling hot, but a warm breeze had blown in from the west. Red and gold burned across the horizon. It was a stunning sunset, and if he had been in a better frame of mind, he might've asked Rose to share it with him, but he couldn't. Their shared pain was so deep it was difficult to pretend there was anything good in this world.

He walked to the bunkhouse to wash. It wouldn't do to sit at his sister's table like he had just rolled around in the mud. He may not care he stunk to high heaven like pigs in muck, but he was pretty sure the others at the table would appreciate him smelling more like clean soap.

Stepping inside the empty kitchen, he heard voices at the end of the hall. He picked up a pitcher of water and a platter of warm bread and carried it with him to the dining room. He might as well be useful.

Elizabeth waved him to her side. "James, you're just in time. Sit next to me."

He placed the pitcher and the bread on the table before bending and kissing her cheek.

After a few moments of chaos, everyone

settled into their seats. Ben's brothers Michael and Luke had come to visit, but the mood was solemn, with Anne and the children still missing. As they ate, Elizabeth tried to keep their spirits up, especially for Vicky's sake. Vicky missed her cousin Tommy and didn't understand where he had gone.

When dinner was over, Elizabeth gave Vicky and Jimmy over to the nanny. They were making do with rooms on the main floor that hadn't been damaged in the fire until they could rebuild. The adults left for Ben's study. It would be cramped, but at least it had been undamaged and was far from the children's ears.

Everyone made themselves comfortable, but the tension was thick. Ben stood, resting against the cold fireplace, an untouched glass of whiskey in his hand.

"I've news I wanted to share," Ben said.

"You've found Anne?" Katy asked, interrupting him, hope in her eyes.

Ben's gaze was solemn. "No, I'm afraid not."

She swiped away the tears.

"Katy, all of us hate that we don't know what happened, but we will find them."

"It's been weeks," she cried. "Why hasn't anyone seen them?"

"I wish I knew. What I can tell you is I received a promising telegram today from a sheriff in Idaho."

"What did he say?" James asked. "Has he seen them?" He stood, his heart in his throat. If he could give Rose even a bit of hope, it might pull her from her despair.

"There've been reports of a woman and children secluded high in the mountains. No one has seen 'em, so the sheriff is wary of the information."

"Then why send the telegram? Is he trying to make things more difficult for this family?" James asked.

"I'm not sure of his intent other than to let us know what he's heard."

"What are we supposed to do with this? We don't have any idea it's Anne and the children," James said.

"You're right, we don't, but the notices we sent said to send any information that might be related. He's just doing his job, tryin' to help."

"He could help if he found the cabin and discovered if it was them," Michael said, disappointment in his voice.

"His telegram said if he had more deputies he would, but he doesn't have the manpower, and with fall coming, he doesn't want to put anyone in danger. They're predicting an early snowfall this year," Ben said.

"What about the danger Anne and the children are in? I'll leave at once and see if there's any truth to the information," James said.

"No," Elizabeth said. "You don't know that it's them."

"I have to try," James said.

"What if you go and it isn't them?" Elizabeth asked. "Then you'll have wasted all that time."

"I can't sit here any longer. Rose is barely speaking to any of us. She's wasting away. If I don't try, we'll never know for sure. This is the first piece of news that sounds promising."

"I'm sure we'll receive more information if we give it time," Elizabeth said.

"How many more weeks do we sit here and wait?" James said, anger rising in his tone.

"I don't know," Ben said. "The sheriff said it was a rumor and wasn't sure it was reliable."

"Rumors start somewhere, don't they?" James said. "And they start with someone seeing something." *Why are they trying to stop me?*

"Let's give it a few more days before you go off half-cocked," Ben said. "I'll send a telegram to the sheriff and see if he can't determine where the rumors came from. The last thing we want is for you to leave and then we hear actual news and can't send word to you."

James sighed. "Fine but send the telegram right away. I don't want to wait any longer than I must."

"Are you going to tell Rose?" Elizabeth asked.

"I don't know. I don't want to get her hopes up and then have them dashed again. She's struggling and this could further push her into the black hole she finds herself in."

"She deserves to know, James. You know what happened the last time you tried to keep her from the truth," Elizabeth murmured.

Chapter 35

The morning sun was bright and warm as James nudged his horse forward. He came in sight of their small cabin. It had been late the night before when they had finished discussing their next steps up at the main house and Elizabeth had insisted he stay. She hadn't wanted his horse to step in a prairie hole and get thrown, or worse. He prayed Rose wasn't upset he hadn't come home last night, but it wouldn't have been the first time he hadn't come home as of late.

Their cabin appeared forlorn. The yard was overgrown, no flowers bloomed, and dry weeds had overtaken the meadow that once was a boon to his heart. They had high hopes and had even named it Thundering Meadows, but now it looked nothing like both he and Rose had imagined. Instead, it looked as if it had no life and he supposed it didn't. Without the children, it was just an old cabin that served one purpose, to put a roof over their heads each night. There was no laughter, no tears. There was nothing.

He didn't know what he was going to say to her or how she'd take the news. He didn't want to get her spirits up unnecessarily, but Elizabeth was right, he couldn't keep this from her. Ben had sent one of the ranch hands into Helena with explicit instructions he wasn't to return until the sheriff in Idaho responded to their telegram. It could be days before they heard, and James was biting at the bit to leave. Despite what he told Ben, he didn't care if the information was reliable or not. Leaving for Idaho would give him something tangible to do. He hated coming home and seeing the despair in Rose's eyes.

James dismounted from his horse, the leather creaking under his weight. Tying the horse to the railing, he walked up the steps of the porch, each step more painful than the last. Every night when he came home, he imagined Tommy running out to him and Rose standing at the door holding little Sarah in her arms. Then every night his dream was shattered when he stepped inside the quiet, still house.

Before reaching the top of the steps, the door flew open and Rose stood there, a small shriek of fright emitting from her lips. She hadn't been expecting him, as he rarely came home during the day.

He rocked back on his heels, not sure what to say. Her big green eyes were wide with fright and something he couldn't name. He raked his eyes over her, taking in the sight of her glowing body and her rounded belly.

Wait, what?

His gaze flew to her mid-section. She cradled it, as if protecting what was inside. If she hadn't been cupping it, he still might not have noticed. She couldn't be that far along, but far enough she was showing. They slept in the same bed and usually within each other's arms, but he had been so negligent he hadn't even noticed.

She shuffled back a few steps and tried to slam the door. She didn't want him to know. Angry, he shoved his boot inside and stopped it. He pushed it open so as not to harm her yet with enough force to prevent her from blocking his entry.

She backed up, taking slow and measured steps, as if trying to decide if she should run or fight. He just looked at her. They were at a standstill. He was shocked, and she wasn't offering any explanations.

After a few moments of stilted silence, he broke it. "Were you going to tell me?"

"Tell you what?" she said, as if she didn't know what he was referring to.

"You're with child, my child."

She dropped open her mouth as her hand rested on her belly. "I'm sure you're mistaken."

"It's obvious you *are* with child, Rose." He pointed to her. "You're protecting what's inside. I can see your rounded belly."

She dropped her hand as if aware she was pointing out the one thing she was trying to deny.

"I've just put on a little weight."

"Has it come to this?" His heart broke at the thought of her not wanting to tell him.

"Come to what?" she whispered.

James struggled to hear her. He stepped closer but halted when she retreated from him. She hit the kitchen table with her backside and it rocked under her weight. The plates from her morning meal clattered from the disruption. She touched the table and scooted around it as though she needed to put space between them. He didn't want to frighten her, and it was obvious she felt something akin to that.

"Rose, you're with child. We both know you are. There's no point in denying it. I can tell when a woman is with child."

She shuddered and fell into one of the wooden chairs. Tears filled her eyes, but she furiously blinked to keep them at bay. "I didn't know how to tell you. I was worried you wouldn't want this child, not after what's happened."

His anger ebbed away. He couldn't be angry with her, not when she was the mother of his children. "No, Rose. Of course, I'd want our child." He sighed. "I shouldn't have yelled at you."

She leaned forward across the table, held her head in her hands, and shook.

"What is it? What's wrong?"

She lifted her head and looked at him, the despair in her eyes even worse than before. "How can I be happy to be with child when Tommy and Sarah…"

"Shh." He came around the table to her side. James grabbed a chair and sat heavy in it before he pulled her into his arms. "It's all right to be happy you're with child."

"But…"

"No." He placed his finger on her lips. "We *will* find Tommy and Sarah. They're going to need their momma healthy and strong for when we bring them back to you. They wouldn't want you to be unhappy about this new one." He gently placed his palm against her belly, and he felt it. It was subtle, but strong. The baby kicked. His baby kicked and love spread through him.

He raised his eyes to look at her, and she tentatively smiled.

"Yes, he kicked," she said.

"He?" he asked.

"Yes, well…" She gulped and wiped at her tears. "I don't know, but in my dreams, it's a little boy, your little boy."

He didn't know what he had done to deserve such a wonderful woman. He hugged her close. She rested against his shoulder, and they sat there for a long moment.

"Why are you home early?" she asked, a log shifting in the fireplace sending sparks flying. "You rarely come home during the day, not since…"

James didn't let her finish. He couldn't keep this from her any longer. "I have something to tell you."

She stiffened in his arms, but he rubbed at

the small of her back until she relaxed once again. It had been so long since they had done more than sleep together. He wanted to savor it for as long as possible.

Whispering, he said, "It's not bad news, I swear."

"Has something happened? Is there news of Tommy and Sarah?" Anticipation filled her eyes and although he didn't want to snuff out any hope, he didn't want to give her hope when it might not be warranted.

"Nothing has happened, but we received some interesting news."

"What news?"

"Ben got a telegram from a sheriff in Idaho."

She pulled away slightly but gripped his shirt, pulling and tugging. He gently removed her fingers and kissed the top of her knuckles before he placed her in the chair next to his. He was anxious and didn't want her to sense it.

"We don't know if the information is reliable. When the children"—he paused and rubbed at his eyes—"when the children were taken, Ben asked the Marshal in Helena to send out notices to all the sheriffs and marshals along the rail and telegraph lines hoping one of them would see something or hear word. This sheriff in Idaho heard rumors concerning a woman with children high in the Rockies."

She opened her mouth, but he held out his hand to stop her. "No one has seen them. We don't know if it's them. It's only a rumor."

"But it's the first bit of information we've gotten." She had brightened significantly with the news.

"Maybe, but we shouldn't put too much stock in rumors," he said.

She stood, looking around the room frantically. "I'll pack my bag. I'm going to Idaho."

"No, you're not."

She turned and glared at him. "Yes, I am." She brushed past him, but he grabbed her elbow to stop her. She wrenched her arm from his grasp. "Don't."

"Rose, you can't go. You aren't in any condition."

"Don't you tell me what type of condition I'm in. Your babies weren't taken." The words were harsh and unforgiving.

"They're my children too," he said, trying to be patient with her. "I love them as much as you do. You aren't the only one who lost 'em."

"I don't care what you say. I'm going." She braced her hands on her waist, daring him to stop her.

"No." James tried to pull her close when she slapped him across the face.

Her face was red with shock when she realized what she had done. "Oh, no." Horrified, she covered her mouth with her hands. "I didn't mean to do that."

"I understand, but you're not going to Idaho. I'm going." His face stung, but it wasn't intentional. She didn't have a mean bone in her. She was only reacting to the tumultuous situation.

"No, I have to go," she cried.

"I don't think so. I don't want to be mean or insensitive, but it's better if you stay here. Ben sent another telegram asking for more information. He wanted me to wait 'til we heard from the sheriff, but I don't want to. Something tells me time is of the essence. It's late August and it'll take me a few weeks to get there. The snow will start soon in the Rockies, sooner than in the valleys, and if we can't find them, it could be months before we see them again."

"I'm going with you," she muttered.

She was one stubborn woman, and she was bound to be furious with him, but this was one area where he would not budge. She was too precious to him, and he couldn't take the chance she would get hurt on the trip. "No, you're not."

"I have to," she pleaded with him.

"No. You can't take the chance. I could get stuck in the mountains for months, and I can't take care of you and our child while I'm looking for them. Do you want to take the chance of giving birth to this child in the same, if not worse, conditions than when you delivered Sarah?"

She glared at him. There was truth in his words.

"If I find them, it'll be hard enough to get them home without having to worry about you." He hated to be so harsh, but she had to understand his position. "Do you want to do that?"

"I can take care of myself." She stood with righteous indignation.

Realizing he was walking on dangerous ground, he said, "I know you can, but it'll only make me worry more. Please don't do that to me."

Rose opened her mouth, but then stopped as his words sunk in. For a long moment, she stared at him before nodding in defeat.

"I promise I'll find them if it's the last thing I ever do. I won't come home without them."

Chapter 36

September 1900

James pushed back the brim of his hat as he tugged on the reins of his horse in the mining town of Gibbonsville, Idaho. It had taken him longer than he would've liked to get there, but he had done his level best to get there as fast as his horses would travel. The two extra horses trotting behind him were the only reason he had moved as fast as he had once he left the train depot on the border between Idaho and Montana.

Gibbonsville was a bustling town, even in

mid-September. The temperatures were dropping, and snow was in the air. If he didn't find Anne and the children soon, he'd be stuck in Idaho for the duration of the winter.

Dismounting, he tied the horses to the post in front of the sheriff's office. Ben had sent a telegram ahead of his arrival and the sheriff should be expecting him. He climbed the steps but hesitated at the door. This was the second time he had stepped inside a jailhouse in recent months, and he had sworn he would never enter one again after he had been released. The only saving grace was he was entering as a free man and not as a criminal, although it didn't make him any less uncomfortable. Too many poor memories were at the surface bubbling hot and heavy.

Shoving back the emotions threatening to overwhelm him, he had to remember why he was there. This was about his children, not about him. He opened the door and stepped inside the one place that made his skin crawl, but he'd do it without complaint.

"Be right with you," a tall man said. He finished digging deep inside a tall gun cabinet before focusing his attention on James. "Howdy, you aren't from around here, are you?"

"No, sir, I'm not. Name's James Dodson."

His smile diminished as he realized who James was. "I've been expecting you. Please sit." The Sheriff gestured to the chair in front of his desk as he sat across from him, the weight of his responsibilities as a lawman likely wearing him down.

James pulled the chair out and sank into the hard seat of the wooden armchair.

"You made good time."

"I had a couple of horses, so I switched out often," James said.

"I'm sorry you've come to our small town with such a heavy burden."

"Have you heard anything?" James asked, getting straight to the point. He didn't want to be rude, but he didn't want to make small talk either.

"No. I've been asking around, but no one has

seen or heard a word." He scratched behind his neck, settling into his chair.

"Why wasn't this information given to my brother-in-law?"

"It was. I received another telegram from Mr. Seymour the other day, and he'd said you'd left, and it was too late to stop you."

"So, there's no proof Anne and my children are here?"

"No, but there's no news they aren't, either. There are plenty of abandoned cabins high in the mountains and there's no way to confirm they haven't been stashed in one of 'em."

"Can I get a map so I can start searching?"

"That's not the best plan right now." The Sheriff leaned forward, resting his elbows against the wooden desk.

"Why not? I must find them. My daughter is only a few months old and…"

"I'm aware of how young those children are and what's at stake," the sheriff said, his tone growing tense.

"Then what's stopping you?"

"A small thing called the weather. It has started to snow." He waved to the window.

James turned and frowned. In the few minutes he had been inside, a storm had blown in and white flakes were floating to the ground.

"From the way the sky is lookin', we're in for a hell of a storm over the next few days."

"I'm not worried about a storm."

"You should be. Have you ever experienced a winter in the Bitterroot Mountains?"

James stayed silent. He had spent plenty of time in bitter weather but not in the mountains, and he was sure the sheriff could tell that with one cold, hard look.

The Sheriff continued, "It gets bitterly cold and unless you've got a decent shelter and something better than a canvas tent, there's no way you'd survive more than a couple of days up there. It's best we wait 'til the weather clears. Then we can start searching the cabins we can reach."

"That could take weeks."

"It'll take more than a few weeks. We likely

won't be able to reach some of 'em 'til spring. Many of these cabins are on remote stretches of land that haven't seen life in years."

"I can't sit here and wait. What if something were to happen to them?" James said.

"Mr. Dodson, I hate to be curt with you, but we don't know if they're being held here."

"This is the only piece of information on their potential whereabouts we've received in months. It must be them."

"But what if it isn't?"

The sheriff had a point, but he wouldn't admit it. He couldn't give up now, not when there was a chance, they were somewhere close.

"I appreciate your concern, but I wouldn't forgive myself if I didn't at least try."

The Sheriff shrugged and accepted James's insistence on looking for his family. He pushed away from his desk, riffled through papers on a shelf behind him, and pulled out a large map. He placed it down and rolled it out, placing books on the ends to keep it open so they could look at it.

James stood and bent over the map. The sheriff pointed out the areas he should search first.

When done, James asked, "Are there any lodgings in town?"

"Yes, the saloons have rooms available. You can leave your horses at the livery."

James held out his hand. "Thank you, Sheriff. I appreciate your help."

"Don't thank me yet. Let's find your family first."

* * *

October gave way, and November was coming fast. James had logged hundreds of miles searching amongst the countless trails covering the mountainous terrain. No one he talked to had seen or heard of any woman with two young children. It was as though the rumor was truly a rumor, but James refused to quit. He was determined to visit every remote cabin surrounding Gibbonsville. He wouldn't go home to Rose without them.

After another long day of traversing the hillsides, he stopped at the livery in town, left his horse and then trudged through the snow to the saloon where he had a room. Every night he wished he were somewhere else, but rooms were scarce and he couldn't be too choosy. He wanted a night free from music, laughter, and gaiety, but that wasn't to be, not in this mining town where the miners let off steam gambling, carousing, and drinking to all hours of the night.

Stepping through the swinging doors, the dim lights, the heavy haze of cigar smoke, and the loud music greeted him. He moved with determination across the room, scanning it with his eyes, a residual of him always being on the lookout for the next blow. It wouldn't do to be caught unaware, for if he were, something dangerous could happen. James had learned that lesson early on from Elizabeth's pa when he'd backhand him or come at James from behind, a bottle in his hand, the drinking caused his eyes to glaze over, and rage poured from his mouth. It had only been reinforced when he had stepped inside the prison walls, threats coming from everywhere. Never a moment to let down his guard, for if he had, he'd pay the price.

"Well, you're back," she purred, sliding up to him before he could stop her.

It was LeAnn, one of the soiled doves who worked in the saloon. He tried to avoid her, but for whatever reason, she had latched on to him and had made it her life's mission to get him into her bed. He wasn't interested and never would be. No one could replace his Rose, but no matter what he said or did, LeAnn never stopped. Any chance she found to place her hands on him, to whisper in his ear, or sit on his lap, she'd take it. He couldn't count how many times he had to push her away, but she never took the hint that he wasn't interested.

She slid her hands across his arms and up his neck. Before he could stop her, she had plastered her body against his and thrust him against the wall. She latched her mouth onto his and sucked on his lip. She moaned and whisked her hands down his front. "Mmm," she said. "What I wouldn't give to have all of this."

Shocked, he brushed her hand away and moved her aside. "Not now, LeAnn." James didn't want to hurt her, but he didn't want what she was offering.

"Not now, but later?" Her hair hung across her shoulders in a ratty mess and her hot breath smelled of liquor and rotten garlic.

She tried to give him a come-hither look, but only looked desperate. He felt pity for her, but he'd have no other woman besides Rose.

"Do we have to do this again tonight?" he asked, irritation lacing every word.

"Do what?" She once again tried to run her hands along his body.

He pushed away her hands. "I'm goin' up to my room. Can you get Todd to send me up a bowl of stew?"

"I'd be happy to do that for you, Jimmy." Her pet name for him grated on his last nerve. "But I heard something you might want to know." She batted her eyes, trying to look becoming but looking more like a rabid raccoon. Her pupils were red and there were streaks of black from the kohl that had at one time emphasized her eyes but were now smeared from sweat.

"And what is that, LeAnn?" Not that he expected she'd have anything he'd want to know.

"Just something about that woman and youngins you've been looking for," she said as she sauntered away.

"Wait! What?" *Did I hear her right?* "Where are you going?"

"Why, just goin' to ask Todd for your stew." She braced herself against the bar, arching her back so much so that her stays barely contained her. She was trying hard to get his attention, but it wasn't her body that was doing it.

"What did you hear?"

"About what?" She placed a finger in her mouth before running it across her collarbone.

Frustration coursed through him. She thought she was good at playing these come-hither games, but he wasn't interested. He wouldn't give her what she wanted, but he'd play along if that's what it took to hear if she had any reliable information regarding Anne and the children.

"Please, LeAnn. Can you tell me what you heard?"

She huffed, dropped her pose, and plopped on the stool behind her. She swung her right leg over her left, she grabbed a bottle of whiskey, poured herself a glass, and downed it in one gulp. LeAnn wiped her mouth with the back of her hand. "There were a couple of men here last night—"

"Last night? And you waited 'til now to tell me?"

She narrowed her eyes. "You were already rolled up in bed. You don't want me botherin' you after dark."

LeAnn was right. He didn't want her knocking on his door after he went to bed or anytime for that matter. He had made that quite clear on numerous occasions for anything else would have her trying to get him to spend the night, and he refused to give in to her wishes. He wouldn't hurt Rose, not for anything. He had learned from his mistakes and was determined nothing would deter him from making the right choices from now on.

"What did they say?"

"Not sure I remember." Her gaze went to the bottle of whiskey behind the bar.

Pulling a few coins from his pocket, he slapped them on the bar and nodded to Todd. Todd poured her a glass that James pushed to her waiting fingertips.

"Why thank you, Jimmy, so kind of you to think of me." This time she drank the whiskey slowly. She was going to drag out this encounter for as long as she could, for she had gotten his attention and now that she had it, she was bound to hang onto it for as long as possible. "Now what were we talkin' about?"

He would play along. "The men that were here last night."

"Oh, yes." She uncrossed her legs and reversed the position, this time her skirt fell open and revealed the top of her cotton covered thigh. The material was yellowed and worn, but she didn't appear to notice or if she did, it was all part of her show. She patted the stool next to her. "Why don't you sit, and we can talk *about* it?"

James sighed. Gesturing to Todd once again, he asked for a bowl of stew and hot bread and then settled, not on the stool she patted, but another one. If he was going to be there for a while, he needed to put distance between them. Not that he didn't trust himself to keep his hands to himself. It was LeAnn he didn't trust. There was no reason to give her any cause to try any more tomfoolery.

He removed his hat, unbuttoned his coat, and sat facing her. "Can you tell me what you overheard?"

Her smile dropped into a frown. "Always so impatient for answers, aren't you?" She drifted her fingers across the scarred and darkened wood of the bar, drawing circles, lines, and all manner of things.

"Please, LeAnn. They're my children." His voice cracked. He didn't want to show emotion, least of all to her, but the strain of the last few months was wearing on him. If what she overheard could help him find them, he was desperate to know it.

"And is she your woman?" LeAnn spit out, her face turning ugly with disdain.

His eyes grew wide. The spite in her voice was alarming. He wasn't sure if he could trust what she told him, but he had no choice. "No, she's a sister by marriage. My sister's marriage."

Why he clarified that point, he wasn't sure. He didn't owe LeAnn an explanation, but he feared if LeAnn thought Anne was his woman, she wouldn't tell him the truth.

"That certainly changes things, now, doesn't it?" Her smile returned as though she was a cat who had just caught her prey.

He didn't think he needed to say anything. There was nothing he could say.

"It was nigh on midnight when two old-timers came tumbling inside, grinning and carefree, as they had found themselves gold dust up in those mountains." She waved to the area behind them.

"Had they seen them?"

"No, darlin', they didn't say that they'd seen the youngins."

"I don't understand."

"Well, if'n you let me tell you what happened, you'd find out, now wouldn't you?"

He chastised himself. Interrupting her was likely not the right way to get her to tell him what she knew. Just then, Todd brought him a large steaming bowl of stew and a couple of pieces of thick bread. His mouth watered. He hadn't eaten all day and although the food in the saloon was far from fabulous, they knew how to make a mean stew. He picked up a piece of the bread and lathered on the warm butter Todd gave him. Taking a bite, he looked at LeAnn. "Would you care for a piece?"

"No, sugar, I had my fill earlier. Besides, Todd here don't like us eatin' with the customers." She winked at the man standing behind the bar. "Now where was I?"

"Two old-timers…"

"Yes, they come in rowdy, just plum tickled, buying everyone a round of beer and wanting to take their hand on the tables. Now, being the good girl that I am, I sauntered over to them and offered my services, if you know what I mean."

She twirled a piece of hair with her finger, but he pretended not to notice as he took a large bite of the stew and burned his tongue in the process. Swallowing hard, he had a quick drink of the beer Todd had left, the cool liquid soothing the heat.

When he didn't respond, she huffed a bit, but continued. "Them being gentleman, wanted me to keep 'em company, sweet ole men that they were." She giggled, almost like she was a little girl again. "They pulled out their gold dust, got it weighed, plunked down their stake, and began playing their hands. They told me stories of their escapades up in the mountains and how they had run into this cantankerous fella who was drunker than a skunk, they said. He claimed he had lost a woman and children and if'n they saw them wandering around, to send 'em back his way."

James swallowed. The story sounded fantastical, but a kernel of hope built inside of him. Had Anne escaped with the children? He could only pray that if she had escaped that she'd found safety. For any other alternative was too difficult to imagine.

"Now when the ole timers asked why the man had lost his woman, well, he got all persnickety and said that didn't matter none and that he had to find them, or he'd be payin' the price."

"Payin' the price?" James cocked his head to the side.

"I was hornswoggled as well, so I asked 'em about it."

"They questioned the man, and he went ons and ons about how's if he didn't find 'em he wouldn't get paid and if'n he lost 'em, well there'd be hell to pay. The old men were concerned and asked more questions, but he then got angry. His face got red, and he threatened 'em, so not wanting to get into a scuffle, they left the man to his ramblings."

"Did they happen to say where they had seen the man?" This was the first potential clue he had. It didn't seem likely that another woman and children would be lost in the mountains around Gibbonsville. It had to be them.

"Just up in those mountains."

James smothered a disgusted sigh. If she had woken him the night before, he could have questioned the miners himself. "Are those old-timers still around?"

"Nah, they got their fill and ran off first thing this mornin'."

"Damnit!" He hit his fist on the bar, the wood vibrating from the force behind his thrust.

She was startled at the anger in him but scooted off the stool and sauntered to his side. She ran her fingers up his arm. "Did I do good?"

He frowned. He didn't want to encourage her, but he was grateful for the information, such as it was. "Yes, LeAnn. I surely appreciate the information."

"Wanna show me your appreciation?" She brushed her chest against his arm and leaned into him, her lips searching for his.

He pulled back. "No, not like that." Pushing her gently away, he reached into his pocket and pulled out a few more coins. "Why don't you get yourself a trinket?" He put the coins on the wooden bar, grabbed the last piece of thick bread, and scooted around her. "It's late and I need to get a start early if I'm going to find 'em."

Chapter 37

January 1901

James had been on various intersecting trails for days. When he had gotten the promising although limited information from LeAnn, he had been hopeful, but after weeks of nothing, he was trying desperately not to lose hope. Heading out after the last snowstorm, the weather had miraculously held.

He had missed Christmas with the family, but he wouldn't leave Idaho until he had searched every inch of the place. Going farther than he had to date, he was pushing his limits. If the snow started falling, he would be in serious trouble. It was hard enough staying warm with how far the temperatures dropped each night, but he wasn't giving in. The sheriff warned him how treacherous it was, and it was likely pure determination that kept him going. He knew in his gut they were out here somewhere, and he would find them.

The horse plodded along, James's eyes scanning the landscape, looking for any sign of a cabin, any sign of life. He was on what appeared to be a well-trampled trail, so with any luck, he would find a place to bed down for the night that was more than under the cover of trees. He'd prefer something with four walls to keep away the blustery wind that nipped at any exposed skin, but considering how late it was, he'd be better off finding a thick grove of trees instead and praying he wouldn't freeze to death through the night.

The wind kicked up the snowdrifts around him and he shivered. He pulled his collar up around his neck and yanked his woolen cap down across his ears. He urged his horse around a bend when he caught a whiff of smoke and hope threaded inside of him. *Did someone live out here? Would they welcome me inside to warm near their fire?* He had to proceed with caution though, as there were many old timers who lived out here and likely hadn't seen another human in months. They were more likely to shoot first than ask questions.

Nudging his horse with his knees, they moved through the woods until he came upon a large cabin set against the snow-covered hillside. It looked like a place out of a children's storybook. A wrap-around porch surrounded the cabin and a large red barn sat to the side. Well-kept fences surrounded the corral. This wasn't an old trapper's place. Smelling the smoke and sensing a warm barn, his horse picked up the pace.

Stopping well away from the barn, he hollered, "Hello. Anyone home?"

A tall man, covered in thick furs, sauntered from the barn, a rifle held loosely in his hands.

Not menacing, but a warning that James best be clear about his intentions.

James held out his hands to show he was of no threat. "Good evening, neighbor. I hate to be a bother, but I was wondering if I could sleep in your barn for the night?"

"What are you doing way up here this time of year?" the man asked, ignoring his question.

James hesitated. His reasons were his own, but if he were to find Anne and the children, he'd need to trust or at least be congenial for he would never know who might've seen something.

"Long story, but suffice to say, I don't mean no harm. I'll be out of your way first thing in the morning."

A door slammed behind him.

"Is everything all right, Nathaniel?" A familiar woman's voice sounded from the porch of the house.

Nathaniel's eyes moved from James to the woman on the porch. "Yes, Anne, go inside."

"Anne?" James said, swiveling his head

across his shoulder to look at the woman. She was covered in fur but got one look at him, dropped the hood, and revealed her face.

"James? Oh, my heavens. Am I dreaming?" A grin split her cheeks. "You found us."

"Us?" James said, disbelief at seeing Anne alive and well, which could only mean the man standing in front of the barn had to have been the one who had taken her.

He reached for his pistol, but the man had cocked his rifle and pointed it at him.

"Keep your hands where I can see 'em," Nathaniel said. The rifle was pointed straight at James. "If you make any sudden movements…"

"Stop, Nathaniel. He's Sarah and Tommy's pa."

Nathaniel kept the rifle pointed at James, not wavering in his stance.

Anne ran down the porch toward James but stopped at James's curt words. "What's going on, Anne?"

Questions burned through him. She didn't seem scared of Nathaniel, but that made little sense if he was the man who had taken her. Or had she gone willingly with him and had taken his children?

She slammed to a halt and studied him. Her once exuberant expression was replaced with doubt as she likely saw the questions in his eyes. He hovered his hand over his pistol.

"Nathaniel rescued us. He isn't the one who took us or started the fire. I escaped with the children in late September and Nathaniel found us on a trail. With the snow imminent, he offered to keep us at his cabin until spring, when he could get us safely to the nearest town. How'd you find us?"

He stared at her in disbelief. All this time and he finally found them. Nathaniel wasn't a threat. He relaxed and removed his hand from above his sidearm.

"Tommy and Sarah?" he asked.

She pointed to the house. "They're safe inside and have been missing their pa."

He began to dismount, but then his gaze found Nathaniel's, and he hesitated. Nathaniel still hadn't dropped the rifle. Was he supposed to stay on his horse while his children were inside that cabin?

Seeing his hesitation, Anne yelled, "Put your rifle down, Nathaniel! He isn't here to hurt us, are you, James?"

Nathaniel seemed a bit trigger happy to James, but he eventually dropped the rifle to his side.

Anne ran to James and as soon as he dismounted, she gave him a sisterly hug. "I'm so happy to see you. Are you alone? How long have you been out here? Where are my brothers? How is Rose? Is she worried sick?" She peppered him with questions, her excitement over seeing him quite clear. "Was anyone hurt during the fire? I've been so scared someone might've been killed. Are Vicky and Jimmy all right? The man only wanted Sarah and Tommy, and when I didn't let him take Sarah, he made me go with him. I didn't know what else to do, but I couldn't let him leave me behind."

James couldn't focus. Not expecting to find

her, he was afraid this was a dream, and he'd wake and discover Anne and the children weren't within his grasp. He was stunned silent and couldn't find his words.

She tilted her head to the side, her gaze searching. "Are you all right, James? James?"

"What? What did you say?"

"She's excited to see you." Nathaniel's voice drummed over them. "Why don't you go inside and get warm? I'll take your horse into the barn, and you can tell him everything that's happened."

She nodded and pulled James with her to the house. "Tommy's going to be so excited to see you. Sarah too, although don't be surprised if she doesn't take to you right away. She's so young, she might not remember you." Anne continued to ramble as they walked inside the warm cabin.

"Tommy," Anne said.

James scanned the large cabin, taking everything in with one glance, but he zoomed in on his little boy. He sat playing in the corner and didn't appear to hear Anne or if he did, was too excited with the toys in front of him.

"Tommy," she said again. He dropped his toys and scampered to his feet, a bright smile on his face as he reached for Anne. "Guess who's here?" She picked him up and pointed him toward James.

Tommy looked around her, moving his thumb to his mouth. He widened his eyes but James wasn't sure if it was recognition or fear. When James had given up hope Tommy would've remembered him, a bright smile lit his face and he reached his chubby little arms toward him. "Pa?"

Tommy squealed with joy, hugging James with a fierceness he hadn't expected. His heart burst. He had missed this little man.

"Where's Sarah?" he asked, holding Tommy on his hip.

"She's sleeping in the other room. I can wake her," Anne said.

"No, let her sleep. I don't want to disturb her.

Just knowing she's all right is good enough for now."

The door shut closed behind them. Nathaniel walked toward the fireplace, picked up a poker, and stoked the flames, pushed at the smoldering logs, and threw another log on the fire. He then turned to look at them.

"Well, seems we should talk," Nathaniel said.

James stared hard at the man. "Seems we should."

Chapter 38

May 1901

The fresh scent of spring woke Rose from her slumber. She rolled over and smiled. Little Daniel lay sleeping in the cradle next to her bed. He was a voracious eater, and she was surprised he hadn't woken looking for his next meal. She swore she was just a cow feeding her young, considering how much he suckled daily, but she wouldn't give him up for anything in the world. He was precious, more precious than ever.

They hadn't heard from James since late November. The last telegram they'd received said he was still looking and wouldn't come home until he found them. Unfortunately, there was no guarantee any of them were in Idaho. They could be anywhere by now.

The Marshal had interrogated Charles, and he swore up and down he had nothing to do with the children being taken. There had been a trail of money Charles couldn't explain, but no proof they could find that he had taken them. His arrogance and satisfaction at seeing Rose hurt told them he was lying. They just couldn't prove it.

When Sam had woken from his injuries, he couldn't point a finger at Charles. There had been a number of men who had invaded the property, but Sam had only seen a few of them and none of them were Charles.

The private detectives Ben had hired watched Charles like a hawk, but the children never appeared. Whatever Charles had done with them was still unknown. Rose prayed Anne had somehow escaped his clutches, and the children were with her somewhere safe. It was the only conclusion she could live with, for anything else was too difficult to fathom.

The silence was disturbed as Daniel let out a loud screech of hunger. The child was relentless. Sitting, she pulled him into her arms. His nappy was wet. Between his hunger and wet bottom, he was not a happy baby. She smiled, though, because his tears and screams meant he was alive and never far from her arms.

She scooted out of bed and grabbed a dry nappy from the wardrobe and, with a quick efficiency born of having three children, she made him dry and comfortable. His screams died to a slow whimper, and he batted his tiny perfect hands at his mouth, looking for his morning meal.

A breeze fluttered through the open window and she shivered. It was warmer today, but the wind was cool. She went to close the window when she saw a wagon coming down the dirt pathway to the house. She had moved into the main house months before Daniel was born. Elizabeth and Ben had insisted she stay with them once the repairs were finished and James had left. They felt it was safer for her to be around the family. They weren't entirely sure Charles wouldn't come after her next.

She had agreed and as time moved forward, she was glad she had listened. Being around Elizabeth and Ben's sister, Katy, helped her deal with the pain, although seeing Vicky and Jimmy every day had been difficult. They were growing like weeds and reminded her daily of what she had lost, but their laughter helped soothe her broken heart.

When Daniel had been placed in her arms, and when she had looked into his sweet face, all she saw was James. Daniel was the spitting image of his father with his dark brown hair and big brown eyes, even down to the cleft in his tiny chin.

She remembered the moment after she had delivered Daniel. She had been exhausted and worn, but had looked up from Daniel's sweet face and caught Elizabeth's eye. Elizabeth had smiled, her smile similar to James' and her heart broke. Tears fell from her eyes and Elizabeth reached for her hand, squeezing reassuringly.

"He looks so much like James, Elizabeth. What if he doesn't come back?"

Elizabeth's eyes were filled with compassion and love. "He will, I know it. He'd want you to be strong, especially for this new little baby in your arms."

"He would, wouldn't he?" she said, gazing at Daniel. She ran a finger along his face.

"He knows how much you love him and how hard everything has been. He won't give up 'til he brings them home."

Daniel squealed with impatience. She'd been woolgathering. He was restless and needed to be fed. She dropped the curtain when the wagon stopped in front of the house, as her attentions needed to be on the hungry baby. Whoever had come to the ranch would be greeted by Ben. No one got into the house or near it without Ben knowing exactly who they were and why they were there.

They had guards stationed everywhere

around the ranch. Ben wasn't taking any chances. Whoever had taken her children and had set the fires wouldn't have a second chance at doing it again. It was a fortress around them, one she secretly appreciated as it kept her and Daniel safe from harm.

Settling into the rocking chair, she raised Daniel to her breast, and he latched on with as much efficiency as Sarah had the last time she held her. He was her child and learned quickly. She relaxed and kicked off with her foot, rocking back and forth. The motion was soothing.

A soft knock sounded on the door. Staring at Daniel, she smiled. He had fallen asleep. A dribble of milk was on his soft cheek. She wiped it off and then adjusted her nightgown, pulling it closed. She placed Daniel in his cradle and pulled on her wrapper, tightening the sash around her waist before she opened the door.

Her mouth fell open in shock.

Chapter 39

His heart lurched. James thought he had been prepared to see her again, but he hadn't been. Her hair was mussed, her tiny toes peeked out from underneath her wrapper, and her cheeks were pink. If she'd let him, he'd pull her into his arms and never let her go, but he hesitated.

It had been over nine months since they'd last seen one another. Nine months! He shot his eyes to her waist, and it was as flat as could be. His throat closed. *Did she lose our baby?* He couldn't ask that question, but he wanted to.

"James?"

"Rose."

They spoke at the same time and then laughed awkwardly.

"You're home," she said.

"I am."

Silence stretched between them for a long, uncomfortable minute. Neither were saying a word yet drinking in the sight of one another. She was as lovely today as the day he met her.

Swallowing hard, he forced words past his lips. "How are you?"

"I'm all right, and you?" Her gaze bored into him, searching, questioning.

He smiled and shrugged. "Good, as can be expected. It's been too long. I've missed you."

"Did you find them?" Her eyes were wide with expectations.

A smile lifted the corners of his mouth. He could at least give her the good news. Why he had been holding out on her, he didn't know, but if he were honest with himself, he had wanted to be alone with her for a brief moment before her attentions were pulled elsewhere. He was being selfish, but he couldn't help himself. She was everything he had always wanted, and he had missed her dreadfully.

"I did."

She peered around him, her movements shaky, uncertain as though the children would pop out in the next moment.

"Where are they?"

A loud mewing cry sounded from behind her. She swung around, her wrapper fluttering behind her.

He followed and stood in shock when she lifted a bundle from the crib next to her bed. A tiny foot punched through the blanket.

"Rose?" His voice cracked with emotion.

She turned, and looked at the bundle in her arms before a tentative smile appeared. She stepped forward before lifting the precious bundle into his arms.

He stood in awe. "What? Who?"

"Your son, Daniel," she whispered.

"Daniel?"

"Yes, I hope you don't mind, but you told me one night that was your pa's name, so I thought it only seemed right. I hope I made the right choice."

"Right choice?" Awe and wonder filled his voice. "It's more than all right. It's just perfect. He's perfect." James lifted the blanket and looked at Daniel's tiny hands and feet. He was beautiful, and he was his.

"Momma!" Tommy yelled.

Rose startled as Tommy ran into the room. It was a good thing she hadn't been holding Daniel, as she'd likely drop him with shock. Tommy's little legs carried him as fast as they could as he ran straight toward her, his arms outstretched. She swooped in, dropped to her knees, and pulled him into her arms. Tears streamed down her face as she hugged her little boy. She kissed the top of his head, squeezing him with everything she had in her. He smelled just as she remembered, but he had gotten so big. He had grown a few inches and his face was fuller.

"Momma, momma," he cried, pushing away at her.

She had held him a tad bit too tight, and he fought her to let him go. She released her grip and then gently touched his face, his arms and his legs to make sure he wasn't hurt.

"Oh, Tommy," she said. "I've missed you."

Excited to see her but wanting to show her something, he pointed behind him. Anne walked into the room with Sarah in her arms.

Anne bent and placed Sarah on the ground, her tiny legs wobbling as she teetered forward, her steps uneasy. Rose reached for her, but Sarah cried and turned to Anne. Rose was a stranger to her own little girl.

Anne picked up Sarah and comforted her, telling her that her momma was here and just wanted to hold her, but Sarah didn't understand. Large tears ran along her sweet cheeks. Her precious daughter had grown so much in the last year and Rose had missed it.

She tried to smile, but it was difficult. Anne's eyes found hers and reached for her hand. Rose stood and grasped Anne's hand in hers. "I tried to come home, but I didn't know where we were and I..."

"You protected them," Rose murmured.

"Sarah will..."

"Shh," Rose said. "I understand. She doesn't know me, doesn't remember me. You were the one with her, protecting her, taking care of her, and I'm thankful." She swallowed the lump in her throat.

Anne hadn't taken her place intentionally, but in little Sarah's world, Anne was her mother, not Rose.

Rose's legs shook, and she stumbled, but before she could fall, James's arm wrapped around her waist to keep her steady. He held Daniel in one arm, his other around her. The moment was reminiscent of when he had protected her when they had first arrived in Helena after the birth of Sarah. But this time was different. She was stronger and healthier. She turned and held him close. He was solid, real, and with her after so many months of being away. Although Sarah feared her, Rose just had to be patient. Sarah was young, but young enough that with time, she would learn to accept Rose as her mother.

Taking a deep breath, she tried to take a step away, but James refused to let go.

"Please," he whispered. "One more minute." He kissed the side of her cheek, and she nodded.

She didn't want to leave him any more than he wanted her to.

He shuddered and then reluctantly let her go. Anne stood still, holding Rose's daughter, her eyes sad. Rose didn't want Anne to feel bad. She, too, had been taken, and Rose was being selfish for not asking if she was all right.

Taking a deep breath, she pushed away the strands of her hair and tugged at the sash around her waist. "Anne, thank you so much for taking care of my children. How are you? Were you hurt?" she said.

Anne smiled, her relief clear with the sudden dropping of her shoulders. "I'm better now that

I'm home." Anne once again tried to hand Sarah to Rose, but Sarah wouldn't cooperate. She screamed and held tight to Anne, not letting go, her distress evident as tears poured along her sweet, plump cheeks.

As much as it pained her, Rose waved her away. "It's all right. She doesn't know who I am. Let's not force her"—she held her hands out—"as long as you don't mind if she wants to be with you."

"I don't mind, but I hate that she doesn't want to come to you. I never intended for her to become so attached to me."

Rose smiled. "I understand. You've been the only one with her for months. How could she not grow attached to you? I'm thankful you cared for her, for both of them. You are an angel for protecting them."

"I wanted to," Anne said. "There was no way I was going to let that man hurt them. I hope you know that. I tried, I really did, but with the snow and being stranded up in the mountains, I had no choice. I didn't want to put them in any more danger."

Sarah's cries grew with intensity, as though she sensed the tension.

Elizabeth walked into the room and took in the chaos with one glance. With a quiet calm, she said, "Rose, why don't you sit, rest for a moment." She then looked at Anne. "I'm sure you'll want to wash, and Ben sent for the doc to look you over."

"I'm fine. Just tired. We should have the doc look at the children. I did the best I could, but there were a few months in the beginning where I couldn't find enough to eat." Anne's voice broke.

"We can talk through this later, after you've eaten and rested. The most important thing is that you're home. We can worry about everything else later," Elizabeth said. She reached for Sarah, but Sarah wouldn't have anything to do with Elizabeth. Screaming, she hung onto Anne tightly.

"I'm sorry," Anne said. "She doesn't... she won't..."

"No, no. Of course, she's upset. This is new to her." Elizabeth looked at Rose. "Would it be all right with you if Sarah stays with Anne for a while longer? I think we need to get her used to us. She's young and she'll adjust."

"I understand. As much as it pains me, I know Sarah doesn't remember me. Hopefully, with time, she'll get to know me again."

"Oh, she will," Anne said, begging Rose to understand. "I talked to her about her momma Rose and that we would see you soon. I think she's scared, tired, and hungry. It was a hard journey."

Anne was right. There was no reason to push Sarah, at least right now. They had time, plenty of time, now that they were back together.

Elizabeth clapped her hands. "Let's get you and Sarah into a warm bath, shall we?"

Anne nodded.

"Do you want me to take Tommy?" Elizabeth asked, looking at Rose. "I'm happy to get him washed unless you wish to do that."

"No, I can do it," Rose said. Tommy still

remembered her, and she would take care of him. "I just need to get dressed."

"Why don't you do that and meet us in the kitchen? Sophia's preparing his favorite foods. Bring him down when you are ready. That'll give Anne and Sarah plenty of time first."

With that, Elizabeth ushered Anne and Sarah out of the room. Anne looked over her shoulder, clearly pained Sarah was not going to Rose willingly.

But Rose didn't blame Anne. She never would, for she could never blame the woman who had protected her children at a cost to herself. Anne was a hero in Rose's eyes and she would be forever grateful.

Chapter 40

James grimaced at the pain in Rose's eyes when she realized Sarah wanted nothing to do with her. Sarah was over sixteen months now, and he himself had been shocked when he had seen how much she had grown when he found them in January. In the four months he had been with her, she had grown even more. Sarah came to him, but she thought of Anne as her momma, no matter how often the two of them had tried to convince her otherwise. She didn't understand and likely wouldn't for some time.

Daniel squawked, and he was jolted back to the little boy in his arms, his son. He was ecstatic yet subdued. He had missed his own son's birth, yet he couldn't be angry as he had found Anne, Tommy, and Sarah and had brought them home. That alone was a reason to celebrate.

Rose gazed at him and after seeking his permission, she reached for Daniel, holding him to her chest as though it would help her deal with the pain of Sarah's rejection.

"It's all right, little one," she crooned.

Daniel settled almost immediately. She checked his nappy and placed him in his crib.

Tommy was complaining of hunger, and James lifted him up into his arms. "Little man, let your momma get dressed and we can get you something to eat." Tommy pushed at him, and James placed him on the ground. "I can take him downstairs for you."

"No, please stay. I want to keep him near me, if that's all right," she said. "I'll be just a minute." She walked behind the screen in the corner of the room, and with quiet efficiency, changed clothes.

James's spine tightened as he heard her

rustle behind the screen, removing her nightgown and pulling on a clean dress. He hadn't seen her in months and had dreamed of her every night. He had tempered his expectations, but a tiny spark had unfurled in his chest. He prayed they would be able to pick up where they had left off.

A moment later, she stepped out from behind the screen. Dressed in a lovely green dress, her hair pulled away from her face, yet hung in a cascade of curls. It was all he could do not to pull her into his arms right there in front of Tommy and Daniel, but he held himself in check. Now was certainly not the time, but perhaps later when they were alone.

She smiled and self-consciously straightened her skirt. She was nervous, just as nervous as he was, and that calmed the erratic beating of his heart. Perhaps that was a sign of good things to come.

"Shall we get you both something to eat?" she asked.

"Yes, I'd like that," he said.

"Let me get Daniel and we can go downstairs."

"Can I hold him?" James waved to the crib.

She startled, but slowly nodded. He carefully picked up his son. Daniel was waving his little fists, cooing, and kicking his feet. His eyes were round with wonder when James picked him up, but he didn't cry and settled in James's arms as though he belonged there.

James turned and found Rose holding Tommy, a happy smile on his little face. She was staring at her son, wonder in her eyes. Things had finally righted in their world.

* * *

Rose closed the nursery door. Tommy and Sarah were nestled in their beds, clean with full bellies, and happy to be with Vicky and Jimmy.

It had been an unspoken decision they wouldn't discuss the events in front of the children and would keep the conversations pleasant. There would be time enough for all that once the children were put to bed.

Sarah had warmed to Rose, but there was no question she preferred Anne. Sarah let James hold her but as James explained, he had been near her for the last few months, and it had taken some time before Sarah trusted him. Sarah did let Rose tuck her into her little bed as long as Anne stood close by. It was difficult watching Anne care for her little girl, but Anne was only helping because she loved Sarah just as much as Rose did. Anne would make a wonderful mother, of that Rose was sure.

Rose followed Anne and Elizabeth down the newly built stairs and into the recent addition of the house. Rooms were added after the fire and Anne was having a hard time adjusting to the changes, but Rose was sure she'd settle in with her family soon enough.

Ben's brothers, Michael, Luke, and Stanley had been sent messages, and they expected Michael and Luke to arrive soon. Stanley was in Idaho, oddly enough, but farther south from where James had found Anne. He was near a rail depot, and Ben didn't think it should take long for the message to reach him. Rose had met Stanley for the first time in December, long after James had left. He'd had a haunted look in his eyes and was more reserved than his brothers but had been as kind as the rest of the family.

Stanley had traveled to Pocatello, Idaho, looking for closure after what his ex-wife Connie had done to their family. The family prayed he would find the closure he was looking for. They had heard little from him, but they knew where he was and a telegram had been sent.

The three women stepped inside the parlor and Katy gave Anne a hug. Katy had been beyond relieved to have her older sister home and gave Anne hugs every time she saw her, as though she had to reassure herself Anne was unharmed.

Ben poured them each a glass of wine. It had been a long day. Rose sat next to James, wanting to be close to him, to feel his strength, to know he was back where he belonged. He put his arm around her shoulders as though they had never been apart, and she snuggled into his side. Her heart warmed with the thought that he had come home to her.

Once everyone had settled with their drinks, Ben looked at his sister. "Anne, if you'd rather wait 'til our brothers are here before telling us what happened, we'd understand."

"I know you're wondering. I can tell them when they get here, but I don't see any reason to keep you in the dark."

She stood and faced the fireplace for a long moment before recounting the harrowing chain of events that had happened on the day of the fire to the day James found them in January. Rose was shocked and in awe of what Anne had done to save herself and her children. She had to find a way to thank the woman who had risked everything for her babies.

"What I don't understand is why you waited 'til now to come home," Ben said.

"We thought it best to stay where we were, what with the children and the long trek to

Gibbonsville," James said. "We were safe enough in his cabin…"

"Whose cabin?" Ben asked, interrupting.

Anne looked at James and hesitated as though she were weighing her words carefully, and Ben caught the glance.

"What?" he asked. "What are you hiding?"

"We aren't hiding a thing," James said. "It's just… well, um…" Rose took James's hand in hers. He was clearly flustered as there was more going on here than they all realized.

"It's all right, James. I can tell him."

"Tell me what?" Ben said, frustration reddening his face as though he knew Anne was going to tell him something unpleasant.

Rose watched this with fascination. She, too, wanted to know why it took so long for them to return if James had found them in January, but at the same time she wanted to be alone with James, to hold him, to reassure herself that this wasn't a dream, that he had kept his promise and brought her children back to her. He had sacrificed so much to find Anne and her children.

She wanted to love him, to show him how much she missed him, but she held back from climbing into his lap like a wanton kitten. There would be time enough for that later.

"Nothing dangerous," Anne said, "or at least I don't think it is, but you may have a different opinion."

As she sat watching Ben and his siblings, Rose's body reacted to the man next to her. His scent was still the same, and her senses were intoxicated. She snuggled more into his chest, resting her hands on his thigh, heat building beneath her fingertips.

James placed his glass of wine on the table and picked up one hand, rubbing his thumb against her palm. Back and forth, circles and strokes sending waves of heat to her arm and to her belly. Seeming to sense the way she was feeling, he pulled her closer and rested his lips against her hair for a long moment.

After a lengthy pause, Anne asked, "Do you remember Nathaniel Walker?"

Ben's eyes darkened, and he took a visible

deep breath before speaking. "Yes. How do you know... What about him?"

Anne nervously gripped her skirt. "He found me on the trail after I escaped with the children."

"What?" Ben gripped his wine glass so tight it shattered between his fingers.

"Ben." Elizabeth jumped up and grabbed a cloth to soak up the blood from the glass that had broken and cut his palm. "What's wrong? Who is this man?" She pressed the cloth to his hand, trying to stop the flow of blood.

Ben shrugged her away but kept the cloth against the cut. "I'm fine, sweetheart." He tried to smile at her, but it was forced.

Elizabeth bit her lip but stayed silent, seeming to sense something dark and dangerous.

"Someone I never thought to hear of or from again," Ben said through clenched teeth. "What did he tell you?"

"About as much as you are telling me. Nothing!" Anne yelled, pain in her blue eyes.

There was something going on here that was

more than just the history between Ben and Nathaniel, thought Rose. James's arm tightened around her shoulders as though he was protecting her from harm although in this moment, all was right in their little world. They had each other and now that their family was back together again, Rose had no doubt they would work through anything that came their way. She worried about Anne, however, as it was clear Anne was hurting.

"Did he hurt you?" Ben asked.

"No, he didn't. He saved us from perishing in the forest."

"You shouldn't have stayed there."

"And where should I have gone, pray tell?" Anne said, anger and sorrow raising the pitch to her voice. "I had two young children with me. I hadn't eaten in days and was barely hanging on to a thin shred of sanity when he found us. Snow was about to fall, and I was high in the mountains with no idea where I was."

"He should've…"

"Stop, Ben. You weren't there. You have no

idea what I went through, what I had to do. He saved me. He saved us." She paced and her face contorted with a pain Rose recognized. It was filled with a love that was not shared or returned. Anne had fallen for this mysterious man.

"And where is he now?" Ben asked with a curt tone.

"He wouldn't come. Your relationship with him stopped him from returning with us, but he wouldn't tell me why."

"Good riddance, I say," Ben said. "He ain't fit…"

Anne's eyes were filled with a deep pain. "No, he's not. You…"

"Enough," Ben said. "I'll not do this with you. You don't know what that man is capable of, of what he did."

"I know more than you realize," Anne said, tears filling her eyes. "I'm tired. I'm going to bed."

"No," Ben said. "We're not done."

"Ben!" Elizabeth's sharp voice interrupted the tense exchange.

Ben looked at Elizabeth in surprise, as though he had forgotten they were there. Anne took that opportunity to slip out of the room, the door closing behind her.

"Anne, wait," Ben said, but it was too late. She was already gone.

Chapter 41

Rose checked on Daniel. He was fast asleep in his crib. He had slept through the commotion. Luckily, all the children had. As soon as Anne left the room, it was clear emotions were running high. They quickly said their good nights and disappeared into their rooms.

James went outside to check on the horses. She wasn't altogether sure he would come to her room when he finished. He hadn't said he wouldn't but hadn't said he would either. In fact, he had said little.

She was vulnerable and scared and wanted him close, but if he didn't come, she wouldn't blame him. They had been through so much and had been apart for months. His feelings could have changed toward her.

Rose threw another log on the diminishing fire and rubbed her arms. The room had cooled, but the fire promptly flamed high. Making sure Daniel was covered, she slipped out of her shoes when the door to her room opened, and James stepped inside.

He closed the door and caught her in his gaze. She stopped, her movements stilted at the sudden arrival of her husband. He raked his eyes over her, from the top of her head to the tips of her toes. He stood still as a marble statue.

When the silence seemed he unbearable, he shook his head and seemed to come out of his stupor. "I didn't mean to intrude."

"You didn't," she whispered. "I'm glad you came."

He sighed. "Are you?"

Of course, she was but it was clear he didn't know for sure. "Yes," she whispered.

He took a couple of tentative steps forward

but then stopped once again, as if unsure of his next step.

Rose's heart broke at his indecision and hesitation with her. They had grown apart, and she needed to fix it. She wanted to fix it. She went to him until she stood mere inches from him. He tickled her skin with his breath, heat seeming to jump from his skin to hers, causing the hair on her arms to stand on end, as though aware of how close he was. Her heart pounded in her chest, and her breathing was shallow.

She reached to touch his cheek, flitting her fingers across his face, the whiskers from a few days of growth tickling them. Her other hand touched his arm, feeling the strength beneath her hand, flexing his muscles at her touch, but he didn't move.

"I've missed you," she whispered. "You kept your promise and brought them home to me. I'm so blessed to have you in my life." Her eyes had filled with tears, and she tried not to cry. She didn't want him to pity her or be swayed by her tears.

The rough pad of his thumb wiped away a lone tear that had escaped. She hitched her breath at his touch, her belly tightened, and her toes tingled.

"Is it too late?" she asked.

His forehead dropped to hers and he closed his eyes.

She started to step back, but he stopped her. He put his arms around her waist and pulled her close, molding her to him. They were a perfect fit, and she sighed in contentment.

He groaned, moving his lips across her cheek. His breath tickled her ear as he whispered softly, "No, it's never too late, my love."

"Oh, James," she said, clinging to him.

Their hug tightened. His warmth and solidness were what she had been missing for so long.

He pulled away, resting his hands on her waist. He searched her eyes with his, the pain of the last few months noticeable in his gaze. He then swept her up into his arms, sat in the armchair in front of the fire, and pulled a thick quilt around them, covering them both.

"Thank you for bringing them home to me." She brushed her hands against his cheek, then to his neck before resting on his solid chest.

"I wasn't going to come home without them, Rose. They have a part of my heart, just as you do."

She hated asking the question, but it needed to be done. "What if Charles comes back and tries again?"

"I don't know if we'll be able to stop him, but I talked with Ben tonight, and he believes they're close to finding proof Charles was involved in taking Anne and the children. He doesn't know when, but he swears with all the security around the ranch, there's no way he'll be able to get to you or the children. We won't leave them alone, not until he is behind bars." He paused a moment. "We'll stay here at the ranch house and won't return to the cabin or to our own place until he's gone from our lives for good."

"What if it takes years?" she asked.

"Then it takes years, but I don't believe it will. His plan fell apart when Anne escaped with the children. He knows we're watching him. If he's stupid enough to make a move, then he'll pay for it. I can promise you that."

She shuddered both with the realization it wasn't over and that she had someone as sure and strong as James who would do everything in his power to keep her and their children safe from harm. He had kept his promise and had brought them home.

"Now"—his eyes twinkled—"I think we've done enough talking for tonight. I'm sure you're tired. Do you want me to go?"

"No," she said. "I need you tonight." Raising her fingers she fingered the top button of his shirt.

"Are you sure, Rose? I don't want to rush you. You just had Daniel."

She chuckled. "Daniel is four months old, James. I'm perfectly fine. There's nothing stopping you unless you'd rather…"

The words were caught in her throat as he

pulled her in close for a long, delightfully sinful kiss. When he came up for air, they both breathed heavily, their hearts close, their skin even closer.

"I love you, Rose," he said.

"And I love you, James."

"We can do this together. No more secrets?"

"We may fight, argue, and I may throw a thing or two at you, but I'll never stop loving you."

He smiled and kissed her tenderly on the lips.

"I'll never stop loving you. You *are* the best thing to have ever happened to me. I'll do everything in my power to protect you and the children. No matter what life throws at us, know you are my everything," he whispered.

And with that, he showed her precisely what she meant to him. There was laughter, love, passion, and an understanding that whatever happened, they would face it together.

No more secrets, no more accusations, and no more lies, for they had everything they needed with each other and would stay that way for the rest of their lives.

Epilogue

September 1901

James raised the ax before hitting the block of wood, splintering it into two pieces. The sun was high above, warming his skin, and sweat lined the collar of his shirt. Wood piled behind him as he worked his way through the large wood stumps, chopping what they'd need for the winter. They had moved to the small cabin two days ago, and there was much to be done before winter arrived, but they were happy to do it.

They had stayed at the main house for months longer than expected. Ben and James had both believed it made more sense for them to stay where the guards could easily watch over them. Then, ten days ago, the Marshal arrived with the news they had been waiting for.

They had found the men who had been responsible for the fire and who had taken Anne and the children. Sam and Anne were both able to swiftly identify them and once the men realized they had nothing to hide, they were quick to place the blame where it fully belonged and had information to support their claims. Letters, telegrams, and large deposits of cash were tied to Charles and his nefarious plan to come after Rose and the children. The trail of misdeeds was long and would put Charles behind bars for years to come. Not only had he planned on removing Rose's children from her care, but he also intended to kill Rose. Being in Spring Creek when the children were taken was likely what had saved her life.

One letter from Charles was so detailed in his plan, Ben and James thought it best not to share the information with Rose. James shuddered to think how she would've reacted if she had known the details of what Charles planned to do with her before killing her slowly and painfully. It was enough to know Charles was going to pay for his crimes and could never hurt her again. They had finally caught him and were transporting him to Helena where he would stand trial.

"Pa," yelled Tommy as he came roaring out the front of the house, the door slamming against the wall with the force of his excitement.

James placed the ax behind the stump he was using to cut the wood and squatted as Tommy jumped into his arms. "Momma said you take me to play with Vicky."

James smiled.

"Now, young man," Rose said as she stepped outside, Daniel in her arms, with Sarah plodding next to her. "I said no such thing."

"Tommy," James said, looking into his son's dark green eyes. "Are you telling a fib?"

Tommy's eyes widened. "No, Pa. Momma said you'd let me play with Vicky."

James laughed.

"I said you could ask your pa if he'd take you to play with Vicky, but I didn't say he'd let you."

Tommy scrutinized them both as though trying to decide what the difference was between what he said and what his momma had said. He looked at James. "Pa, take me to play with Vicky?"

"I don't know, son. We have much to do before winter sets in. Maybe in a few days we can go to the main house."

Tommy's eyes widened and filled with tears. James's heart tugged. He didn't want to see Tommy cry, but before he could open his mouth and change his mind, Rose said, "Tommy, I was going to make cookies. Would you like to help me?"

Tommy's lips lifted into a bright smile, and the tears promptly disappeared. He pushed at James. "Let me down, Pa. I have to helps Momma with cookies."

Rose's suggestion had stopped a tantrum from starting, and he chuckled inwardly at how well Rose tended to their children.

James placed Tommy on the ground. He scampered up the front steps and yanked open the door. "Hurry, Momma, we gots to make cookies."

"I'll be inside in a minute, Tommy. Why don't you find me a big bowl and wooden spoon and place it on the table?"

"Yes, Momma," he hollered, his voice fading as he ran inside the house.

James chuckled as he walked toward the love of his life. Sarah teetered on her feet and stepped toward him, her balance not quite steady even after walking for a few months. He swooped her up into his arms and tickled her tummy, her laughter loud as she batted at his hands.

"Tommy's missing Vicky something fierce."

"We can go there tomorrow for a visit," he said, shifting Sarah more comfortably on his hip.

"No, he needs to get used to not seeing her every day," Rose said. "Besides, there's plenty for us to do, and we don't need to go up to the main house anytime he gets a hankering for it."

"Momma," yelled Tommy.

Rose smiled. "I can distract him with cookies and other activities, but Daniel needed to be fed and Sarah was fussy as well."

"Send him outside with me next time, love," James said. "I can keep him occupied."

"I know you can, but with you chopping wood, I didn't want to send him out until you were done. He asked if he could play with Vicky and when I told him he could ask you, he ran out the door so fast I couldn't stop him. I think he thought you'd take him as soon as he came outside," she said, laughing.

"If we didn't have plenty to do, I might've taken him."

"I'm well aware. The house is still dusty and dirty from being empty for so long. We've only been here for a few days and there's plenty to do."

James held out his hand, and she placed hers in his.

"There certainly is, but we can always take the time to go see his cousin, if that's what you'd like to do. I know you enjoy spending time with Elizabeth and it was hard leaving."

"Yes, I do, and it was hard, but I wanted to be in our own home and coming back is comforting to me. Tommy'll get used to us being out here, and we'll see them often, I'm sure."

Rattling wheels echoed from behind them. James turned and watched in the distance as a wagon rumbled along the dirt road, hitting the many holes and divots that had grown in size on the dirt path in the year since they'd been gone. One of many tasks he needed to make time for. It wouldn't do to have a broken wheel, or a jarred neck for him or anyone in their family.

"Momma," yelled Tommy once again.

Rose sighed but smiled. "I better get inside before Tommy pulls out the flour and makes a mess of my kitchen. Give me Sarah." Rose shifted Daniel to one arm and reached for Sarah with the other.

James shook his head. "I've got her. I'll keep her with me and bring her inside if needed. Go get to Tommy before he finds the eggs next."

She laughed and followed Tommy. If they weren't careful, they were likely to have another mouth to feed and soon, although he wouldn't be too upset with another little one. He didn't want to overwhelm Rose with the care of too many children, but she had whispered in his ear the night before that she wouldn't mind more.

The wagon clattered to a stop with Ben, Elizabeth, and Vicky inside. James grinned. Tommy would be thrilled to see his friend and cousin.

Vicky reached for her pa's arms. Ben lifted her and placed her on the ground. She raced up to James and asked, "Where's Tommy?"

"He's inside with his momma. Go on in."

Vicky smiled and with feet as quick as Tommy's, she ran up the stairs and inside, although she didn't let the door slam as hard as Tommy had in her excitement to see him.

"Where's my namesake?" James asked.

Elizabeth straightened her skirt and raised her head, a sparkle in her eyes after Ben helped her from the wagon. "He was sleeping, so Anne offered to watch him for us."

"Is everything all right?"

"Yes, yes. Everything's fine," Elizabeth said. "We wanted to see how you were settling in and to give you the news."

James eyed them. "What kind of news?" He didn't want to give Rose any more bad news. She'd had her fair share of that over the past few years.

"Where's Rose?" Ben asked.

"She's inside with Tommy and Daniel, making cookies."

"She should hear this too," Ben said.

"Now I'm getting concerned." Sarah pushed, wanting to get down. James placed her on the ground but held her hand to keep her from running away. She was a fast little thing when she saw something she wanted. Too many times he had stopped her from chasing after bees and reaching into a hive full of them. She was fascinated with any creature that flew before her eyes. Butterflies, beetles, and rollie pollies could keep her entertained for hours.

"Nothing to get concerned over," Ben said. "I believe Rose'll want to hear this."

"Let's go inside then." James walked with Sarah and clasped her hand as she climbed the steps. Ben and Elizabeth followed in their wake.

Pulling open the door, he gestured for Elizabeth and Ben to go inside, where they found Rose, Tommy, and Vicky at the kitchen table. Both Vicky and Tommy had large bowls in front of them, mixing their cookie dough, or whatever Rose had given them to mix.

Rose smiled when she saw them and wiped her hands on her apron before moving a wayward curl behind her ear, leaving a flour mark across her cheek. She must've put Daniel down, as her arms were empty.

James let Sarah's hand go. She toddled to her toys and plopped onto the ground, pulling out her doll. Her babbling words interspersed with the ones he recognized tumbled from her mouth. She was a happy child and had finally accepted Rose. It had taken some time, but with a lot of love and patience, Sarah called Rose Momma.

"Elizabeth, Ben. What a pleasant surprise! Can I get you something to wet your lips? It's still a bit warm outside."

They both shook their heads.

"Rose, they've come to share some news," James said.

"Oh." She frowned and hastily wiped her hands on her apron, likely more out of sudden nervousness than any uncleanliness.

Elizabeth held up her hand. "No cause to worry, but we thought you'd want to know as soon as possible."

"Rose, why don't you sit," James said.

Rose's face had gone pale, and he wasn't sure where this was leading. The last thing he wanted was for her to be hurt.

Elizabeth looked at Vicky and Tommy. "Why don't we all go sit in the other room? The children are occupied, and we can have a moment to ourselves."

Once settled, Elizabeth and Ben looked at each other before Ben said, "The Marshal came by this morning." Ben looked carefully at Rose. "While on the trail to Helena, Charles managed to escape, and holed up in a small cabin with a gun he'd stolen. When they caught up with him, they surrounded it, and he came out waving his gun, shooting wildly at the law, yelling and cursing at those who were there. He was killed."

Rose stiffened as Ben continued to tell them what had happened. A few of the men sustained a few injuries but nothing life-threatening and no one else had been killed.

"There's something else," Ben said. "Seems the real reason Charles was trying to get the children was that your late husband had inherited quite a sum of money when their parents passed. Charles hid the information from his brother until the day he died. From what they've been able to gather, they believe Charles had something to do with your late husband's death. Nothing for sure, but when they talked to a few men at the logging camp, there were a few events that lead them to believe he might have caused his death to keep Joseph from getting any of the money."

Rose gasped.

"He believed by killing you and laying claim to the children, he'd be able to funnel the funds into his own pocket."

"I don't understand," she said. "He killed Joseph?"

"It's what the Marshal believes, but there's no way to know for sure now," Ben said.

James was shocked. He took Rose's hand in his and squeezed. Her skin had grown cold and clammy.

"I know it's a lot to take in, but appears you are now a very wealthy woman," Ben said.

"I don't want it," she said. "I want nothing from him."

"Love," James said. "We understand you wouldn't want anything from him"—he held up his hand as Rose sputtered—"but think about what Joseph would've wanted. If you are uncomfortable with taking the money, we can consider putting it into a trust for Tommy and Sarah. They are Joseph's children, and I'm sure he would've wanted to make sure they were taken care of."

Rose considered his words for a long moment. "Can I think about it?"

"Yes, yes, of course you can. Nothing needs to be decided today, but we wanted to let you know what transpired. You have plenty of time to decide and if you're comfortable with it, our family lawyer, Mr. Parker, will be more than happy to guide you through any decisions you need to make."

Ben then explained that the law was asking if Rose would identify Charles's body, although they were reasonably sure they had the right man.

"I wasn't sure how you'd feel about that, so I told the Marshal I'd be happy to identify him. I certainly saw him enough in the courtroom," Ben said.

"No," she said, conviction in her voice. "I

must do this, so I can see for myself that he is gone and is no longer a threat to my own."

James reached for her hand. "Rose, I don't know if that's a good idea."

She looked at him and squeezed it. "It'll be fine. I'm stronger now that I have you next to my side."

His heart burst for the woman beside him. She *was* stronger and showed him how strong she was every single day.

They made plans and the next day, Rose and James went to Helena to identify the body. It was difficult for her to look upon the man who had taken her Joseph and tried to take her children, but with James near her, she'd quietly but firmly told the marshal it was Charles once she saw the body.

As they stepped out of the undertaker's office and into the sunlight, James stopped and lifted her chin with his finger. "Are you all right, my love?"

She smiled, a wide smile so full of love it blew

his breath away. "Yes, yes, I am. Let's go home to Thundering Mountain Ranch."

"Don't you mean, Thundering Meadows, our small but wonderful meadow?" he asked.

"Why, yes, James. I do."

My Dear Readers,

If you've loved James and Rose's story turn the page for sneak peeks of *Thundering Ridge* (book 4) and *Thundering Snow* (book 5) the next installments in the *Thundering Mountain Ranch* series where the Seymour family grows with each happily ever after.

All my love, Nicole

A Sneak Peek

Thundering Ridge

Justice, love, or both... Can he find the peace he's looking for or will revenge ruin his forever?

Luke Seymour, cowboy turned aspiring reporter, left his family's ranch to find justice for his Pa's murder. After eight long years, he finally catches a glimpse of the woman who started it all. Beginning a search of parlor houses in Helena, Montana, he attends an auction where his heart stops, his palms sweat, and his interest in one young lady makes him forget for just one moment why he is there.

Louisa, desperate and alone, agrees to an auction that threatens to rob her of her innocence. With courage and desperation, she stands in front of the wealthiest men in town, leaving her wants and wishes behind.

In a life-altering moment, Luke offers Louisa a chance at a new beginning, a respectable position as his housekeeper and cook. Not knowing if she can trust him, she looks deep into his green eyes and decides his offer is far better than the alternative. As their lives intertwine in a booming frontier town, their bond strengthens, but Luke's relentless pursuit draws danger close and he stands to lose everything. Can he find a way to bring evil to justice or will his relentless pursuit endanger the one woman who has buried herself deep into his cowboy heart?

Thundering Snow

Old wounds, unexpected love, and a chance at a new beginning.

For years, Stanley Seymour has been running from the pain of marrying the woman who killed his pa. One night, a spirited and determined young woman lands squarely in his lap, altering the course of his future.

Charlotte McVicker, accompanied by her aunt, refuses to surrender to her grandfather's plans. When she finds herself embroiled in a bar room brawl, she turns to a dashing stranger.

Charlotte's aunt seizes the opportunity to play matchmaker and convinces Stanley to help them. Stanley finds himself unable to refuse. Both Charlotte's quest and Stanley's guilt will bring danger close. They find themselves caught between ruthless people and a desire to find what is missing in their lives.

Amidst the rugged landscape of Idaho, Stanley and Charlotte's world's collide, sparking a journey of adventure and the possibility of love blossoming in the unlikeliest of places.

Thundering Ridge

June 29, 1900

Luke stuffed the latest piece of news securely in his shirt pocket, and he salivated at what it meant. Hot sweat trickled from his forehead and cheeks, and he wiped it with a worn rag as he finished the morning newspaper run in the basement of the three-story building.

As the typesetter and occasional journalist, Luke straightened his back and stretched his long arms above his head, lifting the sweaty hair from the back of his neck. He had returned late from his brother's ranch the night before and his muscles ached from the quick trip, but he'd still headed into work early to get the day's run complete. Glancing at the clock, he grimaced. He hadn't had the opportunity to talk with Walter, the editor and owner of the *Helena Gazette* and time was passing quickly.

Luke's muscles bulged as he pulled the last of the newsprint into a thick pile and tied it with twine. "Frank, that's it. We're done for the morning. I need to find Walter. As soon as I'm finished, I'll come back and help you in cleaning."

Frank nodded and picked up the broom to sweep the floor. Walter insisted on a clean press room, and it was a daily part of their work to make sure things were in tip-top shape before they left for the day.

Picking up one stack of newspapers, Luke said, "I'll let the newsboys know they can come and get the rest of these on my way up to see the boss."

"Thank ya kindly, Luke," Frank said. "The missus wants to know if you'd like to come for dinner one day next week. She thinks you ain't gettin' enough to eat." Frank laughed, his grey eyes twinkling.

Frank's wife had been determined to find Luke a wife, and she tried to feed Luke every chance she got. No matter his protestations that he wasn't searching for one, she continued to parade eligible young women in front of him with the hopes he'd set his sights on one and settle down. Until he had avenged his pa's death, he couldn't in good conscience put the woman he married into harm's way. He hated to burden Frank and his wife with his problems, so he smiled and indulged her interference knowing full well he wouldn't court any woman until the time was right.

"I'd like that. Tell her to pick a night and I'll be there." Frank's wife was a kind woman with a good heart, not to mention a great cook, and that alone was reason enough to go. His own cooking was abysmal. He would always appreciate a well-cooked meal, no matter the circumstances.

Frank nodded and continued to sweep up the

scraps of paper that were scattered across the floor.

Luke jogged up the stairs, through the spotless front office, to the outside porch where the newsboys sat waiting for the go-ahead to gather the newspapers and sell them. Walter had bought the building just after it was built two years before and it contained the latest modern conveniences of gas-lighting and indoor plumbing. Sometimes, he was afraid he'd track dirt inside the office and Walter would have his head.

Handing the newsboys the stack in his arms, he told them the rest were ready for delivery and then walked up the second set of stairs to Walter's office. A second office was further down the hall, unused at the moment. Luke had been hoping for a permanent promotion to journalist. With any luck, that office would become his when he finally proved himself worthy. He rapped on Walter's door with his knuckles and waited for permission to enter.

"Come in."

Luke opened the door. The sunlight poured in through the dirt-streaked windows, nearly blinding him. Stacks of newsprint lined the far edges of the room. Past issues of various newspapers were stuffed into the tall filing cabinet behind Walter and lay scattered across his desk. It was a wonder Walter could get any work done with the number of papers blanketing the surface.

"Got a moment, Walter?"

Walter raised his eyes from the ledger in front of him and gestured for Luke to come in. Picking up his cigar, Walter sat back in his chair, the leather creaking with movement.

Luke settled in one of the plush armchairs Walter had on the ready for paying customers. Luke likely shouldn't be sitting there, but he didn't think he had much ink on him. Walter didn't seem to mind, as he hadn't told him to get up.

"I kind of have an odd question to ask, Walter."

Walter chuckled. "I can't imagine you asking

me anything I haven't heard before. Go ahead." His blue eyes twinkled as he took a puff from the thick cigar that sat between his pudgy fingers. Walter wasn't a small man or a big one, either. He was average size, but he had a large presence. Not afraid to state his opinion on most anything, Walter was a relatively decent man who had given Luke a chance.

"Before I ask the question, I best explain some things about my family and what happened in the summer of 1893." Luke had never told Walter anything about the woman who had caused so much pain and havoc, but considering what he'd just discovered, it was about time if he wanted Walter's help.

Walter nodded thoughtfully. "Go on, then. I don't have all day."

"Yes, well… my older brother, Stanley, married a woman by the name of Connie, or leastways that's what we knew her as. Stanley met Connie in the spring of 1892, and after a few months, they were married. At first, she tried to fit right in with the family, but then things seemed to change. She became demanding and tried to make all these plans to change the ranch."

Luke's gut clenched as he remembered her determination to change the way his pa did things, her snide remarks when she didn't get her way, and the way she chastised his ma over the smallest of things. It still made him sick to his stomach to think about what she had done.

"Pa didn't take to her ideas and things became tense between 'em. Then, Ma and Pa got sick – real sick. Ma went first and then Pa. Pa had been recovering and then he was gone sudden-like. I thought it was strange and part of me suspected Connie, but I had no proof." He rubbed his hands together, a chill running up his spine. "Come to find out, she had everything to do with it. She convinced a ranch hand to smother him to death while he rested on his sickbed." He swallowed back the thick lump in his throat, the heartache very much as real today as it was seven years ago. His voice gruff, he continued, "Then, she manipulated Pa's will to make it seem like Stanley had inherited everything, kicked me and my brothers off the ranch, and then tried to have Stanley killed. Thank the heavens above, she didn't succeed. Stanley survived the attempt."

Walter's eyes were wide with shock. "That's quite the tale. I knew your pa died, but I never knew it was murder."

"Yeah, it's not something I tend to share."

"What happened to her?"

"She managed to escape and disappeared for years."

"So why are you sharing this story with me?" Walter's blue eyes were piercing, contemplative. "I'm sympathetic, but I'm not sure what you need from me."

While they had a good relationship, Luke and Walter weren't the best of friends and rarely saw one another outside of work. Luke shifted uncomfortably in his chair. "My oldest brother, Ben, sent out inquiries, and he received a letter from a friend of his in Texas. We think she might be involved or had been involved in a fancy parlor house." Luke reached into his coat pocket and pulled out the worn and creased letter Ben had given him the night before.

Ben,

I made some inquiries. Connie's real name is Bethany Constance Ashland. She grew up in a Houston brothel. In 1890, when she was nigh on 20 years of age, she left the brothel. It's believed she moved to San Antonio.

She married an older, infirm gentleman in late 1891. He passed six months after they tied the knot and his death was quite suspicious. The law had been questioning her about her husband and a couple other men she was suspected of killing when she disappeared. They followed her trail for a while but then lost track of her.

If she's anywhere in Helena, I'd suggest you look in high-end parlor houses. She ain't one to live simply, and seems to crave attention and money.

Hope you find this information helpful. I wish you and your family the best.

Norman Petterfield

Walter finished reading and handed the letter back to Luke, his face unreadable. "Does this have anything to do with the black eye you were sporting a few months ago?"

Luke folded the paper carefully and placed it back in his pocket. "Yes. I thought I'd seen her a few times but wasn't quite sure. We never expected her to return to Helena. Toward the end of April, I saw her again and followed her. I was careless and paid the price with a shiner. Since then, I swear I've seen her but haven't been able to track her. Ben gave me this letter last night."

"So, what can I help you with?"

Luke shifted forward in his chair and braced his hands on his knees before raising his eyes to Walter's. "From the letter, it sounds like I need to get myself into a few of the parlor houses in town. It never crossed our minds she might be a lady of the night, so I'd like to start looking there. I can't see her belonging to anything other than an exclusive one, but I doubt I'm part of the clientele that gets a coveted invitation."

"And you think I am?" Walter chuckled ruefully.

Luke's collar suddenly felt tight. He raised a finger to loosen it. "Not exactly, but you know plenty of people, and I hoped you might be able to wrangle me some invitations or point me to someone who could."

Sitting back fully in his chair, the cigar held in one hand, Walter gazed at Luke for a long moment. "I'll see what I can do. Not making *any* promises, but I'll put out some feelers and see what snaps back. Might cost you, though."

"I understand." Luke let out the breath he hadn't realized he'd been holding. "Thanks, Walter. I appreciate it."

"You're welcome. Now get back to work. I don't pay you to sit here idle."

"Yes, sir," Luke said, scrambling to stand.

With any luck, Walter would come back with good news. He was determined to find information on Connie or Bethany, or whatever her name was. With any luck, they would find her and make sure she paid for what she'd done. That way, she couldn't harm anyone ever again.

Thundering Snow

March 1, 1901

Stanley slammed his empty tankard of beer onto the scarred, sticky table and swiped the white foam from his upper lip. He waved and caught the attention of the bartender. He gestured for a new beer, and the man nodded. Within minutes, a full tankard was delivered.

He slouched low in the rickety wooden chair, his back against the saloon's rear wall near a large, black wood-burning stove. Although the heat from the packed bodies was enough to warm the skin on the coldest of nights, he still shivered. He'd lost count of the beers he'd had, but it didn't matter. Regardless of how much he drank, it couldn't erase what his former wife had done to him and his family.

A fight had broken out. Two men crashed into tables, glass mirrors, and even other men. They grappled with one another in an attempt to gain the upper hand. Beer splashed, food was flung, and tankards fell to the floor as the two men broke chairs, tables, and windows. Other men scattered, either trying to avoid the melee or having a reason to join. The bartender and a few burly men rushed to break up the fights, but it was clear those involved weren't to be stopped.

Brawls weren't unusual in the small railroad town of Pocatello, Idaho. It had been officially founded a mere seven years earlier and was bustling with activity from the railroad, establishing it as the Gateway to the Northwest. Stanley had been traveling for years, and it was the latest stop to hang his head, no better or worse than any other town he had visited in his pointless quest to find the woman who had ruined his life. Stanley should have been thrilled that Connie was truly gone, but he was still angry and even more so at his brother. It should have been Stanley who'd ended her, not Michael.

The fight continued to rage in front of Stanley, but it didn't stop him from imbibing his beer. He had no skin in the fight and was content to watch it play out. Entertainment in town was limited to the women in the saloons, gambling in the game halls, or attending church services on Sundays. Not that attending church was entertainment, but one couldn't be too choosy.

Suddenly, a soft body encased in light pink silk crashed into his table and then tumbled into his lap. A full, curvy warm one who smelled like his ma's rose-scented perfume. She had a head full of light brownish hair streaked with yellow that reminded him of the stalks of wheat after a fruitful harvest.

Startled, he dropped his tankard, spilling what was left onto him, the woman in his arms, and the floor. She screeched with outrage. He didn't know why, but considering he hadn't held a woman in his arms in quite some time, he wasn't inclined to let go.

Her frilly dress seemed out of place for a saloon, but who was he to judge the women who worked in them? As he took a good look at her, however, he questioned his initial perception. Her hair was piled high on her head in an elaborate arrangement of curls covered in an expensive hat, and her dress was made of the finest quality of silk.

It was something he hadn't seen since the woman who wasn't really his wife, had worn while he lived and worked on what he thought was his inheritance until he learned she had forged his pa's will, killed his pa with the help of a ranch hand, and cheated on him with the same ranch hand. All of this to take what his ma and pa had labored and built.

The woman's gown, having been pulled down slightly in the melee, barely contained her. He got quite a pleasant eyeful and would've continued to enjoy it until she slammed her sharp elbow into his gut. He grunted and released her. She scrambled from his lap and backed against the wall. She held her parasol in front of him as if she were wielding a sword she'd use to slice a man in half.

He chuckled before jumping out of his chair to get out of the way of the pointy end of her makeshift weapon. Although it would likely do little damage, he wasn't inclined to see what she could do with it.

"Don't touch me, you… you… ingrate," she screeched. The concoction of bows and ribbons that adorned the side of her head fell forward, covering the left side of her face before she shoved it up and out of the way. Her gaze never left his, as though he was the one who had pushed her into his lap.

Two men collided into the table next to them, the fight around them worsening by the second.

"Ma'am," he said, shimmying out of the way. "I certainly don't know what happened, but I can safely say I'm not about to lay a hand on you." He held up his hands to show he posed no threat.

"But you… you…"

Stopping her before she could say more, he said, "I caught you when you fell into *my* lap while I was enjoying *my* beer." He waved to the spilled tankard that rested on its side. "I didn't force you there, nor did I do anything inappropriate for a lady such as yourself." That might have been a slight stretch, as he couldn't have helped but get a handful of her when she landed in his lap. If he had known she was a lady, he wouldn't have taken such liberties.

Her cheeks flared bright red with embarrassment. She continued to hold the parasol in front of her as though that could stop him or any other man from taking what most women offered willingly in a saloon. He was a gentleman, or at least he had been before his life unraveled years before. He'd never take advantage of a woman, but he did see the need to get a lady out of such a place.

"May I be of some service?" He jumped out of the way of another man flying through the air.

"As you can see, things are getting a bit out of hand."

She narrowed her eyes and tilted her head as if contemplating his measure. "I… Just keep back."

"I won't hurt you." He looked down and brushed at the liquid dripping from his trousers and got a whiff of his stench. He hadn't had a bath in days and likely presented as a swine of the worst order. He might be drunk and stinky, but he still remembered the manners his ma had pressed into him when he was but a young lad. "I apologize for my lack of cleanliness and rank odor, but I'd never touch a woman, especially one who wasn't encouraging my advances."

She started to lower her parasol when another body struck him, that time from behind and not of the delightful kind. He stumbled forward and into her bountiful bosom. She dropped her parasol in surprise as he once again got a handful of her soft curves beneath the pink silk. His face was smashed into her chest, and he couldn't help but enjoy the feel and the view. Before he could fully appreciate the woman, she pushed him back, stomped on his foot, and kneed him in the face when he bent forward. He fell back on his hindquarters in stunned and painful amusement.

"My dear, are you all right? Did this swine harm you?" The high-pitched voice then proceeded to smack him over the head with a wooden cane.

He grimaced at the jolt across his head and tried to protect himself, but she didn't stop. His hands smarted from the whip of the cane. Thank goodness she had a horrible aim. If she'd gotten a good whack, he might've been knocked unconscious.

She abruptly stopped and went to stand near the girl's side, clucking like a mother hen. "Why did you come in here, Charlotte?"

He grinned. Charlotte was the name of the woman in pink. He rubbed at the top of his head, searching for any bumps and luckily didn't find much, but his favorite black hat had fallen in the scuffle. It was likely lost in the frenzy occurring all around them. He raised his head and pulled his knees to his chest. He was enjoying the show, albeit at his expense.

Charlotte smiled at the older lady and patted her on the arm. "No one hurt me, Aunt Martha." She jumped as a glass shattered against the wall next to her. "Although I certainly don't look like it, now do I? I got caught in the scuffle looking for Father and fell into this poor gentleman's lap." She didn't seem to be bothered by the fracas blooming at an alarming rate around them.

He shook his head as he was the *poor gentleman* now, and tried to contain the chuckles that threatened to erupt. If he hadn't been there to witness it, he would've thought he was watching a play on the stage of the local theater in Helena. Everything that had happened in the past few minutes had been just as ridiculous as the melodramas put on by the local theater troupe his ma and pa had taken him and his older brother to when they were young. He remembered watching in wide-eyed wonder as the actors exaggerated their movements and their speech to raise laughter from the crowd.

"Where is your father?" Martha asked. "Did you really see him?"

Another plate skittered next to him with what looked like a perfectly good steak and potatoes. His mouth watered. He was downright hungry all of a sudden. He'd have to get a bite to eat at the hotel if he got out of the saloon in one piece.

"I don't know. Maybe." Charlotte tilted her head, a quizzical expression on her lovely face. "I thought I saw him, but I might've been wrong." She pushed at her fallen hat, but it toppled once again. She quirked her lips in irritation.

A chair slammed into the wall behind Stanley, and he jolted from the impact.

"Oh my, poor dear. You keep looking for Marcus, and he doesn't want to be found."

"I know, but I can't help it. I want... No, I need to find him."

He wondered who Marcus was, but before he could ask, a man flew into another table next to them and grunted from the impact. It was time to go. Stanley jumped to his feet. Enough of his woolgathering. He had to get these women to safety—if they let him.

He glanced at the floor and saw his hat under the crumbled remains of the table. He bent, swiped it up, and slapped it on his head. Didn't want to lose that. Grabbing each woman by their elbow, he said, "As much as I'd like to continue to watch you two engage in this tete-a-tete, I think we should leave."

"Unhand me, you—" Martha pulled at his grip, but he didn't let go.

"Yes, I know. I'm an ingrate, swine, wretch, blah, blah, blah."

Martha looked at him in shock, opening and closing her mouth like a baby bird waiting for its mother to bring it a worm to eat.

"You can berate me later, after we get you to safety." He pulled them toward a door next to the bar. The saloon had erupted into a full-fledged bar fight with bodies and furniture flying every which way. It was a wonder they didn't get hurt.

"My parasol," Charlotte muttered, trying to pull away, but he held fast.

"Sorry, ma'am, but I think your parasol needs to be left behind. Unless, of course, you want to ask the men lying on top of it to gather it for you?" She swung her chest across his arm to look behind them, irritation on her face. "I'm sure they'd be happy to help a nice young lady like yourself."

Charlotte gasped but stopped fighting him. She let him lead her out the door and into the back room of the saloon. He practically threw the two women inside before he slammed the door shut behind them. He grabbed the nearest chair and positioned it under the door handle to keep men from coming after them. It wouldn't hold for long but would perhaps give them enough time to find a way out in one piece.

The door jostled as someone tried to get in, but the lock and chair held for the moment.

Fluttering her hand in front of her, Martha took great breaths, her rapid breathing causing her chest to rise and fall from exertion. She struggled to gain her composure and plopped heavily in a chair next to a worn, wooden table that held empty bottles of liquor. "Young man, I don't know who you think you are, but—"

"Shh, Aunty Martha. He saved us from that disaster out there." Charlotte waved her arm toward the door and what lay beyond.

Martha pointed her cane at her niece. "We would've never been in here if you hadn't once again chased after a man who looked—"

"Enough." Anger flashed in Charlotte's eyes. "We don't need to air our dirty laundry in front of Mr…?" She stared at Stanley with questions in her eyes.

"Seymour," he said, bowing his head. "Stanley Seymour's the name."

"Mr. Seymour," Charlotte said. "Thank you for saving us, although you certainly didn't act the gentleman when we first met."

He laughed, as her words were in direct contrast to what had happened just moments before.

"I don't understand what is so funny, Mr.

Seymour," Charlotte said, affronted by his laughter. She rested her hands on her hips.

Tears leaked from the corner of his eyes with the force of hilarity that suddenly overtook him. Bracing his hands against his knees, he took a couple of deep breaths to calm the chuckles racking his frame. She didn't think he was funny, but he sure did. "I didn't act the gentleman."

"No, you certainly did not. Why you… you had your hands all over…" Her cheeks were bright red. She was quite adorable with that blush, not to mention her plump red lips just begged for a man's thorough attention.

"I caught you when you fell into my lap, and then I was pushed into your…" He waved toward her bosom.

"Oh, you're insufferable," Charlotte muttered. "Maybe you aren't a gentleman if you have to mention—"

"I never claimed I was a gentleman." A wide grin lifted his cheeks. A grin he hadn't had in quite some time. That woman was the first to make him smile, and he would enjoy it no matter how long it lasted.

* * *

My Dear Readers,

I hope you enjoyed the two sneak peeks. You can find *Thundering Ridge*(book 4) and *Thundering Snow*(book 5) at all of your favorite retailers.

If you'd like to learn more about me or my novels, sign up for my newsletter at www.nicoleneiswanger.substack.com.

All my love, Nicole